HEAVEN ADJACENT

Center Point
Large Print

Also by Catherine Ryan Hyde and available from Center Point Large Print:

Allie and Bea
The Language of Hoofbeats
The Wake Up

HEAVEN ADJACENT

A Novel

Catherine Ryan Hyde

CENTER POINT LARGE PRINT
THORNDIKE, MAINE

This Center Point Large Print edition
is published in the year 2019 by arrangement with
Amazon Publishing, www.apub.com.

The text of this Large Print edition is unabridged.
In other aspects, this book may vary
from the original edition.
Printed in the United States of America
on permanent paper.
Set in 16-point Times New Roman type.

ISBN: 978-1-64358-263-4

Library of Congress Cataloging-in-Publication Data

Names: Hyde, Catherine Ryan, author.
Title: Heaven adjacent / Catherine Ryan Hyde.
Description: Center Point Large Print edition. | Thorndike, Maine :
  Center Point Large Print, 2019.
Identifiers: LCCN 2019018085 | ISBN 9781643582634 (hardcover :
  alk. paper)
Subjects: LCSH: Farm life—Fiction. | Sculptors—Fiction. |
  Women lawyers—Fiction. | Mothers and sons—Fiction. |
  New York (State)—Fiction. | Domestic fiction. | Large type books.
Classification: LCC PS3558.Y358 H43 2019 | DDC 813/.54—dc23
LC record available at https://lccn.loc.gov/2019018085

THREE MONTHS AFTER
THE MOVE

Chapter One

When Somebody Hands You a Fish

Roseanna was standing under the barely warm water in her tiny, cold makeshift shower when the bell at the gate began to clang.

She cursed to herself a few times, under her breath but out loud, rinsing off more or less all at once and grabbing a towel. She stepped out into her shabby and small add-on bathroom, toweled her hair briefly, then wrapped the towel around herself.

Roseanna stuck her head out the bedroom door, leaving most of her body still in hiding. From there, through the living room window, she could see a young man of twentysomething standing at the gate. He was looking around and—puzzlingly—even up over his head. As though something tangible and remarkable were about to materialize close by. Or above.

"I'll be there in a minute!" she bellowed.

She could see by his reaction that he heard. But he never seemed to get a bead on the direction of the sound.

She trotted down the steps of her little farmhouse, the porch stairs sagging limply under her weight, then headed for the gate. She was still a bit huffy and she knew it. She could feel the ball of irritation tucked under her ribs.

"Peace and quiet," she muttered to herself under her breath. "Solitude. Still don't think it's too much to ask."

She took a deep breath and tried to let it all go before she spoke.

He was a nice enough looking young man. Cleancut. He reminded her of her son, Lance. A little bit, anyway. But he seemed somewhat greener regarding life in general—what Rose-anna's mother had used to call wet behind the ears.

"I'm sorry I got you out of the shower," he said.

"What can I do for you?" she asked, without addressing whether he was or was not forgiven.

"I was hoping to get your story."

"My story."

"Yes."

"You want to know why I made the metal animals."

"I want to know everything. Why you left such a successful life in the city. And a really comfortable lifestyle. Why you chose a place like this that's so . . ."

He paused. Looked around again. Looked at her little farmhouse, with its faded paint and saggy porch. At her barn, huge and imposing, but looking like a good wind could end its upright life once and for all. His face took on a humble expression. He seemed to realize he had painted himself into a verbal corner—that there was no polite way out.

"How do you know what I left behind?" she asked him, feeling her eyes narrow.

Generally the people who stopped here knew nothing beyond what they saw with their own eyes. Oh, perhaps they'd heard that she had a reputation as a colorful local, and that the animal sculptures were worth a look and a few photos. Some had even been told that they could talk to Roseanna about their lives—that a visitor might be asked whether his life had turned out the way he'd dreamed it might, and a conversation of some depth might ensue. But no one had come by who knew anything about the past she had so unceremoniously left in the dust.

"Well, you know," he said. "Word gets around."

"Not a good enough answer." Her tone fell somewhere between firm boundary-setting and an impenetrable brick wall.

"A couple of people came back to the city who'd been talking to you, and, well . . . it just seemed like an interesting story. You know. Human interest."

She looked up and over his shoulder and noticed, for the first time, that a van sat parked across the road. It was not empty. It contained a passenger. A man who looked to be in his late forties, playing with an expensive-looking camera.

"Wait a second," she said. "Wait just a second. Are you telling me you're a reporter?"

"Yes, ma'am."

"From?"

"The *New York Times*."

She spun on her heel and headed back to the house. "Goodbye," she said over her shoulder, the word accompanied by a backward wave.

"No, wait!" he called. "Don't go yet. Give me two minutes to make my case."

Roseanna stopped. For a moment she did not turn back to face him. Instead she regarded her own property. The little girl was out and around, she saw. Chasing the short-haired brown dog, who was chasing the chickens. The old man was chopping wood, which Roseanna had asked him not to do. He was eighty, and the last thing she needed was for him to have a coronary on her property. They never thought of things like that, these people. These squatters. They never thought about legalities. About the extra burden she faced by virtue of owning the land.

Just before she turned back to face the reporter, she saw the young male squatter, the veteran—Nelson, his name was—walking back up the hill from the creek. Two good-sized trout hung from a stringer in his left hand.

She turned back to the gate. Moved a step or two closer.

"Fine," she said. "Take your two minutes. But I'm telling you right now it won't do you a bit of good."

The young reporter swung her gate open and stepped onto her property. Which she had not asked him to do. And he handled the gate a bit stridently, she noticed. He seemed not to understand that everything on her farm needed to be used gently. Like its new owner, none of it had been born yesterday.

Roseanna heard a car door open. The photographer across the street was stepping out of the van. The reporter spun to face his partner, shook his head, and used his hands in a kind of cutting motion. A universal, nonverbal *Don't*. The older man stepped back into the van and slammed the door.

"So, here was my thinking," the reporter said, walking up to Roseanna and standing too close. "An awful lot of people are in the city right now, living the kind of life you left behind. I think they'll want to hear your reasoning. Some will think you're crazy. I won't kid you about that. But others, it might really strike a chord. Like I said. It's a human interest thing."

"I find it hard to believe that welded metal animals are interesting enough for the *New York Times*. And I wasn't exactly a household name in my old profession."

"You're missing the point of the thing," he said.

11

"It's the sudden shift in life direction. Walking out of your life and leaving everything behind. I didn't think my editor would go for it, but I was wrong. It fascinates people. Probably because so many people have thought about it or wanted to do it. Like I keep saying. Human interest is all it takes."

"Well, this human is not interested," she said.

"But you seem to like to share your thoughts on life. From what I've heard. You seem to want to get people to open up about whether they're really happy."

"So?"

"So . . . wouldn't you like to reach thousands of people with that same message?"

"No," Roseanna said simply.

"Why not?"

"Because I don't want my family to know where I am. Or my colleagues. My former colleagues, that is."

"They don't know where you are?"

It was an incredulous question. Unguarded. She looked up into the young man's face. He looked a bit hurt, for reasons she couldn't quite sort out. As if he were the family being held at arm's length. He was still standing too close to her. Not respecting her personal space. She took a giant step backward, holding one hand as a stop sign to ensure he would not follow.

While she was taking him in, deciding he was

more like thirty but with a baby face, she could hear the little girl shrieking, and the dog barking, and the splitting maul whacking down onto wedges of firewood over and over again.

"I text and phone them," she said, feeling annoyed. By the noise, but also by the fact that she knew she didn't owe him this information yet had not found her way out of paying it. "Some of them, anyway. But if they knew my exact location, they'd show up here and try to drag me home."

A silence. If you could call shrieking children and barking dogs and thumping splitting mauls silent.

"No law says we have to give your exact location," he said.

For a moment, Roseanna didn't answer. She was considering it, and she could feel it. And he seemed to feel it, too. It drew him in closer again, as though she had left a door ajar and he was preparing to dart through it.

Just then Nelson, the young veteran, tapped her on the shoulder. She hadn't known he was there, and she jumped.

"Sorry to startle you, miss," he said.

Then he handed her a fish.

"Oh," she said, taking it from him. "Thank you."

It was a rainbow. A headless rainbow trout, carefully cleaned. Its shiny side gleamed in the sun.

"I took the head off the way you like. And I cleaned out that gut cavity real good. Did everything but eat it for you."

"Thank you," she said again.

Nelson tipped his sun-faded hat and backed away.

She looked up at her intruder again. The reporter.

"I have to go," she said. "Somebody just handed me a fish."

"Oh. Okay. You have to go put it in the fridge. I understand. I'll wait right here."

"No, you don't understand at all." She heard a second swelling of her own irritation. He undoubtedly did, too. "First of all, your two minutes are up." They very likely weren't, but she said so all the same. "Second, when somebody hands you a fish, you don't put it in the fridge."

"You don't? I would think that's exactly where you put it."

"Well, then, you don't know much about the subject, do you? This fish was alive and swimming not ten minutes ago."

"You don't know that."

"Excuse me?" she asked, her voice rising to a screech. The dog stopped barking and the little girl stopped shrieking. The old man, who was a touch hard of hearing, did not stop splitting wood. "I do so know it. Why would you say otherwise?"

"Well . . . he was down there fishing for . . . we

14

don't know how long. Right? That's my point. Could have been hours. And he could have caught that fish the first moment he was down there."

Roseanna rocked her head back and stepped away from him again. "See, this is the problem with people like you. You don't know what you don't know. You've never been fishing, have you?"

"No. But I know how to figure basic lengths of time."

"When you fish, you carry something called a stringer. Might be a chain with gill hooks on it. Might be just a cord with a ring on the end that you thread through the gill and back on itself and . . . oh, why am I explaining all this to you? It doesn't matter. You don't care about stringers and I don't care about educating you, and anyway your two minutes are up. What I'm saying is, you put the fish on a sort of . . . leash and put it back in the water. Alive. You don't take it out of the water until you're ready to walk home. Which takes not ten minutes."

"Oh," he said. And for a brief but blessed moment he seemed genuinely abashed. "I guess you're right. I didn't know what I didn't know. But you still have to put it in the fridge."

"Absolutely not. If you've never experienced eating a fish that was alive ten minutes ago, I guess you can't understand."

"So where do you put it if not in the fridge?"

"A frying pan. And then my stomach. Now if you'll excuse me . . ."

She turned and walked up onto the porch, still holding the fish. In both hands, because it was slippery. He darted up the steps to open the front door for her.

"Thank you," she said.

But then he followed her inside.

"If you don't mind my asking," he said, "who are all these people?"

Roseanna sighed deeply. And a bit more audibly than necessary. "Not a day goes by that I don't ask myself that same question."

"No, really. It was a serious question."

"It was a serious answer," she said.

"I think you might need to keep that photographer of yours on a leash," she said, leaning closer to the window.

The man was walking among the sculptures—all of which were located distinctly on her property—doing what photographers do best. He was staring up at the giraffe, and when he broke free of that obsession and stared into the iron eyes of the lion, the lion looked for all the world as though he were staring back.

"I think he just figured everybody takes photos of the metal animals."

"Oh really. Is that what he figured?" She

paused. Watched the photographer for another few seconds. Caught him sneaking a shot of the side of her house and another of the little girl and the dog. Meanwhile she could hear the fish sizzling in oil in the frying pan near her left elbow. It sounded like crispy trout skin, if crispy trout skin had a sound. "Most of them take pictures from the road unless I invite them in."

"Want me to talk to him?" He moved closer to her and peered into her frying pan. "Wow," he said. "That's a lot of oil."

"I like the skin crispy. Not that it's any of your business how much oil I use when I fry a fish. But, there. I told you. Besides. I'm trying to gain weight."

He laughed a sputtery laugh, as though she had just told him a grade school joke and he was attempting to find it funny.

"Nobody's trying to gain weight," he said. "Unless they're . . ." Then he paused, seeming to realize he had backed himself into another conversational corner. She was not problematically thin. "Nobody's trying to gain weight," he said again. As if that simple repetition would free him.

"Wrong. *I* am. It was one of my first goals when I moved here, but it's not working out as well as I'd planned. I eat enough. More than I ever did in the city, believe me. But then I work most of it right back off again."

"Why would you want to . . . ," he began. And never finished.

He was still standing too close. She hated that. *Whatever happened to personal space?*

"Because I can. Because in my old life I never could. Or never felt I could, anyway. And now I can. It's a freedom. I like freedoms. Now to answer your question, yes, you should go have a talk with him."

"Who?" he asked foggily. He had clearly forgotten the question. Then he seemed to clarify matters on his own. "Oh. My photographer. Yes. I'll just go do that now."

He moved for the door. Not the kitchen door, because there wasn't one. Her tiny house was more or less one room, except for thin walls creating a miniature bedroom in one corner. The kitchen was more like a nook in the opposite corner. He moved to the front door of her house.

Then he stopped, turned back.

"Before I do, I just wanted to ask you . . . what inspired you to make them?"

"The animals?"

"Right."

"No comment. If I answer that, then you're interviewing me, and I haven't agreed to an interview. And anyway, they weren't even my idea. They were the kid's idea."

He stared at her for a moment with his mouth open. If she'd had to guess at reading his mind, she'd have figured he was trying to decide if that had been a joke, and whether he should laugh.

Eventually he seemed to tire of the effort.

"That little girl who doesn't look any older than six or seven? Made all those huge, complicated sculptures?"

Roseanna noted a slight burning smell, and quickly flipped her trout with a spatula. Just in time, too. When somebody hands you a fish, you don't waste it by burning it in the pan. And, of course, if she had, it would have been all this reporter's fault. That was the trouble with . . . well, everybody.

"She's five. And I didn't say she *made* them. I said they were her idea. You know how children stare up at clouds and decide they look like teddy bears and elephants? Well, she did that with . . . wait a minute. Now you're interviewing me again. And I haven't agreed to that."

"Sorry," he said, but she wasn't sure he looked it. "You just go ahead and eat your fish, and I'll go talk to my friend."

He ducked out the door, and she sighed out a breath she hadn't realized she'd been holding.

She flipped the trout onto a plate, sat down on the couch, and began to carefully separate the fillets from the small bones.

She watched out the window, but she couldn't see the reporter or his photographer friend. Not that she wanted to. She would have been more

19

comfortable knowing where they were, but she never really cared to see anybody roaming around her place. And yet here the roamers all were.

Long after she had finished eating and cleaned up the dishes, he still hadn't come back. Which was quite a long talk to have with a photographer. She'd had in mind something short and to the point. More like "Stop that." Something efficient.
This much of a delay had to make one wonder.

She found the reporter fellow down on one knee in the hard dirt, talking to the little girl. Or, more accurately, listening. You couldn't talk to her much, that kid. You'd say one sentence and then she'd blast off on some tangent that seemed endless, made your brain hurt, and added up to nothing. Meanwhile, good luck getting a word in edgewise.
"Whatcha doin'?" Roseanna asked in a sing-song voice, tapping the reporter on the shoulder so he'd know which one of them she meant. It was a tone intended to help genuine irritation pass for lightheartedness, at least to a five-year-old. For the adult listener it was hiding her anger in plain sight, to put it mildly.
"Oh," he said, jumping to his feet. "I was just talking to her."
"Talking to her?" she asked, staring at the note-pad in his hand. "Or interviewing her?"

The little girl, obviously bored by them, ran away again. This time she chased the chickens and the dog chased her, seeming troubled to have his job stolen. Shrieking ensued.

"Just talking," the reporter said.

"When I talk to a five-year-old I hardly ever take notes."

"Look . . ."

For a long, strange moment they just stared off into the distance together. As though he had meant the word quite literally. She looked out over the rural farmland, the evenly plowed fields. Down the steep hills to patches of tall forest. The stream that ran through her acreage gleamed in the sun. It was summer, and everything looked a bit browner than it had when Roseanna first saw it and fell in love with the place. But it still struck her as a particular sort of heaven.

The reporter startled her by speaking again.

"Here's the thing. I don't have to write up anything I've got so far. I'll only do it with your permission. But I'm talking to all these people, and I'm taking notes, because I believe you're going to give me permission. I know you don't think you are. But *I* think you are."

"Do you, now?"

"I do."

"And why do you think that?"

"Because I talked to a couple of these people—"

"Like which ones?"

"Like David."

"There's no one here named David."

"Sure there is. You know. The guy who handed you the fish."

"Nelson. His name is Nelson David. And it irks him when people get that backward."

"Oh. I'd better correct my notes on that, then. Speaking of names, I'm Evan Maxwell."

"Maxwell Evan. Got it."

She didn't go on to tell him her name, because he must have known it. He knew what kind of life she had left behind in the city. Hard to arrive at that depth of research without a name to google.

Evan barked a short, uncomfortable laugh. Scratched behind his ear with the pencil he'd been using to note the meaningful thoughts of a five-year-old. "Now that you mention it, I think he did say Nelson David. But I thought he was doing that military thing where you do last name, comma, first name. He was in the military, you know."

"I know he was in the military." Her fuse was burning low again, and she could feel it. And they could both hear it. "You don't have to tell me all about him. He *lives here*. But you're evading the question. Why do you think I'm going to give you my blessing to write about me? And this place?"

She began to walk back toward the house as she spoke, knowing he would follow.

He followed.

22

"Because of what Nelson and the old man told me. I'm sorry, I can't remember the old guy's name. It's in my notes."

"Martin," she said.

But it didn't stop him flipping the pages on his pad.

They passed the ancient, massive barn, imposing and tall with its tin roof and weather-beaten wood sides. The makeshift chicken coop. The tiny shack that could almost have been a large tool shed, but had ended up being a squatter's cabin for her original two squatters. At least it was well tended—unlike almost everything else on the property—with curtains in the windows and flowers in a neat bed out front.

Still Evan was flipping through his notes.

"Oh well," he said as if giving up on something. "I can't find it now. But here's the gist of it." They stopped at the foot of her porch stairs. Evan looked up at the old farmhouse, seeming amazed to see it there. As if he hadn't noticed that they had been moving, approaching it. "They all said they stopped out front to look at the animal sculptures. Originally, I mean. When they first stumbled on this place. And you wanted to talk to them. You purposely got them talking about their lives and asked them all these questions. You wanted to know if their lives had turned out the way they'd expected. If they were as happy as they'd thought they would be."

He paused. As if his point might already be made, but he was waiting to see.

"All? Nelson and Martin aren't really an 'all.' More of a 'both.' "

"I might have had a few words with Melanie and . . . I forget the husband's name. That couple who live in the tent."

"They pretty much all live in tents."

"Oh."

"So what's your point?"

"I think you have something important you want to say. I think you found something here. And you want to share it. I think you want to ask questions that might lead other people to the same place you reached yourself."

Roseanna shook her head. Walked up the six old, saggy wooden steps to her front porch.

Evan followed. The stair risers creaked ominously.

"Yeah, just my luck," she said. "They'll all end up in the same place I reached myself. That's exactly what I'm afraid of and why I don't want to do your interview. That's exactly what keeps going wrong. I wanted to encourage them to find their own place. Someplace that was almost heaven *for them*. I didn't mean they should all look at *this* place that way."

"If you wanted them to go," Evan said, "you would have asked them to."

She paused on the porch. Looked around. Other

than the running, shrieking girl, she saw only Martin, quietly stacking firewood.

"Martin!" she called. But apparently not loudly enough. *"Martin!"* she bellowed, and he turned around. Moved closer to the house to hear, pulling off his big leather work gloves. "How many times have I asked you to leave my property?"

Martin's face fell. He scuffed in the dirt with the bright red high-top sneakers he always wore. "Oh dear," he said. "We're back to that again? I thought you'd more or less gotten used to me by now."

"No, I didn't mean . . . I meant, Martin, *tell this young man* how many times I've told you to leave. *In the past.*"

"Oh, oh. I see. I got it now." Martin smiled then. It was an uneven thing, the smile. A bit sardonic, but not without good humor. "Oh, hundreds. Well. Maybe I'm exaggerating." He raised one hand in a sweeping movement as if to brush hair out of his eyes. Which was silly, since he had no hair to speak of, or to sweep away. Just a raggedy ring of it down around his ears, now overgrown for lack of a barber nearby. "Dozens, at the very least."

"Thank you," she said loudly, and walked inside.

Needless to say, Evan followed. Even Roseanna might have been forced to admit she—possibly—wanted him to. Because it was clear that he would, unless she expressly forbade it. And she did not forbid it.

They stood together in her drab and tiny room of a house.

"Let me ask you one question," he said, looking around. "Whether I do this story or I don't, I just really want to know this for myself. This little house you live in . . ."

He stopped talking and allowed his eyes to rest on one aspect of her homelife after another. The potbellied wood stove. The blanket-covered old couch. The bedroom so small that if you fell down in it, you'd have to plan your direction of fall carefully to avoid hitting the opposite wall. The "light fixture" in the middle of the ceiling that involved a hanging bulb with a chain as a pull.

"You left a pretty opulent lifestyle," he said. "You had money."

She flopped onto the couch. He towered over her, still a bit close for her liking.

"How do you know how much money I had?"

"I don't, exactly. But I know your law firm. I mean, it's not hard to find out about the firm. And you were a senior partner. A founding partner."

"Let's see if we can't find our way to a point here, Maxwell."

But she knew the point.

"I can see you coming out here and buying a piece of land like this. It's beautiful country. And

I can understand wanting to get out of the city. I love the city, but I know not everybody does. But I'm thinking you could afford to tear this old house down and build something really nice here."

Silence. For a time.

He sat down on the couch beside her, still with an energy of hovering. Except now he made matters worse by holding his pad in a state of preparation in his left hand, his pencil poised on a blank page. As if she were about to say something brilliant. Timeless.

"But maybe then I wouldn't have been able to afford to live here for the rest of my life and not have to work. And not have to worry about money."

"I see," he said, and almost wrote that down.

"No. Don't even write that. It's not really the whole truth. I probably could have done both."

"Then why?" he asked, sweeping his arm in an arc to indicate the room. "I mean, not to insult you about this place, but . . ."

"I have eyes, Max. It's a dump."

"Why not make it into something better?"

"Because it's enough."

That sat in the air for a moment. It was unclear, at least to Roseanna, who would speak next. Or when.

As it turned out, she did.

"Because it's everything a person needs to live

a decent life. It has a stove for heat. A fridge to keep your food cold and a stove to cook it when you're ready to eat it. It has a bathtub and a shower to get you clean after your chores and a bed to lie down in at the end of the day. And that's all a person really needs. And I think the whole trouble with us is that we think we need so much more."

"It's nice to have more than just the basics of survival."

"Is it? Maybe. I don't know. I think it's a trap. We have all this 'stuff.' And we think we need it. But it never feels like enough, and we only end up working to defend it, and to get more. And we have all these labor-saving devices. So now we have this life that's almost entirely devoid of labor. A few centuries ago, there was work involved in everyday survival. And I can't know this for a fact, Max, but I have a really strong suspicion that not too many people were neurotic back then. Who had the time for it? Now we spend our spare time getting addicted. To drugs or alcohol, or our smartphones, or the internet, or checking our email, or shopping for all that 'more stuff' we think we need."

She paused. Looked up to see him scribbling fast.

"This is good," he said. "Not totally new thinking, but good. Don't stop."

"I'm still not sure I want you to use this. And

28

I'm not sure you ever explained why you're so convinced that I will."

"I told you. You want people to know your thoughts on all this. You've discovered something that's important, and you care enough to want to share it with other people."

"Nuh-uh," she said. "That won't fly, Max. I'm an attorney. I've been an attorney since before you were born, buddy boy. Compared to you, I practically *invented* that ploy."

"What ploy?"

"The one where you appeal to someone's ego. I don't care about that stuff anymore. Whether I'm looked upon as wise or not. I don't need to be right at this point in my life. I don't care what other people choose to do. I just know what I want to do now."

"Then why did you bother having those serious talks with these people when they came by? If you don't care about them?"

A silence.

During it, she looked out the window and watched clouds scudding across her fields. Watched them touch the top of CPR Hill, the peak they had to summit when any kind of cell phone reception was needed.

"So what if I do, then? Care?"

"If you have questions about life that you want other people to hear, what better place to ask them than the *New York Times*?"

She laughed, quick and bitter.

"Just my luck, Max, everybody who reads it will come pitch a tent on my property. And my son and my former law partners will find me and drag me home. And then everybody in the world will live here, which it almost already feels like they do. Except me. I won't. I'll have been dragged away."

"We don't have to give your exact location," he said again.

Roseanna sighed.

She looked out the front windows to his van to see if the photographer was staying put. He wasn't. The van was empty. So he could be anywhere, taking pictures of anything.

"Another question," Evan said, startling her slightly. "You said you asked these people to leave over and over. And they didn't. But you could have forced them to leave. As the legal owner of the property, it wouldn't have been hard at all. So why are they here?"

Roseanna sighed again. It seemed to be a pattern setting up. One of many.

"They thought I'd found something really special here. And I thought so, too. And I didn't feel right depriving anybody else of it. Just in case it turned out we were right."

Chapter Two

The Fresh Egg Arbitration Department

Roseanna had finished her morning chores and stepped back into her house for another breakfast when the first knock came at her door.

It was nine days after the reporter had come and gotten her story. She knew because she'd been secretly counting—inwardly wondering how long it takes a thing like that to come together. Partly dreading publication and partly looking forward to reading it. But mostly dreading it.

She threw her front door wide.

Nelson was standing on her porch, hat in hand. His face, his eyes, his very aura were filled to overflowing with roiling aggravation.

"Melanie collected three eggs out of the field this morning, miss, and I just know they were mine. I'm really convinced this time. I've been paying extra attention to who lays what and where they lay it."

Roseanna sighed and worked very hard to keep her eyes from rolling.

"Nelson. We've been through this before."

"I know you say you don't want to get in the middle. But we don't seem to be able to work this out on our own."

"Well, you're just going to have to. Maybe go into town and get some chicken wire and build a run for yours?"

"Free range is very important, miss."

"Free range is a whole entirely different thing, Nelson. Free range is a counterreaction to chickens in tiny nesting boxes, being forced to lay eggs without ever being able to see the sun or turn around. It doesn't mean the chicken has to be able to run indefinitely without hitting a fence. Trust me on this, Nelson. If you limit their pecking by, say, a couple hundred feet, they're just as free range as they always were. But that's not the important part of what I told you before when this came up. Here's what matters most: I am not the court of egg ownership. I am not King Solomon for the laying community. Do I look like the arbiter of eggs? Do something to work it out. Separate your birds somehow. Or feed them those dye packs the banks use on stolen money. Just, whatever you decide to do, keep it away from my house. Okay?"

Nelson frowned.

"Okay, miss," he said. "Sorry to bother you, I guess."

He turned and trotted off her porch and down the steps.

"You know I was kidding about the dye packs, right?" she called after him.

He waved a hand in the air without turning around.

• • •

It might have been two minutes later when the second knock came, or it might have been three or four. With no working clock in the house, it was hard for Roseanna to judge time. But clearly not much of it had elapsed.

She stomped to the door, deeply irked about having to spend one more minute of her morning talking about chickens. And somebody else's chickens at that.

"Damn it all to hell!" she spat, and threw the door wide, not knowing if she was cursing at Nelson or his nemesis, Melanie.

As it turned out, she was cursing at neither.

Standing on her doorstep, fist raised to knock a second time, was her thirty-year-old son, Lance. Under his arm he held a folded section of newspaper, which she could only guess was the *New York Times*.

"Lance," she said. Which was an unimaginative thing to say. But in the moment, it was all she had. Then, without thinking, she added, "That reporter fellow swore he wouldn't give my exact location."

The little girl and the dog had apparently followed him almost to her door. They were standing uncharacteristically still behind him, just in front of the porch steps. The girl broke her pose, ran up onto the porch, and tugged at Lance's sleeve.

"Who are you?" she asked in her screechy, windup-toy voice.

Lance didn't answer. He looked to Roseanna, who craned her neck to look up into his face. Lance was very tall.

"Why is there a child tugging at my sleeve?" he asked.

"Probably because she wants to know who you are."

Lance sighed. He looked down at the girl with an exaggerated tucking of his cleft chin.

"I'm her son," he said, and pointed at Roseanna, which caused him to drop the newspaper on her porch.

The little girl scooped it up and handed it back to him.

"Her *son?*" She sounded astonished. As if she'd just been told this tall, solid man was Roseanna's alligator or her jet plane.

"Yes, yes, her son. Why is that so hard to believe?"

"You're too big to be a son."

"Sons can be any size they want. Sons get bigger and bigger and turn into grownups, but you still call them your son."

For a second or two the girl continued to gaze up at him in wonder. Roseanna did not interfere with their delicate negotiation, figuring they would work it out between themselves.

Then the little girl's spell seemed to break suddenly.

"Oh," she said, and ran down off the porch to

rejoin the dog, who had been patiently waiting for her to return.

Lance watched her go.

Then he turned back to Roseanna, his eyes on fire with accusation and resentment.

"You have a *dog?*" Apparently this was the first he'd seen of the dog. On the final word, his voice came up to a full-throated shout.

The little girl moved to the bottom of the stairs again to see what the fuss was about.

Roseanna opened her mouth to answer him, but the girl beat her to it.

"You don't like dogs?" she asked Lance, clear in her tone that such a situation could not possibly exist in her fabulous world.

"I love dogs," Lance said.

The girl extended her arms into a cartoonishly expansive shrug. "Then why is that bad?"

Lance turned back to his mother again. She could tell by his face that he had been careful to bring a certain amount of composure to her door, and that he was quickly reaching the end of that supply.

"You should probably come in," she said.

"You have a dog?" he asked again as she handed him a freshly brewed cup of coffee.

He was sitting on her couch. There was no kitchen table. Nowhere else to sit. He seemed calmer now, but no less aggrieved.

"I wouldn't say that, exactly."

"Oh. I see. That wasn't a dog. My mistake. Hippo? Bird of some sort?"

Roseanna smiled a crooked smile and sat near him on the couch with her own coffee. He had learned that type of sarcastic riff from her, and she knew it.

"I concede that it's a dog. I'm only suggesting that your assessment that I 'have him' might be going too far. Might be more like him having me."

"Always the attorney," he said, and took a sip. "Oh. This is good."

"Why do you sound so surprised?"

"I don't know." He looked around the room. Up over his head. As if the very environment, the very atmosphere of the room were poison. "Just that everything here is so . . ."

He never went on to say what it was. Then again, he didn't need to.

"It may surprise you to hear that good coffee made in shabby locations still tastes like good coffee."

Lance rubbed his eyes before answering. As if all this could have been a bad dream. "I didn't mean it like that."

"How did you mean it?"

"I'm going to change the subject here, Mom. A minute ago I was standing on your porch, and you opened the door, and what did you say to

36

me? 'The reporter swore he wouldn't give my exact location.' Like you didn't want to be found and were sorry to see me standing there."

"Well, of course I didn't want to be found. We've talked three times on the phone since I was here, and you asked me where I was every time and every time I avoided telling you. I mean, take a hint, honey. But I certainly didn't mean to sound like I was sorry to see you. I'm always happy to see you."

"Wow," Lance said, and sipped again. "That's got to be the mixed message of the century."

"You're right. I'm sorry. Let me clarify by asking you a question. What was your goal in driving out here this morning?"

Lance sat back on her couch for the first time. Sighed. "To talk you into coming home."

"And *that* is why I didn't want him to give my location."

He closed his eyes briefly. Offered a sad little smile. "Right. Got it. Have you seen this yet?"

He held the section of newspaper in her direction.

"No. And I'd like to."

She took it from him. Glanced at the photos of the iron giraffe and lion.

"He didn't give your *exact* location. Just said it was in Chudley."

Roseanna laughed a strange, snorting laugh that surprised and embarrassed her. "Honey, only

37

about three hundred people live in Chudley. And most don't have iron zoos. So I would say that's damn well exact enough. Wouldn't you?"

"Well, I'm here," Lance said.

They were lying on the scuffed and worn-down hardwood floor in broad daylight, each covered with a light blanket, their elbows about two feet apart. They were staring at the ceiling and not napping.

It was an old ritual. When Lance had been little, he'd resisted going down for naps so violently that Roseanna had taken to lying down on the floor with him and joining him in the process.

"So, Mom," he said, breaking several minutes of fairly comfortable silence, considering the circumstances. "What were you thinking?"

"Did you read the article or didn't you? Because I went into my reasoning in that interview."

"I guess I was hoping . . . you know, being your son and all . . . that I might get a more personal version of events. In-depth, you know? Something not available to tens of thousands of subscribers."

"Yeah, I see where you're coming from on that."

"This is about Alice, isn't it?"

"Maybe partly. I won't pretend that didn't factor in."

"How could you get a dog now, after I'm

grown? How many times did I beg you for a dog?"

"Two hundred and nineteen."

"You didn't seriously count."

"No. I'm estimating. But it's somewhere right around in there. Look. Honey. I didn't ask for him any more than I asked for all these human squatters. He just showed up. Living in the city . . . back when you wanted one . . . a dog would have needed to be walked three or four times a day—"

"I told you I would do that!"

"Lance. Sweetheart. With all due respect, sons have been telling mothers that since the beginning of recorded history."

"You never gave me a chance to prove I would have been different."

"Or I never gave you the chance to find out you were more like other boys than you thought you were."

"I'm going out to meet this dog," he said.

He threw off his blanket, rose, and strode to the door. Lance had a way of covering a great deal of ground in just a few steps. Which made her new house a very small place for him indeed.

One hand on the antique copper knob, he turned briefly back to her.

"If you don't want these people here," he said, "you don't have to have them. Tell them to move along."

"I'm thinking it'll be better if they figure out a new direction on their own. The problem will solve itself."

"How can you be so sure?"

"Except for the mom and the little girl, they live in tents. The first good freeze should clear this place out nicely."

While he was gone, Roseanna had more than enough time to cook and eat that second breakfast.

Then she stepped out of her house in search of him, worried that he might have driven away without saying goodbye.

She found him in the iron zoo, being towed around by the little girl. The girl had one of his hands in both of hers, and was putting her whole weight, her whole body, and apparently a great deal of her spirit into pulling him desperately from one animal to the next.

Roseanna watched, smiling to herself.

She couldn't hear what the little girl was saying, but she seemed to be in full-on tour guide mode, pointing up at the second animal she and Roseanna had ever created together, and saying quite a bit about it.

Roseanna figured she was telling Lance it was a "hippobottomus." She knew the right word for the animal, that little girl. She had been corrected a dozen times. But she seemed to like it better her own way. The sculpture had a huge, round posterior made from a couple of antique tractor wheels. So it was not a bad joke. For a five-year-old.

She moved closer to hear what the little tour guide had to say.

But when Lance saw Roseanna standing nearby he turned to her with a look in his eyes that felt positively scorching.

He stomped back to the house without a word spoken.

"What's wrong with him?" the girl asked.

"Not sure. He might still be mad about the dog."

"How can he be mad about a dog if he loves dogs?"

"Because he wanted one for himself."

"He should just go get one, then. They're all over the place."

"Good thinking," Roseanna said. "I'll go tell him we say so."

She found him sitting on the edge of the unrailed porch, his long legs dangling. Swinging them back and forth like a very big little boy.

"What did I do *this* time?" she asked, walking up onto her porch and settling on the spongy boards behind him. She leaned on his back. She thought—feared—he would pull away. He didn't.

"You babysit that little girl?"

"Did she tell you that?"

41

"Yes. If you must know. I asked her where her mom was. She said she was at work. I said, 'So who looks after you?' She said sometimes Melanie and sometimes Martin but usually you."

"And this is bad because . . ."

"Oh, come on, Mom. You're a smart lady."

"Not smart enough for this one, apparently."

"You don't even like kids."

"No. That's true. I don't. I find them immature."

"I was raised by a nanny because you couldn't find the time."

"Ah. I see. All sorts of stuff is coming up and out today."

"I'm going home now," he said, and pushed off the porch.

He landed on his feet in the dirt of her yard, and she nearly fell off after him, but she caught herself. He raced to catch her out of reflex, but by then there was no need.

"Think about what you're saying," she called to him as he turned to stamp away.

He turned again. Stamped back. It was amazing how much he reverted to his childhood self when he was angry. And how cowed she felt by his anger.

"Fine. You tell me," he said. "What am I saying?"

She worked to cover her own intimidation. Not let it show in her voice. "That you're mad because we don't spend enough time together."

"Right."

"So you're cutting this visit short."

Lance stood still a moment, blinking into the sun. As if recently wakened from a deep sleep. Then he dropped his head into his hands. When he lifted it again, Roseanna saw that he was laughing. Which seemed like a damned good start.

He walked over and leaned against the porch, quite near her, and she draped an arm over his shoulder and felt her tension drain away.

"Look," she said. "I get it. I was not mother of the year during any of the eighteen years I raised you. I'll be the first to admit that I probably shouldn't even have tried to be a mother. I'm glad I've got you, kid. I'll never regret that. But it wasn't really fair to you. And I'm sorry for that. I genuinely am."

They fell silent for a moment. A hen skittered by close to Lance's feet, and he brushed it away with the toe of his shoe, as if it frightened him. Which seemed odd.

"I sense a 'but' coming," he said.

"*But* . . . my darling boy . . . we're not dead yet."

"Meaning?"

"Meaning if you want a better relationship with me, here I am."

"Yeah. Here you are. That's exactly the problem. If you were in the city we could spend some quality time. You know. Even though we never did before."

"If I was in the city, I'd be the same person I'd always been, and we wouldn't have a chance to do something new. You want to spend time with me, spend time. You want a better relationship? We'll make one from scratch. Right here, right now, buddy boy. Stay."

"Stay?"

"Yeah. Stay. You know the word? Even most dogs know it."

"Don't even mention dogs."

"And that's another thing. You're thirty years old. You want a dog? Stop complaining and go get one. Hell, even the five-year-old suggested that."

"But I'm gone all day. I work."

"So?"

"It's not fair to the dog."

"Oh, that's bull. Go pull one out of the pound. Get one who's on his last day before they take him to that room at the end of the hall. Ask him if he'd rather go into that room and never come out, or go home with you and have to wait for you to come back from work before he collects his loving. Small price to pay for being literally saved."

Lance didn't answer for a long time. Just stared off over the hills.

When he did speak, dogs seemed to have left his mind completely.

"I can't stay here. I have the business."

"Darren and Annie couldn't manage it while you take a little sabbatical?"

Another long silence.

"Maybe," he said. "I'm not sure."

"You're not sure they can manage it? Or you're not sure you can let them?"

"I hate it when you do that."

"What? Guess correctly?"

"Pretty much. Yeah. Okay, I see your point, Mom. I do. And it's only a few hours from the city. So I'll come around more often. And we'll figure out how to be two adults together. Maybe. We'll have a go at it, anyway."

"That wasn't really the request. But I suppose I'll take it."

"I can't *stay*."

"Why can't you?"

"Because I have a life."

"People take little vacations from their lives all the time."

He peered around at the house, his eyes narrowing. Whether it was a reaction to the sun in his eyes or the sight of the house itself was hard to say.

"Any good four-star hotels nearby?"

"If by 'nearby' you mean New York City . . ."

"I love the idea of it. And thank you for offering. It means a lot to me that you would want that. But I have to go home."

• • •

They sat cross-legged on her porch boards, facing each other, each holding a hand of playing cards. They were playing gin, just like in the old days. Except in the old days he had been easy to beat.

"So you have playing cards," he said, squinting as he gazed into the distance, waiting for her to decide what to discard.

"That's a bit of a memo from the Department of Duh. Don't you think?"

"I meant . . . in that article you were talking about only having what you need to get by."

"To live a decent life, I think I said."

"So no decent life without playing cards?"

"You know I like to play solitaire when I'm thinking. But, anyway, you're missing the point, honey. My point was that I wasn't going to spend the lion's share of my life savings building a dream home that I could live without. And also that I wasn't going to work hard all day at a job I hated just to be able to afford more stuff I don't need. I honestly think a person can make her way through the world with a deck of playing cards and still be traveling fairly light. Don't you?"

She pulled a card off the stack. Then she frowned at her hand of cards for a moment and discarded a five.

"I didn't know you hated your work," he said.

"Of course I hated it. Who wouldn't?"

"Then why did you do it all those years?"

"Now that, my son, is a question for the ages. It's more or less what I came out here to try to answer. Why do we do work we hate all our lives? Somewhere earlier on the road somebody must have made us feel that we didn't have an option to do otherwise. I'm sure it gets psychologically complex."

"Gin," he said, and laid his cards faceup on the rotted boards. The wind nearly took them away.

Roseanna held them down with one hand and examined them. Not because she thought he could not be trusted. It was just what you did. It's how the game was played.

"Damn," she said. "I used to be able to beat you ninety-nine percent of the time. We'd play game after game after game, and I can only remember you winning maybe two times."

"I was a kid. What did you expect?"

He gathered up the cards, shuffled, and began to deal again.

"Hey, wait," she said.

His hands stopped moving.

"No, I didn't mean literally wait and don't deal."

"Oh," he said, and began tossing cards again. "What, then?"

"If we played all those hundreds of hands of gin, how could we never have spent any time together?"

"I didn't mean we never spent any time together. I didn't say that."

She picked up her hand of cards and arranged them. It was a lousy hand but she tried not to let on.

"What did you mean, then?"

Lance sighed. For a few moments he stared at his hand without speaking.

Then he said, "I guess I felt unwelcome. Like you'd rather live alone."

"Oh, there's no doubt I would rather have lived alone. Still would. That's just me, darling. I was hoping you wouldn't take it personally."

"I didn't."

"Then what's the problem?"

"Today I do. That's the problem." They stared at each other for a moment. Then he cut his eyes away. "All my life I've been thinking, well, that's just my mom. It's just how she's always been. She hates dogs and people and she just wants to be by herself."

"I don't hate dogs," she interjected. It was half a joke and half just a simple statement of fact.

He went on as if he hadn't noticed. "And then I get out here, and you have a dog. And you're letting all these people live with you. And I guess I wonder why they rate if I never did."

"Oh, honey. You rated. Besides, I can't stand all these people. I'm just waiting for them to go away and leave me alone. And I tried to get you

48

to stay, too, but you weren't having any of it."

"Great," he said. "You keep it a secret where you are, and then when I finally find you, you're living with six people, a kid, and a dog. And the offer is that I get to be the ninth if I want."

"It's five people, a kid, and a dog. You could be the eighth if you wanted. Isn't that better?"

Unfortunately, Lance did not smile.

"You had a chance to live any kind of life you wanted, Mom. You got to choose all over again. And now it seems like everything you said you wanted wasn't true. You even have a kid here. And you babysit. And I'm sorry, but it makes me jealous. I've been walking around here all day feeling jealous. Does that make me a terrible person? I mean, is that really petty?"

"Well, that's not my call to make, baby. It either is or it isn't, but whatever it is, it's the way you feel. You can put any kind of judgment you want on the way you feel, but that won't make it go away. Unfortunately you can't insult your feelings out of existence. Trust me. People try all the time. If it worked, we'd know about it by now."

He drew a card, discarded, and laid his hand down faceup again.

"Gin," he said.

"You have *got* to be kidding me. You draw one card and you have gin?"

"What can I say? I'm lucky in some games and unlucky in others."

49

She did not attempt to delve more deeply into his veiled sarcasm.

It was nearly eight in the evening, with a view of the sun just touching the western hills through her living room windows, when she voiced her opinion that it was too late for him to drive all the way back to the city.

"Just stay one night," she said.

"Where?" he asked, looking around her little house.

"My couch. Or there's a motel in Walkerville."

"Hmm," he said, as though it were a truly momentous decision, and one best not entered into lightly. "Is the motel in Walkerville better than what I'm seeing around me right here?"

"Not a great deal, no. And there's no mother to talk to while you're trying to fall asleep."

"Sold," Lance said. "I'll take the couch. But then in the morning I have to go."

"That's fair enough."

"I have to make a call," he said, standing up from her couch and digging his phone out of his jeans pocket. He tapped it a few times and then stared at it closely, frowning.

"You can get reception," she said. "Just not right here in the house."

"Oh. Thank goodness. Because I have to call . . . someone."

Roseanna pulled herself up off the couch and

walked with him. Out the door and onto the porch, where the orangey light of sunset turned this whole arena of farmland and raw nature into a spectacle. It was a sight that made her suck in her breath and thank whatever had created her for the chance to stand here and see it unfold. It happened that way every night.

"You might not like this part," she said, pointing at the big hill down the road. "That's CPR Hill. You have to go to the top of it. There's a little scrambling involved here and there."

Lance just stood beside her on the porch and stared.

"You'd best get a move on," she said. "It's not one of those trips you want to make in the dark, believe me."

"And you call it CPR Hill because . . ."

"It stands for cell phone reception."

"Ah. Got it. Good. That's a little less terrifying than what I was thinking."

It was pitch-dark by the time he came back in. Roseanna was in bed but awake. It was strangely comforting to hear her son come through the door. It was a connection to the one part of her past she was not inclined to discard.

She had left a candle burning on the steamer trunk coffee table. To guide his way in.

"I left you a pillow and some blankets on the couch," she said.

"I see that. Thanks."

"Everything okay at home?"

"Yeah. It is. Sorry I was away so long."

An extended silence. Roseanna could see, by candlelight, Lance stripping down to his boxer shorts and climbing under the blankets. He leaned over and puffed out the candle.

"You trying to sleep?" he asked.

"Not necessarily. Why?"

"It's barely nine o'clock."

"I know. When you live out in the middle of nowhere like this, you tend to rise and set with the sun."

"I'm not sure if I can go to sleep this early."

"We could talk."

But then for a strange length of time they didn't.

"See, this is the problem with getting to know each other better," he said. "It's not that I don't want to. I just never know where to start."

"Here's a possible starting point," Roseanna said, and pulled a big, deep breath before continuing.

A tightening in her chest almost stopped her. It was a foreign feeling, to be so afraid of words addressed to her own son. And, in another very real way, familiar. She had stood at this threshold many times, and each time she had let that clench of fear stop her. Turn her around, steering back into simpler territory. This time she felt like maybe she would keep going.

"You're thirty years old. Any time now you

could say, 'By the way, Mom. I happen to be gay. And my significant other's name is Blank. And he's a great guy for the following list of reasons. And maybe I could bring him around to meet you at some point.' "

Another long silence. Though, oddly, she noted it did not feel uncomfortable. There was no tension in the room that she could feel. The energy was more like that of a soft sigh.

"And you've known about this for how long?" Lance asked after a time.

"Since you were four."

"What did I do when I was four? That was so telling?"

"You didn't *do* anything, honey, you just were. It's just what you were. I'm not going to say something hopelessly stereotypical. You didn't play with dolls or listen to show tunes. It was just part of who you were. I can't explain it any better than that."

"Did it bother you?"

"Not at the time, no. Later it bothered me. Because I kept waiting for you to take me into your confidence and you never did."

Roseanna stared out the window at the moon. It was a mere sliver, hanging in the sky over CPR Hill. It seemed to be listening. Which was a silly thing to think, and she knew it. But it felt that way. And it wasn't just the moon, either. This was a moment between a mother and a son, two people who could find each other belatedly or blow their chance yet again—maybe forever this time. And in that important moment Roseanna felt an odd sensation, as if the whole universe understood the significance and was holding still, anxious to see how things would turn out.

He still wasn't answering.

So she added, "I just really hope you don't think I'm such a blockhead that you can't share a thing like that with me."

"No," he said. His voice was soft. It sounded aware of the gravity of the moment, like the moon and the rest of the universe. "No, I didn't think that. I just . . . I guess I just felt like it was . . . fairly . . . personal. And it didn't seem like . . . I mean, we didn't have much of a precedent for getting that personal with each other. Really, when did we ever talk about private things?"

Roseanna's brain and belly tingled as she let the question soak in. She didn't answer, because no answer would come.

"Wow," Lance said. "We really are in trouble, aren't we?"

Still Roseanna had no answer. She tried, but it was too much to sort through. She might have one. Eventually. But it had been a long and trying day, so she accidentally fell asleep instead.

When she woke in the morning, Lance was sitting on the end of her bed, in boxer shorts and a

T-shirt, staring out the bedroom window at more or less nothing. His shoulders slumped under the weight of whatever concerns had brought him into her room.

"Okay," he said quietly. "Okay."

"Okay what?"

"Okay I'll stay. I'll go home this morning and grab some things and make some arrangements, and then I'll come back and we'll figure our stuff out."

She sat straight up in bed. "Really? For how long?"

"Oh, I don't know. As long as I have to, I guess. Until we dig out of this mess we've gotten ourselves into. Or until I can't stand it any longer. Whichever comes first."

And in that moment Roseanna felt . . . well, contradictory emotions. She felt elated at the idea of another chance with her son, and touched that he cared enough to upend his life in the effort. Around and underneath all that, a voice suspiciously like her own was saying, *Great. One more squatter. And this one will be living in the house.*

And before that moment had even faded there came yet another knock at her door. It seemed rather astonishing in Roseanna's overloaded brain.

"Want me to get that?" Lance asked.

"Sure. If it's anybody who wants to talk about

the ownership of eggs, tell them to hit the road."

"Eggs. Got it."

He strode to the door, still in just boxers and a T-shirt, and swung it wide.

Roseanna sat up in bed and saw the one person in the world she least wanted to see on her doorstep. It was Jerry, the only senior partner in her old firm now that she and Alice were both gone.

"Hey, Jerry," Lance said, as if it were not an utter disaster to find Jerry on the porch.

But then, to Lance, maybe it wasn't.

"Lance," Jerry said. A bit cautiously. As though that might or might not be Lance's name. "You swore you didn't know where she was."

"I didn't," Lance said. He was either calm or doing a great imitation. "I found out the same way you did."

He pointed to the newspaper dangling from Jerry's hand.

"Is she here?"

"I'm not even decent yet," Roseanna bellowed from under the covers. "Holy crap, Jerry. What did you do? Drive out of the city at three o'clock in the morning?"

"I'll just give you a minute, then," Jerry called in to her.

"Should I ask him in, Mom?"

"No," she said. "You should treat him like a person complaining about eggs."

"Eggs?" she heard Jerry ask, in that irritating tone of his. The one that made your subject sound like cartoon fiction, and belittled you for merely discussing it.

Roseanna sighed and tossed the covers back. She grabbed her robe off the hook and threw it on, stomping to the door.

"I *knew* better than to talk to that Maxwell guy," she muttered to herself as she stomped. "Stupid, stupid, stupid." Then, to Lance, "I've got this, honey."

Lance peeled away and Roseanna faced the trouble head-on.

Jerry was wearing his glasses halfway down his nose. He looked as if he hadn't combed his hair in days, which was unlike him. He wore a camel-hair coat on a nearly sixty-degree morning.

"I'm not coming back," she said.

"Well, that's going to get awkward."

"Yeah, for you."

"No, for you, Roseanna. Look. Consider this a courtesy call. Twelve years we worked together. I could have just served your attorneys and let them pass the papers on to you, but it seemed too cold. So, yes, I left at three in the morning to see if I couldn't find you based on this article. I wanted you to hear it from me first. I wanted to give you another chance. I know it threw you, what happened with Alice. It threw all of us. But life is still life, and it goes on. You're in breach of more than one contract with us, and I know you know it."

"Right. That's why I have attorneys now, to sort all that out. Come to some agreement that satisfies all involved."

"It's not nearly enough," he said. "What they're offering." He had dropped into a tone that she had only heard him use with the opposition. A deepening of his voice. A threatening edge. "You need to come back and fulfill your commitments. If you don't, we'll be taking you to court for most or all of the money you think you're going to live on for the rest of this"—he backed up a step, gazed up at her house—"fantasy life of yours. I wanted to give you the respect of telling you this myself. We're colleagues. I even thought we were friends."

"Really? Because I never got that." There was some nervousness. She could only just barely feel it, but it was there. It was tucked deep in her lower intestines. She tended to keep things rattling around down there until she was more pre-pared to deal with them. "But really, I'm moved. It's always very sweet when an old friend chooses the personal touch when they sue you."

Jerry shook his head slowly. Took off his glasses and rubbed his eye with the back of one hairy hand. "I'm doing my best here, Roseanna. But you don't answer my calls or texts. You don't call in. I don't know what attitude you expect me to take."

"Look," she said, "I'd invite you in, but . . . I just really don't like you anymore. I never liked you a great deal, and now your stock has taken a hit with me, so . . . drive carefully."

She swung the door shut. She leaned on it for a minute or so, poking at the feeling deep in her gut. Making sure she could trust it to stay put.

When she turned around, Lance was sitting on the couch staring at her. The fear in his eyes made her own fear jump up into the base of her throat.

"Can he really cause all that trouble?"

"Oh, attorneys can always cause trouble if they get it in their head to. He can bury me in legal fees if nothing else. Coffee?"

"Please."

She moved into the kitchen to make some.

"Whatever," she said, running water for the coffeemaker. "Doesn't matter. I own this place free and clear. If I have to live on nothing, then I'll live on nothing. I'll grow vegetables and eat eggs. Nothing he does can make me go back."

"Can he take this property?"

"Yes," she said, and stopped moving, the coffee forgotten. "Possibly. But I'm trying not to think about that right now."

THE MOVE

Chapter Three

The Little Bird That Changed Everything

The alarm shrieked. Roseanna woke up.

What choice did she have, really, what with all that shrieking?

She slapped the top of the clock, which silenced it. Then, as she did every weekday morning, she formed her thumb and index finger into a revolver, took aim at the offending machine, and fired. She even imitated the kick of the weapon, and pursed her lips to blow away imaginary gunpowder smoke.

As it had done every morning for the last three decades or so, the alarm clock survived the mock execution.

She had tried a gentler, quieter alarm clock, but it had served poorly. Nothing short of a shriek could pull her from her dreams.

Roseanna sat up in bed, silently nursing the discomfort of her need to ignore the day coupled with her obvious inability to do so.

She gazed out her bedroom window—the one that looked over Central Park East—with a wistful sort of energy. She was lost in her head, and at first did not see much of anything. But then something caught her eye.

63

She saw the little bird that changed everything.

She had no idea what variety of bird it was. Nor, really, did she care. It wasn't a big, ungainly pigeon of the sort one normally sees in the city. It must have been some small feathered thing that lived in the park. Her late friend Alice would have called it a "little brown jobber" as part of Alice's habit of labeling various things whose labels were unknown to her.

Why it had crossed Central Park East to peck around on her windowsill, Roseanna would never know.

This she did know: for just a split second, she considered the world from the point of view of a small, brown, unremarkable bird. The feeling that came up—no, it did more than come up; it flooded her, overwhelmed her senses—was one of undeniable envy.

A bird did not carry the weight of . . . well, anything. With the possible exception of finding food and avoiding miscellaneous predators, its day was free. Its life was free. It was not crushed by the responsibility of other people's losses. It was not required to pore over law books or take meetings or mollify angry clients. Had anyone tried to force such burdens on it, it would simply fly away.

It could fly away.

Roseanna rose and shrugged on a robe.

She tucked her smartphone between her ear and shoulder and carried it into the kitchen, telling it, as she did, to ring her office. While it rang, she poured a cup of the lifesaving coffee that had brewed on a timer.

Her secretary answered.

"Roseanna Chaldecott's office," Nita said, her wispy little voice official and cordial as always.

"It's me. I need you to do something for me."

"Anything. What can I do?"

"Tell the others I'm not coming in."

A brief silence fell on both ends of the telephone line. Well, the wireless line, if such a thing can be said to exist.

"Oh dear. Are you sick?"

Roseanna sighed. "I started to say I was. I was going to say that. But why am I lying to my own firm? It's not like I'm subordinate to anybody. Call it a mental health leave. Just be honest and tell them that."

"That's good," Nita said. "You *should* take some time."

"Excuse me?"

It was unlike Nita to editorialize or otherwise inject herself into their brief conversations. So, when called on it, Nita clammed up immediately.

While Roseanna waited for Nita to get her act together, she split a bagel and popped one half into the toaster.

"I just think that's something we all support you on," Nita said after a time. A trifle sputtery. "It's something that's come up. Not that it's my place to tell you this. But ever since Ms. Cummings . . . you know. Since we lost her . . . It just seems like some time off might do you good. I hope you don't mind my saying so."

Roseanna did, just a little. But she knew she probably shouldn't. And she knew the slightly ruffled feeling would shake out over time.

So she only said, "I suppose I don't."

"I'm not sure a day will do it, though," Nita added.

"I'm not sure it will only be a day."

It was something Roseanna had not known until the moment she heard herself say it. Then again, it was so obvious—something that would have been so easy to know, had she been paying attention. If only she'd had a few more sips of coffee and a couple more minutes to wake up.

"So . . . ," Nita began. Then she paused, as though praying not to have to ask more.

"Yes," Roseanna said. "So. As in, 'It is so.' "

"What would you like me to tell them as far as . . . *time duration?*"

"I would go with the fact that you don't know. Since you don't."

"Okay," Nita said. "Got it." But she sounded as though she didn't want what she got.

Roseanna clicked off the call before Nita could ask any more questions.

She popped the toaster mechanism up, took the cream cheese out of the fridge, and smeared the tiniest layer of the white heaven onto the toasted surface of her bagel half. It was a layer so thin that one would have to be standing fairly near the bagel to notice it.

She carried the scant breakfast into her bedroom, took a bite, and stared out over the park. It was a dreary day outside. A rainy spring day that made the street shiny, yet at the same time made the rest of the world dull and gray.

The bird was gone. Flown away, which is what she had found so remarkable about it in the first place—that enviable ability. But its little feathered being had not been forgotten.

Roseanna pictured it briefly.

Then she walked into the kitchen, fetched the cream cheese again, whacked off a good quarter of the brick with a butter knife, and spread it on the rest of her bagel. Or maybe "flattened slightly" would have been a more apt description. It sat on her breakfast easily an inch thick in most places.

Roseanna took a rudely massive bite, closed her eyes, and sighed.

She could have taken the Lincoln Tunnel. Or the Holland Tunnel. She didn't.

She had never liked tunnels under bodies of water. They felt dank and claustrophobic and vaguely dangerous. She just had never really focused on the feeling before.

Besides, a tunnel wasn't scenic enough. And she was enjoying driving her Maserati through the rain—the shushing of the tires on wet pavement, the swish of windshield wipers. The sound of the heavy drops as they drummed on the roof.

She drove many miles out of her way to the George Washington Bridge.

Then again, what exactly was "out of her way"? She had no clear idea where she wanted to go. The "way" was wherever she decided it should be.

There was plenty of traffic on the bridge, but not in her direction. Cars were pouring into the city, not out of it.

Roseanna powered her driver's window down, even though it spattered her with rain to do so. She didn't mind getting wet. It was refreshing. It was counterintuitive. In many ways, it was counter-adult, which appealed to her. Like a little girl who splashes joyfully in puddles before she grows up to be sober and mature and decides it's more reasonable to walk around them. Fewer laundry bills. Less drying time.

When had she begun making bargains with life to avoid extra trouble, and, with it, any joy whatsoever?

She turned up the volume on the stereo and clicked through to her favorite track on her favorite CD, the "Flower Duet" from *Lakmé*.

Bumped the volume up again to a virtual blast. She leaned her head back against the rest and allowed the rain and the music to enter her gut and change her. She almost closed her eyes, but that would not have been wise. But it was a struggle to override the tendency. She looked up at the sweeping cables, arching down and then back up again to the towers. She looked at a rainy Manhattan in her droplet-spattered side-view mirror.

Roseanna looked at the faces of the city-bound drivers as she zipped by, squinting her eyes against the rain.

They looked . . . well, maybe they didn't look like anything different or special. Maybe Roseanna was not even close enough to tell. But in her head, they looked like her. Like the way she pictured herself, based on the overriding feeling in her gut. Or, at least, the one she had just shaken off.

Still feeling somewhat childlike, she cupped one hand around her mouth to yell something at them. Something they were too far away to hear, and that the rain and the road noise would have swept away in any case.

For a brief moment, Roseanna thought it would be a taunt.

Suckers!

But no such word came out of her. Because she felt sorry for them. She empathized. How could she not? She knew exactly how it felt to be them. She always had. She only just now, in that very moment, understood how to be anything else.

"I'm sorry!" she shouted into the rain, vaguely aimed at traffic on the other side of the bridge. "I'm sorry our lives didn't turn out the way we wanted!"

The words faded into nothing. Went nowhere.

Roseanna stopped at a café in rural New Jersey. Because it struck her suddenly that she could. She could eat a meal that was utterly unscheduled. Having already eaten breakfast, she could eat another breakfast. She could do anything it came into her head to do, no matter how utterly it defied the rules she had lived by all her life.

She parked the Maserati in the nearly empty parking lot, close to the diner's door. When she stepped out, she could barely feel the rain. It had slowed to a light mist—the kind that builds up fast on your windshield at sixty miles per hour, but, when you're standing still, barely registers at all.

She stuck her head through the door.

A tall, solid woman in a tan waitress's uniform leaned on the counter, staring through the front picture window into nothing. There was not much in this corner of New Jersey to see. She was about Roseanna's age. Fiftysomething.

There were no other diners in the place.

"You open?" Roseanna asked.

The woman pulled her attention around to Rose-anna slowly. As if much effort were required.

"Yeah," she said. "Of course."

Roseanna walked to the counter and sat.

"This is going to sound like a rude question. I hope you won't take offense."

She could see the waitress retreat into herself. She watched it happen in the woman's eyes.

Her name tag said "Rosie." Which was interesting. And odd. And maybe even meaningful. As if something or someone were leaving a breadcrumb trail along Roseanna's path.

"I think I've heard them all," Rosie the waitress said.

"Is the food here good by any objective standard?"

"Yeah. We make a decent breakfast and lunch. Our customers like us. We're popular."

Roseanna looked around the diner, as though she might see some patrons she had previously overlooked. "So where is everybody?"

"This is a working-class neighborhood. They clear out in time to get to work at nine. Unless they go to work at seven. And they don't get off for lunch until noon. Then there can be a line out the door."

"Got it," Roseanna said, and picked up a menu.

"But I guess not everybody needs to get in to work in the morning."

Roseanna looked up from her menu to see the

waitress staring through the glass door at her Maserati.

"Oh, I wouldn't say that. I'm supposed to be at the office right now like everybody else."

"Something tells me your office is not like everybody else's," Rosie said, still staring at the car.

"Be that as it may," Roseanna said, her eyes still fixed on the breakfast options, "I work. Or, at least, I did. After this I'm not so sure. I think I'm . . ." But then she paused, not sure she was willing to share much of her life with this stranger. Then again, she thought, why not? Why shouldn't she? In half an hour she would drive away and probably never stop in this part of the world again. What better person with whom to share information than someone about to be left behind forever? "I think I just ran away from home. I realize I'm a bit old for it. But I guess . . . you know. Better late than never. You still serving breakfast?"

The clock behind Rosie the waitress's carefully coiffed head claimed it was just after ten thirty.

"We serve breakfast all day."

"Good. I'll have the number three. Eggs over easy. Hash browns, not home fries. Rye toast. And can I get all bacon instead of two bacon and two sausage?"

"Sure. Whatever."

Rosie wrote down the order on a pad she'd

pulled from her apron pocket, with a pencil she'd pulled from behind her ear. Just like the waitresses do in movie diners in the old classic films. She tore the order off the pad, clipped it onto a hanging stainless steel wheel next to an infrared heat lamp, spun the wheel until the order faced the kitchen, and rang a bell by slapping her palm down on it.

Roseanna jumped slightly. It was sharp and cutting, that bell. It reminded her of her alarm clock, except that it finished startling her more quickly.

She realized for the first time that she was not alone in the diner with this waitress. She couldn't be. Someone was picking up her order and cooking her breakfast. Not that it mattered who all was in the building. It just caused her to shift her perceptions. Everything seemed more vivid somehow. More sharply defined. She felt strangely aware of her focus on everything.

Rosie the waitress pulled up a tray of bright red ketchup squeeze bottles and began to fill them, through a funnel, from an industrial-sized tub. "So what made you decide to run away from home?" she asked without looking up from her work.

"A little birdie told me to do it."

"Okay, never mind. I just thought you seemed like you wanted to say. Like maybe you seemed to want to bring it up. But it makes no difference to me. I just thought it was one of those moments. You know. Like bartenders have. People confide. I get that a lot. More than you would think."

A brief silence passed, and the rain let go again. All at once, battering the windows and the roof. It was so loud it sounded almost like hail. But it was rain in huge, weighty drops. Roseanna looked out at her car and watched the image of it turn muted, faded by the wet glass, as if it were melting. As if the whole world were melting.

"I had a best friend," she said. "Her name was Alice. Alice Cummings. I met her in law school. We went to law school together. And that was not anytime recently, let me tell you that. We were in our twenties. This was over twenty-five years ago. A quarter of a century. Hard to believe, but it's true. We'd been best friends that long."

A gust of wind threw rain against the window with a noisy slap, blotting out the world beyond the diner almost completely.

"So Alice, she was a worker. She was like me, only even more so. When we got out of law school we worked for a couple of firms not a mile apart in Manhattan. Then we started our own firm together. And we built it up into something, too. Took years, but we gave it everything we had and we made it work. I got married and had a kid. But not Alice. She just kept working. She never took vacations. For her, it was all about retiring. She believed you work your whole adult life, from college to retirement. You put away enough money to do it right—to retire in luxury. And then you enjoy life. You put off the fun of your life until after you retire, and then you bask in the fruits of all that labor."

Roseanna sat watching the rain in silence for a moment. Not going on with the story. Not sure she ever would. There had been no obligation to begin this story. There was no obligation to finish it. She was writing these new life rules as she went along.

"I can't help noticing you're talking about her in the past tense," Rosie the waitress said, wiping ketchup off her hands with a well-bleached white linen towel.

For a time, Roseanna didn't answer. But a minute or two later—which is a lot of silence when you're sitting in the middle of it—she heard herself say more. Even though she hadn't really planned to.

"A month and a couple of days ago we were in the Brandt meeting—sorry. An important client. Alice stands up at the end to shake this guy's hand, and down she goes. Like a sandbag. She just swayed for a second like she was drunk all of a sudden, then crashed. Hit her head on the edge of the conference table going down. But that wasn't the issue. It was a stroke. She'd had a massive stroke. Fifty-three years old. She was going to retire at fifty-five."

She looked up to see the waitress staring into her face now. Because of that, Roseanna looked away.

"She died on the spot?"

"No. Not exactly. She was alive when we got her to the hospital. But not much beyond that."

"Sorry," Rosie the waitress said, but it was a weak-sounding thing. A word that made it painfully clear, by its tone, that words could do nothing to fix this.

A plate of breakfast thumped down on the counter in front of Roseanna, at the end of Rosie's hand.

Oddly, she had not lost her appetite. Not at all. If anything, reliving the whole ordeal was making her hungrier. She dug in enthusiastically.

"You look like you haven't had a good meal for a while," the waitress said, watching her eat.

"You could say that."

"How long since you've really eaten?"

"*Really* eaten? About thirty years. That's how long ago I started dieting. And once you start dieting, if you really overdo it, and keep it up pretty steadily, it just ruins your whole metabolism. You get to a place where you have to eat like a bird to stay slim, and the more you do it, the more you have to do it."

Roseanna's eye itched suddenly. She reached to scratch carefully underneath the lower lid with one well-manicured fingernail. Then it struck her.

She was wearing no makeup. She could directly rub her eye. She placed the pad of one index finger on her eye and ran it back and forth, hard, until the itch was satisfied.

Freedom, she thought. *Freedom everywhere.*

She pitched back into her food. That other form of freedom. She broke the gooey orange yolk of an egg with a crust of rye toast and soaked up as much of that richness as she could before taking a bite.

"So, anyway," she said, "job number one in my new life: putting on weight. Who the hell cares? Who am I trying to impress? I want to eat. People eat. It's time for me to eat like everybody else."

As she stood at the cash register paying her check, she found herself staring at the waitress's name tag.

"That's an interesting coincidence," she said.

"What is?"

"Your name being Rosie and all."

"Your name is Rosie?"

"No."

"That's not much of a coincidence, then. Is it?"

"Well, it's close. My name is Roseanna. But I always insist on people saying it out. No nicknames. A couple of people have tried to call me Rose or Rosie. Never more than once, though. Not unless they want it to be the last word they ever say."

Rosie the waitress shot her a skeptical glance as she counted change into Roseanna's palm.

"So what you're saying is . . . you think I have a terrible name?"

"No. Not at all. It's a fine name. It's just . . . informal. It's a way of people saying they think they can treat you informally. View you as . . . familiar."

"Then I would say . . ." The waitress paused. Trailed off. As though she never planned to tell Roseanna what she would say. "Now that you've run away from home, you might want to think about a nickname."

"That might be a bridge too far," Roseanna said, almost without considering her words. Then, remembering the feeling of freedom everywhere, she added, "But I guess I could think about it."

On her way out the door, as she passed her well-cleaned plate, she left the waitress a fifty-dollar tip. On a nine-dollar breakfast.

Chapter Four

Why More People Don't
Run Away from Home

Roseanna stood beside her car, waiting. Looking around.

She had gotten off the main thoroughfare a good hundred miles back. Begun driving byways and smaller roads. In her head, she figured she would let herself be guided—that she would drive the Maserati until its tank of gas was exhausted. And when she could go no farther, well . . . somehow she had allowed herself to believe there would be significance to that place.

There was a problem, though. She had imagined a gas station nearby.

There did not seem to be one.

Roseanna looked around again, and began counting her problems. There were several. Focusing only on one had been wishful thinking.

She couldn't see much of anything. That felt like a problem. The rain had stopped, but she was in the hills, or maybe even the foothills. The Adirondacks were around here somewhere. Her spatial relationship to them was hard to gauge. But in place of the rain, her location was socked in with fog. Dense, white. Cold. A little frightening. She estimated her visibility to be something like twelve feet.

So Roseanna quite literally did not know where she was. Not only did she not know what to call it, or where to locate it on a map, she couldn't even visually assess it. She had no idea—if she drove forward, if she stepped off the road—what surrounded her. She could be standing at the edge of a thousand-foot drop-off and would not know. It made the little hairs stand up at the nape of her neck.

And there was another pressing problem. Yes, she had her phone. And her phone could pinpoint her location. It could advise her of the closest gas station. Call a tow truck or the auto club to bring her some gas. Except at the moment it could do none of those things. It was getting no reception.

Roseanna shivered in the gray for a moment longer, feeling as though the world had disappeared. The fog was so thick, and had nestled so tightly around her, that she had lost all visual bearings. There was no horizon. No sky. Even the point at which the road met the fog was nearly impossible to decipher.

Shaken, she decided to wait in the car.

Before she could even reach out for her door handle, a movement caught her eye. She jumped, thinking only of danger. Her first instinct was to plunge into the car and lock the doors. But she froze for a split second. And in that split second, the movement clarified itself.

It was not danger.

It was just two people. A couple. A young man and woman, maybe twenty, walking along the road, hand in hand, bundled up against the wet coolness. A shaggy brown dog danced ahead of them, along the road in her direction.

She felt saved.

"Excuse me!" she called.

The couple walked up to her and stood a few feet away.

"Car trouble?" the young man asked. He had a waterproof hood over his head, with the string drawn tightly to keep moisture out. He looked like a face floating on the road alone, independent of the rest of a body.

"I'm out of gas. Not completely out. I could start it up. But I think my range at this point is something like five miles or less."

"Oh, you won't find a gas station that close to here," the young woman said. She wore a rain hat with an absurdly wide brim. The wisps of dark brown hair surrounding her face drooped limply, saturated with fog moisture.

"Where am I?"

"You're in Chudley," the young man said.

"I don't know where that is."

"No," he said. "Unless you live around here, nobody really does."

"I'm not sure how to get out of here. I'm not getting any cell phone reception."

Both young people pointed ahead down the road and slightly right.

"There's a hill just a few hundred yards from here," the young woman said. "Hard to see in all this fog. But you'll see if you walk down the road a bit. We're just in a dip where we're standing. We have hills all around us here. But if you walk to the top of that hill, you'll get good reception. And you can call a tow truck to come bring you some gas."

"Okay," Roseanna said, thinking it did not feel okay.

They were about to walk on now. She could feel it. She could tell. She didn't want them to, but they clearly would. As if that tiny bit of information had set her up, and she'd do great on her own.

"We'll come by again on the way back," the young man said. "Make sure you got out okay."

"Thank you," Roseanna said.

It didn't feel like enough. But it would have to do. She would have appreciated an offer more like . . . well, maybe the couple taking her phone and running it to the top of the hill for her. Making that call. But what they had offered—to check on her situation on their way back—was a reasonable amount of help to offer a stranger.

Still, as they walked away, Roseanna felt strangely abandoned. Stranded.

As their backs disappeared into the white mist, she realized they likely had not intended to be rude or unhelpful. They had simply perceived Roseanna as a woman capable of solving her own problems. Someone who could walk her phone up a hill and make a call.

And really, she thought, *isn't that what you want to be? Don't you want them to be right?*

She sighed, and set off down the road in search of a hill that could not be seen with the naked eye.

"So this is why more people don't run away from home," Roseanna said. Out loud into the blank wall of fog.

She had found the hill in question, and was walking toward the top of it. But it was not as easy a task as it had sounded in the verbal instructions.

First of all, it was steep, which required a heart and lungs in good condition, which Roseanna did not possess. So she had to take only three or four steps at a time. Then she would stop. Lean forward, bracing her palms on her knees. Gasp for air. Take a few more steps.

Perhaps more of a problem was the mud. The rain had left the hill mucky and slippery. Roseanna was wearing sensible shoes, by Manhattan standards. Slip-on boat shoes of the sort that could be worn without socks. They even had a bit of tread on their rubber soles. But it didn't help much. The mud simply adhered to them, building up into a thick, heavy clump on each shoe that made it hard even to lift her feet. Then, as she placed each foot down again, the mud on her shoe against the mud of the hill provided a system more like makeshift skis than any sort of traction.

She picked up a stick when she spied one, and used it to scrape the soles of her shoes every few steps. Still, she could not shake the feeling that one wrong step would send her sliding and tumbling to the bottom of the hill. She had no idea how far down that might be, because she could only just see her hand if she extended it as far as her arm could reach.

And she was shivering, because her light coat was not sufficient against the wet chill.

A sensation of panic was rising in her gut, and fast. She felt exposed.

What if the fog cleared and she could no longer see the road, or her car? What if she was lost out here? Forced to spend a night in the elements? How cold would it get in the wee hours, waiting for someone to find her? Would it rain again?

In the midst of this jumble of panicky thoughts, Roseanna failed to notice that she was no longer stopping to gasp. She still had to scrape mud at regular intervals. But the walking was not taking her breath away.

She stopped. Glanced around. The earth on all sides of her seemed more or less level.

She pulled her phone out of the pocket of her light jacket, woke it up with her thumb.

Three bars of reception!

Roseanna laughed out loud. And, with the sound, all the panic left her. Just like that.

As she was finishing her phone call with the cavalry—whose role in this instance was played by a semi-nearby AAA repair shop with tow service —Roseanna raised her eyes and looked back the way she had come.

She gasped audibly.

The fog had cleared. Or, more accurately, it had allowed a hole to form in itself. The sun above her was warming the fog into a kind of filmy Swiss cheese, leaving a space for Roseanna to view her surroundings.

"This is it," she said out loud.

It was a strange thing to say. Even Roseanna thought so. Nonetheless, it's what came out of her mouth in that moment.

The earth dropped off below her feet into a valley of farmland—mixed crops of various shades of green planted in careful grids. Dividing the planted fields lay strips of forest, tall trees stretching up out of the earth, swaying in a light wind. Streams ran through, their water glinting in the sun at various points along their journey.

On all sides of this pastoral scene rose more hills. Deep, healthy green hills. Green like a pool table, only better. More natural. A huge bird sailed on a current of air above this heaven. Maybe large enough to be a hawk or an eagle. Roseanna knew nothing about birds, so she didn't know. Still, birds were playing a larger than average role in her day. There was no denying that.

It's hard to find a particular place when you don't one hundred percent know you're even looking for it, Roseanna thought. She silently congratulated herself on that unlikely accomplishment.

She glanced down at her phone again. It had, rather rudely, downloaded two texts and six voicemails. Wincing slightly, she clicked through to the texts.

One was from Jerry, the only other senior partner now that Alice was gone. Roseanna could read the first lines without opening it.

> Honey, we understand, but this is not the way to solve it. What about the Neiderman case? When—

She didn't click on the message to read the rest. The second was from Nita.

> OK, not to sound panicky or anything but all the other partners are freaking out. If you could—

She clicked back to home, then to phone and voicemail. All six messages were from Jerry.

Roseanna held her finger down on a button until the prompt came up to power off the phone. She slid her thumb as indicated and the screen went dark.

Then she slowly, carefully made her way back down the muddy hill.

By the time she arrived back at her car, the donut hole in the fog had closed again. But it was a light, misty thing, this fog. It no longer felt dense and impenetrable and scary.

Roseanna leaned on her car before realizing its roof was soaking wet, then stood beside it waiting for the tow truck to bring her gasoline.

It would be a longish wait. Forty-five minutes to an hour, the man on the phone had said.

The beautiful hills and valleys were gone again now. That hurt a spot in Roseanna's chest, the absence of them. In that moment she would have done almost anything to get them back.

All she could see was a pale farmhouse surrounded by a plain, unpainted board fence. The house was a faded off-white, porch boards and roof sagging under years of weight and wear.

And, in front of this, she saw a real estate company's "For Sale" sign.

Roseanna stared at the sign for a moment before it fully registered in her brain. When that inner click happened, her head snapped up. She walked around her car and approached the sign—warily, though it would have been hard to explain why if anybody had stood nearby insisting on an explanation.

On its white four-by-four post the sign offered shiny, brightly colored printed flyers in a Plexiglas holder. She slipped one out and looked at both sides of it. There was not much of it she was going to be able to absorb without her reading glasses. Which were in her purse. Which was in the car.

But she saw overly flattering photographs of the farmhouse and a couple of other raggedy buildings. And she read, "Loman Realty is pleased to offer a very special property," because it was in larger type at the top of the page. And she saw "27 acres," because somehow the numbers ran together less than letters. In fact, the word "acres" was a guess on her part, though a likely one.

Roseanna walked toward the front porch of the house.

It was a small house. Tiny, really. Just about big enough to hold one decent-sized room—a rectangular box of old, dry wood with a window on either side of its ancient door. The porch had no railing. Just wood pillars holding up a roof, and six unrailed steps leading up to it. Its boards squeaked and sagged further under Roseanna's weight.

She walked to a window, shaded her eyes,

and peered in, realizing as she did that someone might be living here. But no one was. That much was clear. She could see furniture—couches and tables and what might have been chests of some sort—covered with old sheets and an air of abandonment that she might have been adding to the scene with her own imagination.

The slightly peeling wallpaper was a faded floral pattern.

In one far corner sat a nook of a kitchen with appliances—sink, stove, old-fashioned fridge—that might well have been fifty years old or more. In the other far corner a tiny room was partitioned off. A miniature bedroom, maybe? In the middle of the living room sat a potbellied woodstove on a brick pad.

Roseanna drew back from the window and walked down off the porch again. She began to wander about the property, carefully circumventing the mud puddles.

There was a barn, as the flyer had indicated there would be. A huge, cavernous thing with a tin roof peaking maybe twenty feet or more off the ground. It didn't look any too sturdy as buildings go. And there was an outbuilding of some sort. A little shack that looked as though it could serve as a guesthouse.

She began to cross the muddy field to examine it, but something stopped her. It was more carefully tended than anything else on the property.

It had flowers growing in a tilled bed out front, and lacy curtains in the windows. A welcome mat in front of the door. Someone might be living there, as unlivable a space as it appeared. Maybe a caretaker during the sale process?

It reminded Roseanna that she had no permission to be on the premises, and she hurried back to her car.

The tow truck driver looked to be about sixteen. He was wearing only a short-sleeved T-shirt and jeans, as though there were no such thing as damp or cold. He obsessively combed his long hair back along his head with his fingers, even as he poured five gallons of gasoline into her Maserati from a red plastic gas can. He chewed gum with a similar vigor, snapping it at intervals in a rhythm that ground on Roseanna's nerves.

"So where did you drive from?" she asked, hoping that encouraging him to speak would break up the maddening gum snapping. "Where's your shop located?"

"Walkerville," he said. Just that one simple word. It seemed to bore him to say it.

Then he went back to snapping.

"Is that where this Loman Realty is located?" she asked, holding the flyer out for him to see.

He did not look.

"Yup," he said, more or less simultaneously with a snap of gum.

Roseanna wondered how he managed to do both those things at once. Also why.

"Any advice on how to find it?"

"It's on the main drag," he said. "Everything's on the main drag."

Then he looked up at her for the first time. As if he had wakened up, located his interest in . . . well, anything. He looked at the flyer in her hand, then at the property. Then he returned his attention to pouring the very last bit of gas.

Roseanna expected him to say something. Ask questions. Maybe whether she was really interested in a place like this. And, if so, why?

He asked no questions.

He secured her gas cap, charged her credit card, tipped the brim of his raggedy baseball cap, and drove away.

Chapter Five

Rhinestones and Impossibilities

Roseanna woke in the morning all on her own initiative. No alarm clock.

She was in a room at the Value Motel in Walkerville, though it took her a moment to piece together her recent history and arrive at this conclusion.

She lay awake in bed for a few minutes.

She had been sleeping in her underwear, for lack of anything better to wear to bed. A wall heater blew warm air noisily in her direction, and she was able to lace her fingers together behind her head, comfortably exposing her bare arms. In fact, it was almost too warm.

She stared at the ceiling for a minute or two, then picked up the phone beside the bed and dialed the front desk.

"Good morning!" a chirpy female voice said.

"Right. Whatever. You know how hotels"—she paused, realizing this wasn't a hotel—"and motels sometimes have a few basics on hand in case you forgot them? Toothbrush, comb. That sort of thing?"

"Yes . . . ," the chirpy one said. As if waiting for Roseanna to finish. As if that were not enough information.

"Are you one of them?"

"We have a few things. What do you need?"

"Everything."

"Everything?" Now the voice was de-chirped. Filled with awe and a trace of dread. Apparently she could not fill the void of Roseanna's request. Which was understandable, since the need for "everything" was a hole more or less the size of the world.

"Yeah. Pretty much. More or less everything. I didn't know I'd be stopping for the night. So I have . . . nothing."

"Okay," the voice said, making it clear that it was not okay. "What do you need?"

"What do you have?"

"Oh. Well. Let's see. We have toothbrushes and toothpaste. Plastic combs. Mouthwash. Sewing kits. Mini first aid kits. And . . . cotton swabs, I think."

"I'm not injured," Roseanna said. "And my clothing is in fairly good repair. But I'll take one of everything else."

Then she hung up the phone, got out of bed, and—for the first time in her life as far as she could recall—dressed in the same clothes she'd worn the previous day.

Roseanna walked to Loman Realty because it was only five doors down, and it was no longer raining. So it did not seem worth warming up the car.

She pushed open the swinging glass door and stepped into a nearly oppressive warmth.

The small office held six desks. Only one was occupied by an agent.

She was a woman maybe ten years younger than Roseanna, with ridiculously overstyled hair and glasses with rhinestones in the frames, like the ones silly women used to wear in the sixties. At least, Roseanna had found them silly. She had always looked down on any sort of frills.

She was talking on the phone, the agent. She held one finger up to Roseanna, asking her to wait. Meanwhile Roseanna could smell coffee. She sniffed the air in search of it, found it in a corner of the office. Poured herself a white Styrofoam cupful.

Then she sat down across the desk from the Rhinestone Realtor and stared at her until she finished her phone call.

It sounded as though she were talking to one of her kids. Or maybe a babysitter. Terse orders ensued.

"I have to go now," the Rhinestone Realtor said into the phone. "I'll call you back." Then she turned her eyes up to Roseanna, snapped down the receiver. "Good morning! How can I help you?"

What is it with perkiness in this town? Roseanna thought but did not say.

She pulled the folded flyer out of her jacket

pocket, opened out the folds, smoothed out the creases, and slid it onto the woman's desk.

"This property," she said. "This very special property."

"Yes, it really is. You want to see it?"

"I want to buy it," Roseanna said.

"But first you want to see it."

"No. I've seen it. Now I want to buy it."

"You couldn't have seen the inside of the house."

"Not entirely true. It has windows. Clear glass. So what I'd like you to do now is call up the owner, or whoever is selling it, and put in my offer."

Silence. The real estate lady stared at the flyer. Roseanna sipped her coffee. It was dreadful. Full-on, make-a-face dreadful.

"Before you make an offer, though," Rhinestone said, "there are some . . . factors . . . regarding the . . . condition of the place. And you'll want to know them, because then you can take them into account when deciding on the dollar figure of your offer."

Roseanna took another sip of coffee, because she had been distracted by the conversation and had forgotten it was dreadful. She made another face.

"I know how much I want to offer," she said. "I want to offer to pay the full asking price."

"What I'm trying to . . . tactfully say here . . . is . . . while it's a lovely property with terrific potential, it's a little bit of a fixer-upper."

"So I noticed. Now why not go ahead and make that call?"

"What call?"

"The one I suggested earlier. Where you call the owner of the property and tell him—or her—that you have a buyer who's just offered the full asking price."

Another long silence, during which Roseanna did not sip her coffee. This time she remembered.

"Tell you what," the Rhinestone Realtor said. "I'm free right now. We'll drive out there. I'll show you around the place. And then if you still want me to make that call, I'll be more than happy to do it."

"Whatever," Roseanna said. "It's not going to change anything. But it's your time and your gas."

"I think you'll be pleased with the permitting process in this county," the Rhinestone Realtor said on the drive. "It's not grotesquely expensive to get a permit, as localities go, and you won't grow old and gray waiting for one to come through."

But I'm already gray, Roseanna thought. *You just don't know it because my colorist is a genius.* But people would know soon. That was second on the list for her new life, after putting on weight. Letting her hair revert to its natural gray.

Rhinestone drove one of those massive SUVs that put its passengers many feet up above the road. Roseanna found it to be a weird sensation, looking down onto the roofs of cars like her own. Normal-sized vehicles.

"What do I need a permit for?" she asked.

She sipped at her coffee, and it was heavenly. They had stopped at a drive-through coffee place on their way out of town, at Roseanna's firm request.

"Well, you know . . ."

"Actually, not so much. Hence the question."

"Building permits."

"What do you think I want to build?"

"I figured . . . a house?"

"It has a house."

"Um. Yes. But not much of one. And it's not in very good condition. I mean, it's sturdy enough. But it's . . . old. And it doesn't have much in the way of creature comforts. I just assumed that anyone who wanted that place would want it for the land. It's a beautiful location. People buy properties like that one and tear the buildings to the ground and build their dream home. I just assumed . . ."

Roseanna watched dense stands of evergreens rush by outside her window. She kept her eyes on them as she spoke.

"All my life I've been pretty good at defying assumptions. And now I'm about to get *even better at it* than I've ever been before."

"So you're looking for . . ."

"Heaven." It was unlike Roseanna to say such

a thing, and she knew it. She heard it. Still, that's what she said.

"Heaven?"

"Yes."

"That's a tall order." The statement was accompanied by a nervous laugh.

"Maybe not literally heaven. But something close. Something that will do for heaven until the real thing comes along. I still want to keep both feet in this world. I'm not ready to move on just yet. But I want to get as close to paradise as I can get while I'm still here on the planet. If that makes sense."

She glanced over at the Rhinestone Realtor. Watched frown lines crease into the woman's forehead.

"I'm not sure. What exactly does this heaven look like to you?"

"My thoughts on that are evolving as we speak," Roseanna said. "Up until yesterday morning I lived in a condo overlooking Central Park. And most people would consider that heaven. And maybe at the time I did. But it's in the city. And everything is so complicated. Everywhere you want to go, it's always so hard to get there. And the air is barely breathable. And it's dirty. And there are all these fees and expenses involved with living there. Not that I couldn't afford it. But I had to work hard to afford it. I don't know anymore how I lived in the city. It's strange—I left yesterday morning, and now I look back and I don't know how I lived there. Now I think heaven is more like . . . like just what you need to live a decent life. I looked in the windows of that house yesterday, and I saw just the minimum a person needs to be okay. Heat. A bed. Food storage. Something to cook food on. It does have a bathroom. Right? I didn't see a bathroom. It's not an outhouse situation, is it?"

"It was. Until about twenty years ago. And then the owner had a bathroom added on to the back of the house. Off the bedroom."

"See?" Roseanna said. "Heaven. And I don't need to work just to be able to afford to live there. With the amount of money I've accumulated in various holdings, I can buy the place outright and live there comfortably the rest of my life. Never have to get along with coworkers. Never have to drive in traffic. There's only one problem. The other thing I need . . . the other answer about what heaven looks like to me . . . it has to do with solitude. I've had it with people. I like that place because it's miles from everything. And everyone. I want to be there by myself. I want to be in the world by myself. In silence. And peace. Now that would be heavenly."

"That shouldn't be a problem."

"But there seems to be somebody living in that little guesthouse-type shack out behind the barn. That's why I mentioned it."

"Oh, no," Rhinestone said. "That's impossible."

"Impossible things happen every day. This one seems to be happening in spite of your thoughts on its impossibility."

"I'm sure you're wrong."

"I don't think I am. And if I'm right, I'll need that fixed. Straightaway."

"Oh, that would be very easy to fix, if it's true. I'm friends with the locksmith in these parts. I'd have him come over and change the locks. Today if need be. Problem solved."

They drove in silence for a time. Roseanna was feeling a sense of peace dawning. Things seemed to be working out just the way she had dreamed they might. Though, granted, it was a dream she had not been dreaming long.

"Pardon me," Rhinestone Realtor said, startling her out of her thoughts. "But I forgot to ask your name."

"Rosie," Roseanna said.

"So, here's the thing," Roseanna said as they tracked their way around mud puddles on the way to the guest shack. "I still want to offer full price. Even after walking around inside the house. But I want something in return. And it's not much to ask of the seller under the circumstances, so . . ."

She trailed off because she realized she had no idea whether Rhinestones was even absorbing her words. She didn't appear to be listening. She seemed completely obsessed with proving that no one could be living in this shack, and a bit disturbed as they grew closer to it—now that the visual evidence was stacking up against her.

"Hmm," the agent said, and tried the door of the tiny place.

It swung wide.

Inside Roseanna saw two twin beds made up with ridiculous stacks of blankets. A small electric heater. A bare light bulb hanging from the ceiling. A hot plate, and one of those half refrigerators you see in motor homes.

"I see how you could think someone is here," Rhinestone said. "But I still don't think so. I think they left in a hurry after the owner died."

"Flowers are still in good shape out front," Roseanna said.

"Lately we've had nature to water the flowers."

"Nature doesn't weed, though."

Rhinestones seemed to ignore her logic. "Now what were you saying a minute ago? About something you wanted in return for your offer?"

It took Roseanna a moment to answer. Because she was straining her ears to listen. There was a humming sound, and she was trying to decide if it was coming from the minifridge. It seemed that it was.

"I want to move in right away," she said.

"We can arrange a short escrow. Thirty days, say?"

"Fine. We'll do a thirty-day escrow. But I want

thirty days' free rent while we're waiting for it to close."

A silence fell, except for the humming.

"Well . . . you'd have to get the utilities on."

"I think the utilities are on," Roseanna said.

"Oh, no. That's impossible."

"There you go again with your impossibilities."

Roseanna moved two steps into the middle of the room and pulled the cord on the hanging light bulb. The bulb sprang to light.

She walked another two steps and opened the minifridge. Inside she saw a partial package of hot dogs, a carton of milk, and an open box of baking soda. She lifted out the milk, unfolded the top of the carton, and sniffed. As she had suspected, it smelled fine.

She carried it over to the Rhinestone Realtor, who recoiled at the idea of sniffing it.

"Trust me," Roseanna said. "This won't hurt a bit."

The woman took a reluctant sniff. Then her face darkened.

"We'll fix this," she said. "Right away. Right now. Today."

"You can't exactly change the lock."

"Why can't I?"

"Because there isn't one. Didn't you notice?"

They both turned to look at the door. There was a chain lock on the inside. But nothing that would lock it from outside.

"Well, no matter," Rhinestone said, clearly perturbed now. "I'll call the locksmith and have him put a hasp and padlock on the door. And I mean in the next few minutes."

"That seems harsh."

Roseanna walked around the place as she spoke, but there wasn't much exercise involved. Two or three steps in any direction took her across the room.

In one corner she noticed a dowel suspended horizontally from the ceiling with a few clothes hung on it. More than half were tiny. Barely bigger than toddler sized. And there was a well-worn teddy bear on one of the beds, all but its head covered by the mountain of blankets.

"Okay, now I'm confused," Rhinestones said. "You told me you wanted anybody who might be living here to be put out."

"Oh, I do. Definitely. But when you send some-one packing, there's packing involved. As in, you let them take their belongings."

"If this person wants their belongings back they can show up at my realty office and explain what they've been doing living on this property with-out permission. The very idea . . ."

"I guess that's between you and them," Roseanna said.

She moved quickly to the door. Then she stopped. Turned back. Looked around the room again, realizing what was missing.

"It has no bathroom," she said.

"I don't think it was ever intended for human habitation."

"Right. Probably not. But it's being inhabited all the same. Is that outhouse still around after twenty years?"

"Oh, goodness, no. That was torn down immediately when the bathroom was added."

"Hmm." She looked around for another few seconds, as if expecting the missing bathroom to appear. "How do decent people live in a place with no toilet?"

"Who says they're decent people?"

"How does anybody?"

"I'm sure I wouldn't know," Rhinestone said. With a bit of a self-righteous shudder.

Chapter Six

What Would Your Dead Best Friend Say?

She knew it was Nita's car immediately. Even in the dark.

She looked up, saw the headlights coming toward her, and knew. She had never seen Nita's car before—hadn't even been sure Nita owned one, in fact. Lots of people in the city didn't. So it must have been some "other" kind of knowing.

Then again, Roseanna thought, *before you get too chuffed about your own psychic abilities, bear in mind that this diner is closed. And not many people have a reason to pull into the parking lot.*

It was a Jaguar, Roseanna noted as Nita pulled up under a light post and parked. A golden-colored Jaguar.

Roseanna stepped out. Smiled.

Nita stepped out. Did not smile. In fact, she did not look at Roseanna at all. She just moved around to the trunk of the Jag, opened it, and began to haul out heavy-looking suitcases that Roseanna recognized as her own.

Roseanna stood quietly, watching Nita's breath puff out in clouds, rising up toward the light source on the pole above her head. Still no words had been spoken.

It dawned as a tingling in Roseanna's gut—and

grew into an uncomfortable ball of tension—to see her former secretary too angry even to glance at her face.

"So I guess I was paying you too much money," Roseanna said, hoping to lighten the mood. It didn't seem to work. "I wasn't even sure if you had a car."

Nita's hands stopped moving. She raised her gaze to Roseanna's face. Roseanna knew in that instant that she had been better off before, when Nita had refused to look at her.

"I don't have a car," she said simply.

"You stole this?" Another attempt at humor that fell embarrassingly flat.

"It's Jerry's. It's new."

A stronger tingle to Roseanna's gut.

"He's not hiding in the trunk waiting to drag me back, is he?"

Nita slammed the trunk lid. Hard. Without comment.

"Guess not, then. Why would Jerry loan you his car so you could bring me a bunch of my things? So I can stay away. That seems unlike him."

"I didn't tell him that part. Just that I was meeting you and we were going to talk. I think he figured I would talk you into coming home."

"Got it," Roseanna said.

She stood still in the cold night, in a rare break in the rain, watching Nita begin to transfer the suitcases to Roseanna's Maserati. She knew in some vague and distant way that she should help. But it was so natural to let the people who worked for her do all the heavy lifting. Literally as well as figuratively.

Besides, she felt frozen. Rooted to the spot.

It struck her that she was experiencing the first moment in which she fully absorbed the gravity of this life change. The weight of it. The sheer scope. The implications. And she hadn't seen all that coming, either.

"I guess it seems weird," she said, as Nita began to load up the back seat of Roseanna's car. "You worked for me for eleven years and I didn't know if you had a car or not."

Nita finished the transfer of suitcases without answering.

Then she walked up to where Roseanna stood in the dark parking lot. Stood strangely close. It would almost have felt threatening if Nita had not been barely five feet tall. Her wildly curly hair had deteriorated to a full-on frizz in the humid night. Roseanna watched the wet clouds of their breath intermingle.

"You're saying things in the past tense," Nita said, her elf-like voice a painfully familiar reminder that nothing in Roseanna's new world came with any history attached.

"I guess I am."

"You're not coming back. Are you?"

"No. I'm not."

Nita turned on her heel and walked back toward Jerry's Jaguar.

"Hey, wait. Nita. Don't go like that."

Nita paused and glanced over her shoulder. "How should I go?"

"You shouldn't. Yet. You should stay and we should have a talk." Roseanna took a few steps to close the distance between them. "That's why I picked this diner," she said, indicating it with a hooked thumb thrown back over her shoulder. "I didn't know it would be closed. I thought we'd sit down where it was warm and light and have a good talk. And something to eat."

I should have known it would be closed, she thought. She remembered Rosie the waitress saying, "We make a decent breakfast and lunch." Certainly she hadn't meant that they served dinner, but only breakfast and lunch were good.

"Here?" Nita asked, her voice dripping with judgment.

Roseanna knew she shouldn't be surprised by Nita's reaction. It was the same attitude she would have had herself a couple of days earlier.

"Yeah. Here. Okay, I get it, we're spoiled by great New York restaurants. But I ate here yesterday morning. Yesterday? Yeah. I think it was just yesterday, but that seems strange. Feels like a year ago. Anyway, I just had a classic American breakfast, and it was good. Not fancy, but good. So I guess I thought—"

"You totally don't get it, do you?" Nita asked, stopping Roseanna's diner talk in its tracks. "I thought of you . . . like . . . like you were almost . . ."

Roseanna waited, but it seemed Nita would never finish the thought.

"Like what?" she asked, her voice much gentler than usual.

"Like a mother. Kind of."

"Oh," Roseanna said. And for a long, uncomfortable moment they just stood in the mostly dark, breathing steam. "Well, then I'm a complete idiot. I guess that makes me a real first-class jackass, doesn't it? Because I had no idea you felt that way. None whatsoever. I mean, we got along well enough. I always liked you. But we saw each other outside work maybe . . . what? A couple of times a year? And we never confided or talked about anything personal, or—"

Roseanna stopped talking suddenly. For a moment she stood quietly and allowed a few thoughts to awaken in her.

"What?" Nita asked.

"Ironically, I just realized that's exactly the kind of mother I was. My relationship with my own son is just what I was describing. Just now."

Roseanna looked up to see that Nita had taken to pacing back and forth under the light post. It felt mildly alarming.

"Speaking of Lance," Nita said, "you need

to call him. Tell him where you are. He's been calling."

"Lance called the office? How did he even know I was gone?"

"How could you not *tell him?*" Nita shouted. Shouted. It was chilling.

"I . . . I thought it would take him much longer than this to even figure out I was gone. We only talk a handful of times a year."

"Well, it's possible Jerry might have phoned him," Nita said, seeming calmer now. Though it might have been an artificial calm, because she did continue her pacing. "You know. In case he knew where you were."

"I'll call him," Roseanna said, surprised by how much the anxiety inherent in Nita's pacing was pulling her apart at the seams. "Can we sit in my car and talk for a minute? It's cold out here. And pacing makes me nervous."

Roseanna ran the engine so they could have the benefit of the heater.

She glanced over at Nita, whose face was fairly visible in the dashboard light.

"You have to come back at some point," Nita said. "You know. At least to make some arrangements."

"I wasn't planning on it."

"But you have to sell your condo and make some kind of deal for your partnership, and . . ."

"So what do people do, then, Nita? When they need to make business deals but they don't want to have to be physically present? You should know this. You work for a law firm."

"They get their attorney to do it all."

"Right."

"But you don't have an attorney. Because you are one."

"True. But I know one or two. Hundred. So I'm sure I can work that out."

"I don't get it," Nita said. And sighed. Then a strange noise came out of her. A quiet little thing, like a cross between a breath and a whimper. It took Roseanna a few seconds to realize Nita might be crying. "How can you hate everything at home so much that you can't even go back to do your own packing or sell your own property? How is that even possible since yesterday morning?"

"Hard to believe that was just yesterday morning."

"Don't deflect the question, please."

Through the windshield and off in the distance, car headlights streamed along the interstate. Roseanna watched them in silence.

She opened her mouth to speak, and in that moment the rain let go again. Just all at once like that.

"I guess I feel like it was all strangling me."

"Is this about Alice Cummings?"

Roseanna closed her eyes and listened to the rain before speaking.

"I guess everything is, to some extent. But it's also about me."

"I'm going to say something that I never would have said to you before. Before now I would have kept this to myself out of respect, and out of feeling like I have no right to comment on your life. You're my boss. There are boundaries. But I guess I don't work for you anymore. And I probably won't see you again after tonight. So here goes. I think Alice . . . Ms. Cummings . . . would have been dead set against this. I think if she were here right now, she'd say you're nuts to leave this all behind. Everything you two worked for."

Roseanna sat a few moments longer, her eyes still closed, gently poking at her feelings. Exploring around in them. She did not feel agitated by Nita's comments. Not in the least. She felt surprisingly at peace. It felt like a confirmation that she was doing the right thing.

That felt good.

So few things had lately.

"Yes and no," Roseanna said. Softly. "I think if she were here and still alive . . . and still just who she always was. Then . . . yes. She'd be furious with me. But let's say that wherever she is now, she can still think. I mean, let's say she exists somewhere with . . . you know. A . . .

consciousness. Can you honestly tell me she wasn't smart enough to learn from her mistake? She spent her whole life working for something she never lived long enough to enjoy. If she were here right now with full benefit of hindsight . . . being able to factor in her sudden death . . . well, I have to believe she'd tell me not to make the same mistake. Don't you think?"

Nita never answered. Just sighed. She dug a tissue out of her purse and dabbed at her eyes. Carefully, so as not to smear her makeup.

No freedom, Roseanna thought. *I hope someday you know the freedom I found. Double breakfasts. Rubbing your eye without smearing your mascara. Running away from home.*

"Well," Nita said. And she was resigned now. Roseanna could hear it. "That was my best shot. Those were the big guns, right there."

Nita sighed deeply, a tremble on the out breath. Then she opened Roseanna's car door and stepped into the rain.

Roseanna sat a moment, watching her walk through the downpour. Then she opened her driver's door and stepped out. The rain was torrential, coming down in huge, battering drops. It soaked her to the skin in seconds.

She trotted after Nita.

"Wait," she called.

Nita stopped and turned around. Roseanna caught up to her and wrapped her in a bear hug.

They stood that way for the longest time, dripping in the rain. Cold except for each other. Nita might have been crying again, but the rain was hammering off the tarmac so loudly it was hard to tell.

"A piece of motherly advice," Roseanna said. "I'm letting you down. I get that. People always will. That's not as much of a downer as it sounds. There's a reason people will always let you down. It's because they came to this weird planet to live their own lives. Not anybody else's. Classic case of needs in conflict. You get what I'm saying?"

Nita nodded against her shoulder, then lifted her head and smiled sadly.

"I think so," she said. "Yeah."

Then Nita walked off into the rain. And Roseanna knew she would never see her again. She *could*. Arrangements could be made to stay in touch. But they wouldn't be. And she knew it. And it was okay.

People come into our lives, she thought, *and it's not always a forever kind of thing, and not always meant to be. Not every deal is for keeps.*

Roseanna let herself into the farmhouse for the first time ever, carrying two of her suitcases. She stumbled into the middle of the room by feel, and by moonlight. There was a moon, fortunately. A three-quarters-full thing, hanging in the sky, shining a trace of light through her dusty, rain-streaked farmhouse windows. It allowed her to see the hanging chain for the light, which she pulled sharply.

The light came on, and she looked around. And felt nearly overwhelmed by fear. Bowled over.

It was cold, and she was still soaking wet. She had seen firewood stacked in a lean-to on the property, but she had never built a fire and wasn't sure how. She had stopped for a sandwich on the way home, but there was no coffee for the morning, no food in the fridge.

And she had no idea which of her belongings Nita had seen fit to pack.

She shook the feeling away again and opened one suitcase, lifting out clothes. She carried them into the tiny bedroom. There was a freestanding electric space heater, she noticed. And maybe that would do for her first night.

It was only spring. It would probably feel fine in here all summer, she thought. But when winter came she would have to do something. Maybe get a heating and air-conditioning unit installed outside the corner of the house, with a duct into the bedroom and bathroom.

A knock on the door nearly stopped her heart. It was a big knock. A pounding. And here she was, alone. Alone out in the middle of nowhere. With no phone reception. No burglar-proof locks.

"Who is it?" she called, too loudly, her voice breathy with panic.

"I need the key to that padlock," a young female voice called back.

Roseanna pulled a few deep breaths and tried to convince her heart to settle.

She moved to the door. But she did not open it. Just touched the wood of its surface with the tips of her fingers as she spoke.

"I don't have the key," she said.

"How can you not have the key? You put a padlock on a place. The padlock comes with a key."

She sounded desperate, but not angry. More as though she were about to break into millions of pieces, leaving shards of desperate young woman all over Roseanna's front porch.

"I didn't put that lock on the shed."

"Oh, it just jumped on there all by itself?"

"No. Of course not. That real estate lady had it done."

Silence. Roseanna waited. But nothing more was said. And she heard no footsteps retreating, either. Apparently the young woman was just standing at her door doing . . . what? Roseanna had no idea.

She carefully opened the door.

The girl on her porch was a thin thing, maybe in her early twenties. Her hair was long and thick and wild, not recently combed. A lovely amber color. Other than the great hair, there was nothing about her that would cause a person to look twice. Her face was pleasant but unremarkable.

A child of five or six slept in her arms, head drooped over her shoulder. Lost in that stubborn, nearly irreversible sleep that children do so well.

"So you would be my squatter," Roseanna said.

"Well, I don't know what I'm supposed to do, then," the young woman said, ignoring Roseanna's squatter comment entirely. She seemed to be holding back tears. "The car broke down. And we missed the last bus. We walked two and a half miles to the bus stop to go into town, which means I carried her for two and a quarter miles. And then we missed the last bus home. So I've been walking with her all this way. I've been walking for almost four hours. And she's heavy, you know? And it rained on us half the time. But nobody offered to give us a ride, and we had to get home. And then we get home, and there's a padlock on the door. All my stuff is in there. I can't even sit down. It's cold out here, and it might rain again, and I can't put her to bed, and I can't even get a drink of water after all that walking . . ."

At this juncture of the story the young woman trailed off. Seemingly not so much because she was done recounting the horrors of her evening. More because tears and emotion overcame her and stole the show.

"You want to come in and have a glass of water?" Roseanna asked.

"Thank you," she said, wiping her nose on

the shoulder of her shirt that did not contain a sleeping child. "That would be very nice."

"I may or may not have a glass. This is all a process of discovery. But come on in and we'll see."

"I told the real estate lady that it was a harsh thing to do. Locking up somebody's belongings like that."

They stared down at the sleeping child as Roseanna spoke. The little girl lay sprawled on the couch, cheeks twitching, as if she were smiling at something in her dreams.

"Well, thanks for that, anyway."

"Thing is, you have to understand she was angry because you're living here without permission. There are liabilities involved with a thing like that."

The young woman drained the last of her water and held the glass out to Roseanna.

"Can I have another, please?"

Roseanna sighed. Accepted the glass. Rose to her feet and began the short walk to the kitchen area.

"It wasn't without permission," she heard the girl say. "Macy let us live in that little place. She even let us use her car."

"Macy?"

"The lady. You know. She lived in this house for, like . . . I don't know. Sixty years or something."

"And then she died?"

Roseanna turned on the tap. The stream of water sputtered and hissed with trapped air, as it had while delivering the first glassful.

"Yeah. She died."

"And, sorry as I am to say it, with her died any permission you might have had to use the property."

Roseanna waited for an answer, but none came. She turned off the tap and carried the water back to the couch. Handed it to the young lady, who accepted it without looking up.

"I still need to get our stuff out," the young woman said after a time.

"I'm afraid I can't help you with that. She didn't give me a key. Technically I'm just renting this place until the escrow goes through. You'll have to take it up with her or someone in her real estate office."

"That's in Walkerville."

"It is."

"That's more than thirty miles from here."

"Right."

"So what are we supposed to do?"

Roseanna sighed deeply. Sat back on the couch. She was tired, too. In a different sort of way, but she was. It had been a long, strangely emotional day. It had been scarier than she had allowed herself to consciously realize. She felt barely equal to her own challenges in that moment.

"I realize it must be hard raising a child on your own."

"It is."

"And with not much money."

"You can say that again."

"And I really don't mean to be cold or uncaring. I swear I don't. But the world is full of people in the middle of their challenges. I feel for them. But I'm in the middle of my own. And this really doesn't have much to do with me. Just because I'm the next person to come along and live in the house after . . ."

"Macy."

"Yes. Macy. That doesn't really make this mine to solve. If you know what I mean."

"Right. Got it."

The girl set her now-empty water glass down on the steamer trunk that served as a coffee table. Scooped up her positively boneless sleeping child. She made no attempt to hide her tears from Roseanna.

"I have a phone," Roseanna said to her back as she carried the child to the door. "You'd have to walk it up that hill to get reception. But if you want to call somebody to come help you, I would loan you my phone. You could even leave the little girl here on my couch . . ."

The young woman stopped at the door. Looked back toward Roseanna without connecting their gazes. She shook her head.

"There's nobody I can call. Nobody's going to help me."

She walked out, closing the door behind her.

Roseanna stood staring at the door for a moment. Then she forced her gaze away and returned to her unpacking. Or perhaps it would be more accurate to say she briefly pretended she would unpack again.

She picked up another armload of clothes, carried them into the bedroom. Dumped them on the bed.

Then she walked quickly to the door and opened it, expecting to see the two squatters on their way to the road. There was no one there.

"Hmm," she said.

It occurred to her that the young lady might be out back by the shed, seeing if she could break the lock or climb through a window.

Roseanna picked her way carefully out to the shed in the moonlight.

The young woman and her daughter were there. But not attempting to break in. The woman had simply slumped down onto her own welcome mat, her back up against the locked shed door, her child still sleeping on her shoulder. Still crying.

"I could give you a ride into Walkerville," Roseanna said.

"Well, that's very nice of you. But the office is going to be closed till morning."

"There's a motel."

"I can't afford a motel."

"It's only about seventy dollars."

"*Only? Only* seventy dollars?" Her bitter laughter mixed with her sobs, forming something quite strange. "You know how long my daughter and I live on seventy dollars? I have thirty-one dollars in my pocket and we have to eat on it for more than a week."

Great, Roseanna thought. *You couldn't leave it alone. You had to mix in. Had to make it your problem, too. And now it's a big problem, and you're stuck in it. And this young person who rightfully owns the big problem isn't even working with you here. She isn't even trying.*

Roseanna turned to walk back to the house. But she only made it a step or two before turning around to face her squatters again.

"Okay, fine," she said. "I'll drive you into Walkerville and I'll loan you the seventy dollars."

But "loan" really meant "give" in this case, and Roseanna knew it. She figured they both did.

"So, not to be rude . . . ," Roseanna began.

They were driving along a back road, a shortcut into Walkerville, in the pitch dark. Under more stars than Roseanna had even known existed.

"This is a really nice car," the young woman, whose name Roseanna still had not asked, said.

"Thank you. Are you trying to distract me from asking a rude question?"

"Probably." She sighed. The sleeping little girl on her lap opened her mouth and let out an almost comically loud snore. "But go ahead, I guess."

"There's no bathroom in that little shack."

"No." She stared out the window, though there was nothing to see in the dark. "There's no bathroom. But that's not really a question."

"Right. I was hoping you would volunteer the rest."

Roseanna waited. Nothing was volunteered.

"So you and your daughter go out into the woods?"

"Of course not." There was a hint of fire in her tone now. As if she had finally wakened up to her own defense. As though her state of surrender were wearing off. "We're not animals."

"I didn't mean to suggest—"

"We have a little porta-potty. It sits under the bed. Out of the way. It has a cover. It's sanitary and all. And then in the morning . . . there's a way to dump something right into the septic tank. There's an overflow. A pipe that goes down into the tank. Macy showed me how."

"I see. I'm sorry if it was a rude question. I just couldn't help being curious."

"You're wondering why I can't do better."

"I didn't say that."

"You think I should go get a job. But what do I do with my daughter while I'm working? If I pay for her childcare then I'm working for practically nothing. I'm hardly better off than I was when I was staying home to raise her."

Roseanna saw the first lights of town in the distance. It was a relief. It always scared her a little to motor through the middle of absolutely nothing. They drove without talking for a time. The only sound was the purr of the Maserati's engine and the less civilized roar of little-girl snores.

"So what will you do now?" Roseanna asked as they pulled up at the motel.

"I have absolutely no idea," the young woman said.

She stepped out of the car, slinging the little girl over her shoulder again.

So at least she understood that it was not Roseanna's job to provide a solution. At least, beyond this one night.

Chapter Seven

People Who Hoard Metal . . . and Mouses

It was after eight the following evening, and pitch-dark. Roseanna had just arrived home from her second trip to the supermarket in Walkerville. In one day.

On the first trip she had bought coffee, food, and a few essentials of grooming that Nita had neglected to pack.

Then she'd spent the day noting how many items she had forgotten, but unable to make a list of them. Because a pad of paper—or any variety of paper that she hadn't accidentally left on her bedside table at home—was one of them. And a pencil—that she hadn't broken the point off of while carrying it in her purse—was another. Even a cheap sharpener would have helped a lot.

So she'd driven the sixty-mile round-trip a second time, holding a number of items in her head, spinning them around and around on repeat like a song you don't enjoy but can't stop mentally playing. It was a secret relief, that second trip to town. Because, quite honestly, Roseanna had no idea what she was supposed to do with all this time.

Only as she was driving home from the second

trip did it occur to her that she could have made a list on her phone or her iPad. In which case she might have remembered that the flashlight, which she had remembered to buy, required batteries, which she had forgotten.

She was halfway from the dirt driveway to her front porch when she heard a small noise. It sounded human. A voice. More of a vocalization than a verbalization—in other words, not words. But a recognizable human sound.

The moon had not yet risen, or was locked behind the clouds. And Roseanna had not thought to leave a light on in the house, forgetting it would be dark by the time she got home.

She set her grocery bag in the dirt and began to move, slowly, quietly, toward the barn and the direction of the sound. Not so much with the goal of confronting it. It was more of a reflexive desire to get a bead on what and where it was. Her heart hammered, feeling more and more as though it were sitting in the base of her throat. Then she stopped. Questioned whether it would be smarter just to go inside and lock the door.

Before she could decide, something slammed into her. She screamed out loud, a huge, full-throated shout. The something screamed back, sounding a bit younger and more high pitched.

"Who is that?" Roseanna cried, her voice a terrified screech.

"It's only me," a young female voice said in

return. Roseanna recognized it as the young woman she had put off her property the evening before. "I'm sorry," the young woman said, a voice emanating from a dark shape in a black night.

"What are you doing back here? Did I not make myself clear about this?"

"You did. I'm sorry. I just . . . can we leave in the morning? Not tonight? I was trying to get all our stuff out, but it's late and I don't have a car that runs, and we don't have anyplace to stay tonight, and . . ."

Then she seemed to reach the end of her steam.

Roseanna closed her eyes for a moment. It didn't change the scenery much. She placed one hand over her heart, as if she could hold the shocked organ together manually.

"You scared the living . . . you scared me," she said, letting it go at that.

"I'm sorry."

"Where's your daughter?"

"Inside. Asleep. We need time to figure out a way to move all our stuff someplace else. And right now I have no idea where that could be."

Roseanna blinked her eyes closed again and left them that way for a moment. It felt like a comfort, but she wasn't sure why.

It was quite obvious that the problem this young woman had just outlined could not, and would not, be solved overnight. But she wanted to be done with all of this. She wanted to leave her big scare behind and get back inside, and warm up the house, and feel safe again.

So all she said was "Fine. But just tonight."

In the morning, while Roseanna was making coffee in the surprisingly distressing cold of the house, the young woman knocked.

Roseanna crossed the house in her robe and opened the door.

The little girl was hanging—fairly literally—from her mother's hand. She was reaching up to hold hands, but at the same time leaning her weight on her poor young mother. As if it were all a game. As if she could use her mom as a makeshift rope swing.

Roseanna had never seen the little girl awake and with her eyes open before. She had rosy cheeks and wispy, thin, soft-looking brown hair. Huge eyes. She looked up at Roseanna and smiled broadly, showing teeth that looked tiny and perfect and orderly. Little enamel pearls lined up just so.

Great, Roseanna thought. *The kid's going to be looking at me like that the whole time I'm trying to evict them.*

"Good morning," the young woman said.

"Hi!" the little girl added, and her voice was so screechy and enthusiastic that it hurt Roseanna's ears.

"Good morning. Have you figured out where you'll go?"

"Well . . . that's actually what I wanted to talk to you about. May we come in for just a minute?"

Roseanna looked down at the kid, who beamed up expectantly. Cheerfully. Optimistically. And just like that, Roseanna knew she was sunk. She could have said, "No, you can't come in, because once I let you in, it'll be like feeding a stray cat. I'll never get rid of you." If it had been only the mother on her porch, she could have. But she could say no such thing into the face of this happy child.

Roseanna sighed deeply.

"Fine," she said. "For just a minute." She stepped out of the doorway to allow them by. "Coffee?"

"Yes, please," the young woman said.

"Yes, please!" the little girl shrieked. She probably hadn't meant to shriek it. It seemed to be the way she said everything. She did not seem to have a second, more dignified, tone.

"You don't drink coffee," the mother said, tugging on her daughter's hand. "Silly."

"I don't?"

"No, of course not. You're five."

"How old do you have to be?"

Her mother seemed to struggle with that question in her head for a moment. Then she said, "Eighteen."

"Oh," the little one squealed. "Never mind!"

Roseanna pressed one finger into her assaulted ear, as if that would repair it.

She handed the young woman coffee in one of the late Macy's chipped cobalt-blue mugs. Then she sat on the couch and watched the five-year-old put on a show, with some dismay. Dismay on Roseanna's part, not the little girl's. The kid had clearly never heard a discouraging word.

Every time the young woman opened her mouth to speak to Roseanna, the little girl tugged desperately at her sleeve, bounced up and down on the toes of her pink sneakers, or cried "Mommy, Mommy, Mommy!" Or, in most cases, all three diversionary tactics at the same time.

"*What,* honey?" the frazzled young mother said at last, peeling her attention away from Roseanna.

"I saw a *mouse!*"

"At our house?"

"No, *here!*"

"When?"

"Just *now.* In the *kitchen!*"

"There are mice in the kitchen?" Roseanna interjected.

"Oh, yeah," the young mother said. Roseanna still had not asked her name. Quite purposely. It was not her intention that this be the beginning of . . . well, anything. "There are mice every-where. That's just how it is when you live in the country. Macy used to catch them alive in those 'kind traps' and drive them up into the hills. But I think they find their way back. Either that or more mice just move into the empty mouse holes. You know. It's a place to live."

"Speaking of which—" Roseanna began.

But the little girl interrupted them again with her bouncing and tugging.

"Mommy! Mommy! It was a *gray* mouse! I thought mouses were brown. But it was *gray!*"

"Well, honey, some mice—"

"Only maybe it was just *dusty*. Maybe it had *dust*. Do mouses have dust?"

"You know," Roseanna said before the little girl's mother could answer, "there comes a time in the life of every child when they need to learn they're not the center of the universe."

The young mother sat up rigidly straight on the couch. She looked directly into Roseanna's face, her own face appearing positively scorched.

"In control, you mean." She didn't sound angry. Just measured. Careful.

"Exactly."

"Well, I don't agree. I think the whole problem with this world is that we control our kids too much. What they naturally are just seems too darned inconvenient for us, so we get impatient with it, and we tell them not to be who they are. No good comes of it. Not in my opinion."

"We can't always just do what comes naturally."

"Why can't we?"

As they discussed this, Roseanna noticed that the kid had fallen uncharacteristically silent. She seemed to have noticed the tension in the room. Maybe she even knew that she was the center of that disagreement. She shifted her eyes back and forth from one adult face to the other as if sitting in the stands at a volleyball tournament.

"Well . . . we have responsibilities. We have to learn that life . . ." But then she never finished. Because she realized she was reminding herself of Alice. "So, look. I don't mean to be curt, but maybe we can cut to the chase here. You came to my door this morning to say something."

"Right. I did. I need to ask something of you."

But then she stalled and asked nothing.

Still the little girl stared from face to face in silence.

"My name is Patty," the young woman said when she'd restarted herself. "And this is Willa."

"The chase," Roseanna said. "No offense."

"We don't have anywhere to go. We need time to figure out a place. We'll probably have to move into Walkerville, but I don't know of anyplace that's for rent. I can probably borrow some money from my parents. I hate like"—she glanced at her daughter's watchful face—"like heck to ask them, but I guess I don't have any choice. Willa will be in kindergarten in the fall, and then I can work a part-time job and pay them back. And afford rent. I'll call my folks today, but it'll still take a little time to find a place. I swear we'll be so quiet you won't even know we're here."

Roseanna glanced at the little girl, who looked back in a perfectly unguarded stare. No agenda whatsoever.

"I doubt you'll be so quiet I won't know you're here. You just said yourself that you never put any limits on your daughter."

"I didn't say that."

"You let her be a natural kid. Which is fine. Raise her any way you want. But now suddenly you need her to be quiet. How's that going to work?"

"I can be quiet," Willa interjected. Too loudly.

"Look. Patty. I feel for your situation. But the whole point of coming out here was to find peace and quiet for myself. It's what I've been needing. If this place is not about solitude then what's it about? Who lives in a place like this unless they want silence?"

"I swear it'll just be for a week or two. And we can help you. I can help around the place."

"What help do I need?"

"I could help you clean all that stuff out of the barn."

"What stuff?"

A silence fell. Patty looked genuinely surprised.

"You didn't look inside the barn?"

"No."

"You bought this place without looking in the barn?"

"I'm not going to live in the barn, so who cares what's in there?"

"Okay, fine," Patty said.

She sat back on the couch and sipped at her coffee. Willa ran into the kitchen, probably to look for more mouses.

"I give up," Roseanna said. "Now the curiosity's got me. What's in the barn?"

"Holy . . . ," Roseanna began. But she never finished. Because the little girl was staring up at her and listening. "Why would anyone keep all this . . . ?"

"I think the word you're looking for is *junk*," Patty said.

Roseanna stepped into the barn. But it wasn't easy. You couldn't step in just anywhere. You had to choose an aisle.

In between the carefully constructed aisles lay . . . well, as Patty had said, junk. But it was junk with a theme. It was one hundred percent metal. Fenders and wheels and chains and engines and chain-link fencing and . . . in some cases, it was hard even to tell. If at one time these pieces of metal trash had been something else, something greater, it was impossible for Roseanna to guess at that prior state now.

Now it was simply a sea of stacked metal parts.

Higher than her head in most places. Almost to the rafters in the corners.

Patty and Willa followed her down an aisle. She craned her neck in wonder.

"Why would anybody keep all this?" she asked no one in particular.

"I have no idea," Patty said.

"But it was Macy who wanted it all?"

"Right."

"For what?"

"No idea."

"You never asked?"

Roseanna turned a corner at an intersection in the stacks and was struck with a sudden and disturbing thought. *If there were to be an earthquake right now . . . hell, even a good sonic boom, maybe . . . we'd all three of us be squashed like bugs.*

"I asked," Patty said, holding her daughter's hand and turning the corner behind Roseanna. "But she didn't really like to talk about it. I think she knew it was unreasonable. It was kind of an obsession with Macy. You know. Like one of those people who love cats, but instead of having two or three they have two or three hundred."

"Like a hoarder."

"Yeah," Patty said. "Like that."

"What did all of this used to be?"

"Oh, different stuff. Farm equipment. Tractors and plows and trucks. Bikes. Even a motorcycle or two."

Roseanna ran out of aisle and stopped near the inside wall at the back of the barn. Still staring almost straight up. It was beginning to make her neck hurt.

"But somebody had to take it all apart. And stack it up in here. And Macy was an old woman."

"Not all her life, she wasn't. But anyway, she had farmhands."

"Right. Farmhands. I guess you'd have to, on a place like this."

"That's what I was trying to tell you earlier, back at the house. I can be a helper around this place."

Roseanna chose to ignore the comment entirely.

"What did she think she was ever going to do with all this? It has no use that I can imagine."

"No idea," Patty said. "Maybe just parts. Like an auto junkyard keeps old parts around. If the tractor breaks down or whatever, you can find a spare part."

Roseanna wandered down another aisle and found a corner of the barn, near a side door, that was open and clean. A clearing.

"What's this, then?" she asked Patty. "Was she not done collecting?"

"This is where she used to bring the horse in out of the weather."

Roseanna squeezed by Patty and Willa, which was not easy in the narrow walkway, and made her way back to the open barn doors. She had begun to feel claustrophobic. It was making her a little bit ill.

"This is why that Loman Realty lady kept saying I needed to see the place before I put in an offer." Roseanna stood in the open barn doorway, feeling better to be back out in the light. "Because it'll cost thousands of dollars to have all this junk hauled away. And I should have deducted that from my offer."

"Maybe," Patty said. "But I could help you. I could start hauling stuff out. Maybe borrow a truck, or . . . well, I have no idea who would loan me a truck. Maybe rent one. And start making trips to the dump. I can't move all of it. Some of it, the engines and stuff, are just too heavy for me. Unless I could use a winch or something. But even if I just moved everything that's small enough to move, that would be most of it. Three-quarters of it, anyway. And that would give you plenty of useable space in here."

Roseanna continued to ignore her offer. "Well, it doesn't matter," she said. "I don't need a barn. I wouldn't have cared if the place didn't have one at all. I don't keep livestock. Who needs it?"

"I figured you'd want a place to park your car inside."

"Oh. My car. Well. Maybe. But I'm not sure I'd park it in here. Looks like the first good wind would bring it down."

"Oh, no," Patty said. "It's very strong."

She joined Roseanna in the sunlight in the open doorway. Her daughter did not. Willa continued to skitter up and down the junk aisles, laughing at nothing.

"I know it doesn't look like much," Patty continued. "The barn. But Macy had somebody come out now and then and make sure the structure was sound. The siding . . . you know, the boards . . . they're pretty rotten from the weather. But it has a good concrete base to protect the bottom of the support beams from water damage. And they're in good shape. It's such a pretty car. Expensive. I know you don't want to leave it out in the snow."

"Oh," Roseanna said. "Right."

"The winters are really fierce here. You'd barely be able to dig it out."

It struck Roseanna that there was a great deal she did not know about this property and its geographical location. Maybe it didn't hurt to have someone around—briefly, of course—to educate her about the history of the place. Its inherent dangers.

"I doubt I'll keep that car," she said. And it was odd, because it was both logical and true, yet utterly surprising. She'd had no idea she was thinking it until she heard herself make the declaration. "I mean, who drives a Maserati out here? It's a city car. Meant to drive on paved roads only. It's so low slung you could damage the body on a curb or a parking stop. I'll probably sell it and get . . . oh, I don't know. A pickup truck, most likely." But, as she said it, her resistance to selling the car rose up like a wall and secured itself into place. Maybe she'd buy a truck and keep the car. She could afford to, after all.

"You still don't want to have to dig your pickup truck out of the snow."

"What did Macy do?"

"She had a sort of . . . canopy. Like a carport, but made of tent fabric. But it's dead now. The weather killed it. I think the listing agent had somebody haul it away. It looked terrible. But the barn would make a great garage. You could just rent a truck, and I'd spend a couple of weeks getting all this stuff cleared out of here."

Roseanna stood a moment, feeling the sun warm her back. Listening to the little girl shriek with laughter as she ran up and down the aisles. Wondering why life was always a process of choosing the lesser of two evils. Why couldn't a person have all of what they'd been wanting? Especially after working so hard for it, for so long.

"It's going to be a noisy couple of weeks," she said, followed by an audible sigh.

"I'll teach her not to shriek like that. I promise. We'll make it a game. The Whispering Game."

"Oh, I doubt that," Roseanna said. "But I guess I can put up with anything for a couple of weeks."

Chapter Eight

Metal Cats and Horizontal Horses

Roseanna woke the following morning to a high-pitched squeal. It was outside the house, but that didn't seem to help muffle it much. The windows were ancient single panes with no weather stripping around their frames. The thin walls did not seem to have room for any sort of insulation. Maybe insulation had not yet been invented back when this house had been built.

No wonder it's so cold in here, she thought, and pulled the blanket more tightly down around her neck. The little electric heater was blowing on its highest setting. Had been all night. But there was only just so much it could do.

I'll have to get a bigger, more powerful one, she thought.

And with that she began to drift back to sleep.

Just as the pictures in her mind morphed into nonsensical dream images, Roseanna was jolted by another shriek.

"Damn it!" she shouted out loud, and pulled one end of the pillow over her upward-facing ear.

About two minutes later there came another happy, irritating little shriek. But this time it didn't startle Roseanna awake. Because this time she hadn't been sleeping. She had been lying there waiting, braced to hear it again.

She sighed, and threw back the covers.

As she slipped into her robe she felt a strong draft on both sides of her body at once—a warm one from the heater side and a cold one from the window side. She stepped into her fuzzy slippers and trudged outside, squinting into the early morning sun.

Seeing and hearing nothing, she walked around to the barn. As she approached the barn door, the little girl came barreling out, slamming into Roseanna, knocking the wind out of her with a poorly placed forehead, and stepping on her foot.

"Ow," Roseanna said.

"Willa! Tell the lady you're sorry."

"Sorry," Willa said.

It sounded distressingly sincere. Her little-girl face twisted into deeply felt, heartbreaking remorse, and she looked up into Roseanna's eyes as though her life would end right there and then without the older woman's forgiveness.

Roseanna's heart melted. And she hated that. Hated it. Always had.

"And tell her you're sorry you woke her up," Patty said from an unidentified location. "I mean, did we wake you up? If we did, I'm sorry."

Roseanna opened her mouth to speak, but found she simply was not awake enough yet. She could not respond to all of this.

"So, I got a good start," Patty said, stepping out into the early slant of light. "I can't haul anything away yet, but I've hauled a lot of it out of the barn. I've been putting it around the back, so you won't have to look at it until we rent a truck and a trailer and I can haul it away—"

"I'm not so sure about renting," Roseanna said, waking up fast. "I have to buy a truck anyway."

But as she said this she glanced over her shoulder at the Maserati, parked in the dirt in front of the gate, and realized she was in no way willing to let it go. Maybe she would have to buy a truck, but nobody was forcing her to sell her car. Sure, she had said herself that nobody out in the country drove one of these. *But what the hell,* she thought. *I can be the first.*

"We need more than just a truck," Patty said, breaking Roseanna free from Maserati thoughts. "If all I have is the bed of a pickup, it would take me a year to move all this stuff. I need one of those open trailers you can use to haul."

"Oh. Right. Okay, I guess. But you still need a truck to pull it. Right?"

"Right. I'm sorting the stuff out as I go. If it's too heavy to move, I leave it in. If I can move it out but it's worth selling, it goes in one pile. Or if it's just landfill material, in another."

Roseanna felt a sharp tug on the sleeve of her bathrobe.

"Hey, Mrs. Lady!" Willa piped up. "Hey! I found a cat."

"A cat? Oh no."

"What's wrong with a cat?"

"I don't want a cat."

"It's not a real cat," Patty said.

"I'm confused." Roseanna felt herself over-whelmed by a desire for coffee. Also solitude while she drank it.

"Willa's been looking at the junk and finding shapes in it."

"Oh," Roseanna said. There were certainly more apt things to say, but that's where she landed.

"Come here!" Willa shrieked. "I'll show you the cat!"

She dragged Roseanna around to the back of the barn by her sleeve.

They stood a moment, staring at a constellation of metal laid out in the dirt. Two car fenders, something that looked like a chain guard for a bicycle. A variety of small wheels, maybe from a lawnmower or a wheelbarrow. Several pipes cut to inconsistent lengths.

"See it?" Willa asked.

"Not really."

"You don't see a cat?"

"I'm trying, but . . ."

"Its head is right *there!*" Willa insisted, clearly irritated. She pointed vehemently.

"Oh, *there*. Right. Of course."

"See the cat now?"

"Yes."

Roseanna did not see the cat.

" 'Bout time."

"Well, I would say you are a kid with a very good imagination," Roseanna said, because most of the time children didn't know enough to judge that such statements were not genuine compliments.

"Do *you* have a kid?" Willa asked.

"I do," Roseanna said.

"Where?"

But Roseanna never answered the question. Because she suddenly remembered what she had been forgetting.

"Oh no! I said I'd call him. I said I'd call Lance. And that was . . . what? Three days ago?"

"Who's Lance?" Willa asked, clearly not relishing the distraction.

"Damn," Roseanna spat in lieu of an answer.

"You cursed."

"Yes. I'm sorry."

"You shouldn't curse."

"That's probably true."

"Oh, it's true."

"Will you excuse me, please, Willa? I have to go make a phone call."

"Oh my God, Mom!" Lance fairly shouted.

It was the first thing he said. He did not say

144

hello. He seemed to have skipped hello and replaced it with this complaint, springing directly from what she could only assume was his having read her name on the caller ID.

"I know," she said. "I'm sorry."

She sat quietly for a second or two. Right in the dirt at the top of the hill. A small stone was poking into her thigh, but she didn't bother to move. She was looking out over the farmlands, stunned by the clouds. They looked billowy and white and enormous, like puffy mountains, their bottoms dark and flat. They scudded along fairly close to the earth, leaving imposing shadows sliding across the forests and crop rows.

The wind was up, and it cut through her clothing and made her teeth chatter.

Roseanna realized, just in that moment, that living in her new home was all about feeling exposed—feeling the sun and the wind and the cold. And living in the city was about being insulated. And she had lived in the city all her life.

There was discomfort involved in this new way of being. It made her feel alive. But not necessarily in a good way. Maybe these things just took some getting used to.

"You must've called to say something," Lance said.

"Right. Sorry."

"Why do you sound out of breath?"

"Long story. Not what I called to say. Look, I'm sorry. It's been a very strange time. In a lot of ways. You know how sometimes you get up and walk into the kitchen, and then once you get there you don't know what you went in there for? Turns out there's an actual reason for that. It's some kind of evolutionary thing. It kept us safe, I guess, when we were running from dinosaurs. Once you're in a new environment your mind goes blank. Like a clean slate. That helps us be ready for any challenges in the new place. Or, anyway, that's what I read somewhere."

"With all due respect, Mom, I have no idea what you're going on and on about."

"Sorry," she said, and just watched clouds scud for another few seconds.

"Are you saying you literally haven't had a second to call me?"

"Well, it takes more than a second, actually. I have to climb this little mountain to get reception. It's no small task. But no. That's not what I'm trying to say. I'm admitting that I forgot. I feel incredibly guilty that I forgot. But that's the truth of the matter. I told Nita I'd call you, and then I forgot."

"Then why not just say you forgot? Skip all the evolutionary lessons about evading dinosaurs?"

"I guess I thought I had extenuating circumstances," she said.

Lance didn't answer.

Roseanna looked away from the clouds and down onto her own property. She could see the little girl and her mother dragging metal trash around, but they looked like ants from this vantage point. Every time Patty added a piece of trash to a pile, Willa dragged it away again and added it to her arrangement. Another indecipherable cat, perhaps.

"And I wanted you to know that it really wasn't a matter of not prioritizing you. Because I know you think I don't prioritize you."

"Right, be that as it may, Mom . . . there's something I need to say to you."

"Go ahead."

A brief silence fell as he put the thing together.

"Come. To. Your. Senses. Seriously. Please."

Roseanna sighed, still watching the mother and daughter haul trash, working utterly at cross-purposes.

"Lance, I *have*. That's the thing. I *came* to my senses and that's why I left."

She waited a moment for his reply.

When no reply came, she pulled the phone away from her ear and glanced at its screen. The call had ended. A dropped call, she thought at first. But she was getting a full four bars of reception.

No, the more logical assumption was that Lance had hung up on her.

She rang him back but he never answered.

"I made a *horse!*" Willa shrieked as Roseanna stepped back onto her own property.

The little girl grabbed Roseanna's hand and dragged her behind the barn. Roseanna stood a moment, considering the spot where Willa eagerly pointed.

"Oh," Roseanna said. "A horse."

"I *told* you."

"But, I mean, it really looks like a horse."

"Well, it's a *horse,*" Willa said. "So what else would it look like?"

"Good point, good point."

Roseanna dropped to one knee and examined Willa's work more closely. It was rudimentary but clear. Its legs were made of pipes. Straight pipes. This particular horse was capable only of gaits that did not require bendable legs. He had no hooves. His neck and ears were pipe as well, so he had shaped up to be something of a stick-figure horse. But the metal piece she had found for his head—Roseanna thought it looked like an elongated motorcycle gas tank—looked surprisingly like the head of a fairly cartoonish equine.

"We could make him look even more like a horse," Roseanna said.

"How?"

"We could give him legs that bend."

"How could we do that?"

"We could find some of those pipe fittings that let you put two pieces of pipe together so they can turn a corner."

"I have no idea what that means," Willa said.

"And we could give him a mane and tail."

"Out of what?"

"Maybe some of that chain that's stacked up in the barn. We'd have to have some way to cut it."

"How do you cut chain?"

"I have no idea," Roseanna said. "I'm as new to all this as you are."

"You use a bolt cutter," Patty said.

Roseanna whipped around to see the young mother standing behind her.

"Is there a bolt cutter around here?"

"There might be. I could look. And I just put some pistons in the landfill pile."

"I'm not sure what pistons are in this context," Roseanna said, struggling to her feet and dusting off her hands on the thighs of her pants. "Or what they do."

"From an old engine. I was just thinking they would look like hooves."

"If he had hoofs," Willa shrieked, "he could stand up! And then I could ride him!"

"Honey," Patty said, "if you tried to stand all this up, it would just fall apart. The ground is the only thing holding it together."

"Oh," Willa said. She sounded heartbroken. She wiggled into position and lay down on her side in the spot that represented the horse's back. As if attempting to ride him horizontally. Lying down. "Giddyup!" she shrieked, then frowned and pulled to her feet. "That's no good. We have to glue him together."

"Glue won't hold all this," Roseanna said. Then she looked to Patty in case she was wrong. "Will it?"

"No, I wouldn't think so. You'd have to weld it."

"Well, that's that, then. Unless you know how to weld."

"Not really. But I used to work for a guy around here who welds. Maybe he could teach us."

"Hmm," Roseanna said. "Sounds like a project."

"Yeah!" Willa shrieked. "I think it sounds great, too!"

While Patty hiked to the top of the hill to call the welder, Roseanna sat in the shade of an old maple tree with Willa. They both leaned against its trunk, Willa's shoulder pressed into Roseanna's arm.

"Why are you sad now?" Willa asked. She did not shriek it. She seemed to have slipped into a more nappish mode.

"Why do you say I'm sad?"

"Because you are. You seemed good when I was showing you the cat. Then you walked up the hill. Then you came down and you were sad."

"Oh. Yeah. Right. Well. It's like this, Willa. I was talking to my son. And we didn't exactly get along."

"I'm sorry," Willa said.

Then she scooted her butt a foot or so away and lay down on her side in the dirt, resting her head on Roseanna's lap.

Roseanna stroked Willa's thin, silky hair and thought, *Okay, I'm dead now. It's all over. They're going to stay forever, and there's not a damn thing I can do.*

ABOUT A MONTH BEFORE THE MOVE

Chapter Nine

Scratches and Scuffs of the Heart

Roseanna arrived at her Manhattan law firm offices nearly half an hour late.

When she walked into Alice's office, Alice immediately spun in her chair until she sat faced away from the door. And from Roseanna. She was on the phone, speaking in hushed tones. She did not meet Roseanna's eyes.

This was not a business call. Nor a happy occasion.

When Alice glanced guiltily over her shoulder, Roseanna tried to signal that she would come back later. It involved a vague pointing toward the door she would use for her exit. Alice shook her head and held up one finger.

Roseanna exited anyway.

Three or four minutes later Alice stuck her head out into the hall where Roseanna stood with her back leaned up against the wall, staring at nothing.

"Apologies, darling," Alice said.

"Bad timing. It's my curse in life. It follows me wherever I go."

"Oh, bull. Nobody has better timing than you.

You could have been a stand-up comic. Get your ass in here."

Roseanna walked in.

She sat in one of the buttery-soft leather wing chairs, facing the window.

Alice poured herself a drink. A rather stiff one for ten twenty in the morning, Roseanna thought. About four fingers. Three if it were Roseanna's stubby, sausage-like digits doing the measuring. Alice raised the bottle in a silent offer, and Roseanna nodded.

"Not *that* much, though," she added, this time in words.

Alice set a glass of bourbon near Roseanna's elbow and sat in her desk chair, spinning it around to face the window as well. They sat looking over the Midtown skyline together.

For a surprising length of time, they did so in silence.

"So how's life?" Roseanna asked.

It was a mildly sarcastic question. Clearly life was not so good, but Roseanna wasn't sure if her friend wanted to talk about how good it wasn't.

"I was never a big fan," Alice said.

"Of life?"

"Right."

"In general?"

"Right."

They sat in silence for a couple of minutes more. Alice propped her Jimmy Choo heels up on the windowsill. Crossed one ankle over the other. Brushed her curly hair out of her eyes with one careless hand, meaning Roseanna would have to prompt her friend to check her hairdo in the mirror before the big meeting.

They didn't have all that much time to kill, either. Their appointment to meet with Tyler Brandt was only about seven minutes away. Roseanna kept an eye on her wristwatch as they sat. She wore it with its face on the inside of her wrist, an old habit that allowed her to glance at the time without tipping her hand, either literally or figuratively.

"I got my heart broken," Alice said, startling her slightly. "Yet again."

"Oh." Then Roseanna was not quite sure where to go from there. Being someone's shoulder to cry on had never been her strong suit. Then again, Alice wasn't crying. "I'm sorry to hear that."

"But it's okay."

"How can that be okay?"

"It just is."

"Not in any world I ever lived in."

"I'm not just saying that to be stoic."

"I wasn't calling you a liar. Just explain to me how getting your heart broken is okay. Because I'm not following that."

"Oh, come on, Roseanna. You've been through an acrimonious divorce, so what can I teach you about heartbreak?"

"Maybe . . . how it can be okay?"

Alice sighed. She spun back to her desk and pulled her battered soft-side leather briefcase out from under it. Slapped it hard onto the papers on the desktop.

"It's like this bag," she said, sounding as though the liquor might be going to her head already. Then again, Roseanna had no way of knowing if this was her first glass. "My favorite bag. You know how much I love this bag."

"Your heart is like that bag?"

"Exactly."

"I think you're a little in the bag yourself, hon."

"No, I'm making a serious point here." Alice ran a hand over the straps and buckles. "How many times has Jerry told me I should get a new one of these?"

"I've lost count."

"But I never replace it."

"No. You never do."

"Because it's *supposed* to be beat up. That shows it's had a life. That I *used* it. That I wasn't afraid to put it through its paces. I didn't just put it on a shelf and stare at it. It's not for looks only.

"It reminds me of . . . when I was a kid in Missouri . . . I don't think I ever told you this, because I just now thought of it for the first time in years. My brother got into a big fight in a gas station, and I mean an actual fistfight. Our dad had to go downtown and bail him out of jail. And you know what the fight was about? Well, of course you don't. Sorry. He told a local kid, a teenage guy he knew from his high school, that the guy's truck was 'disco.' I'm really dating myself now, because nobody uses that term anymore. It means it was too clean. It was a jacked-up four-wheel-drive pickup. It's not supposed to be clean. It's supposed to be driven in the dirt. So those are fighting words, if you accuse someone of having a truck that's too clean. It's about more than just the truck. It means the person is a big phony. Like if a Texan says you're all hat and no cattle. You know what I mean?"

"I think so. You're saying hearts are *supposed* to be broken. Not sure I agree, but . . ."

"Right. Otherwise you're not really using them. Which is a very cowardly way to live, don't you think?"

They sat in silence for a minute or so.

Roseanna glanced at her watch to be sure they weren't late for the Brandt meeting. "I didn't even know you were seeing somebody," she said after a time.

"Not really for that long. And it was somebody . . . well . . . too young—that's all I'm going to say about that. I should have my head examined. It's embarrassing to talk about it even. But, you know. We're at that age when we realize we have a few more wild oats left to sow."

"Speak for yourself," Roseanna said, because she considered herself utterly oatless. "So what happened?"

"Oh, the usual. I'm too married to my job."

"Only for two more years."

"That doesn't work with the young ones, darling. It's like saying 'I'll spend more time with you in your next life.' The earth doesn't spin as fast for them as it does for us."

It was nearly time to go. But Roseanna had one more burning question. And it didn't seem to want to wait.

"Why didn't you tell me?"

"What? That I was seeing someone? Or that it didn't pan out?"

"Yes. That."

"Oh, well, what can I say, darling? We don't really talk about private things like that. Do we? I didn't think we did."

"But we're best friends."

"True."

"That can't be a good sign."

"Oh, I don't know, Roseanna; don't read too much in. Being private people is not the worst thing in the world. But I'll tell you what. After the Brandt meeting we'll have a nice long three-martini lunch. And we'll see what it is we've been missing about each other's gossip. Maybe we can do better. Maybe you really can teach a couple of old dogs. You know."

"Okay," Roseanna said. "That's a deal. I'd like that."

And Roseanna *would* have liked that. Very much. She would have treasured such an opportunity, in fact, had it ever come to pass.

THE MOVE, CONTINUED

Chapter Ten

Fishing—as Opposed to Catching—and Knowing What You're Afraid Of

Roseanna was on her way to the barn to do some welding when she noticed him. The young man. He was leaning on her fence, staring at the iron zoo. People did from time to time.

She walked closer to him, but he was too caught up in the animal sculptures to notice.

He looked barely twenty, if that, wearing a battered and faded hat with a brim. Not quite a cowboy hat, but something similar. He lifted it, squinting his eyes into the early afternoon sun. His hair was strangely short. Shaved, almost. He had a serious, intelligent-looking face. He scratched his nearly bare scalp and snugged the hat back into place. By his feet sat a massive backpack, the kind people lug with them when they go out into the wilderness for days at a time.

Then he saw her standing nearby, and he removed the hat again, tipping it to her. "Morning, miss," he called. "Or is it afternoon?"

"Afternoon, I think," she said.

She walked closer, and leaned on the fence from the inside, and they stared at the animals together.

"Interesting what you've done here," he said. "Or I guess I shouldn't assume. You make these yourself?"

"Well, not all by myself. There's a little girl who helped with the creative part of the process. But you don't hand a welding torch to a five-year-old. So I'm the one who welded them together."

"Hmm," he said. "Big job, welding. Kind of a lost art these days. Don't think I ever met a woman welder, though it's all good that you are."

"I'm not sure I'd call myself a welder," Roseanna said. "I'm just learning. If you were to go closer, you'd see I'm quite a bit short of a pro."

"Mind if I do? Oh, not to check up on your work, miss. I didn't mean it like that. I'd just like to see these things up close."

"Be my guest," she said, and pointed toward the gate.

The young man hefted his heavy pack onto his shoulders and walked toward the gate, which Roseanna held open. He held his hand out to her to shake before walking onto her property.

"Sorry," he said. "Where're my manners? Nelson David. First name Nelson, last name David. People get that backwards a lot. And I appreciate it a lot if they don't."

"Pleased to meet you, Nelson," she said. "Rosie Chaldecott."

They walked together into the field with the elephant, and the lion, and the horse, and the giraffe, and the hippopotamus, and walked among them in silence.

"Looks like good work to me," Nelson said.

"You can see all the welds."

"Holds together, though."

"Yes, in fact the little girl rides the horse daily." Roseanna had welded the saddle-shaped seat of an ancient tractor onto its back. "Where's home for you?"

Nelson pointed to somewhere in the area of his own shoulder with a hooked thumb. Roseanna could only think he was indicating a vague direction, and did not understand.

"Where?"

"Pretty much here on my back," he said. "Since I got out of the service, I've just been moving around."

"The service?"

"Armed services. The Army."

"Ah. Got it." *That explains the haircut,* Roseanna thought. "How long have you been out?"

" 'Bout four days."

They walked to the giraffe, and Nelson stared up its long neck, shielding his eyes when the midday sun poured in under his hat brim.

"Still," Roseanna said. "You must be from somewhere. Everybody is."

"True enough, miss. Everybody's from somewhere. Me, I'm from North Carolina. But I'm not so sure I'd call it home."

"Ah," she said. "Now that you say it, I can hear just a trace of the accent."

"Too bad. I did my best to shake it in my two years of duty. I guess I just wanted to leave all that behind me. Lived there with my parents from the day I was born till the day I turned eighteen. Then I joined up because I wanted to get away. Don't get me wrong. I love my parents. They're good people. Each on their own. But put them together and what you get is not good. They fight all the time. Every minute they're together, seems like. And I could never understand why. Life's too short for all that fighting. That's how I see it, anyway."

They wandered over to the lion. Roseanna was particularly proud of the lion—the way she had welded the links of dozens of lengths of chain so they stood rigid in a curving pattern to form the gigantic ruff of mane.

"Because they're not happy," she said.

Nelson looked at her face briefly, then back at the lion. He offered no comment.

"I'm starting to see that we make choices at an early age," Roseanna continued, "when we're too young to know what will make us happy. But they're more or less permanent choices. They don't have to be, I guess. But somehow we end up *thinking* they have to be. It's hard to make a change after so many years, and we don't want to let people down by breaking our promises. But what we do to those poor people is worse.

We blame them for the fact that we're not happy. Because that's easier than blaming ourselves. Because if we blame ourselves, then we have to fix it, and that's a tricky thing."

Nelson's eyes came up to hers again. Briefly.

"Well, I appreciate the close-up look at your work, miss. It's quite . . . fanciful."

"Yes," she said. "It is that."

They moved off toward the gate together. Slowly. The young man didn't seem to be in any hurry to leave.

"Sure would like to see what's involved in the process of welding," he said.

Roseanna lifted her heavy welder's mask and wiped sweat off her brow. The interior of the barn was nicely shady, but did not have the benefit of a breeze. All she had done was weld two pieces of pipe together at an angle, and already she was hot and exhausted. She turned off the torch. The silence felt heavenly.

"So this is something you really like to do," Nelson said, carefully testing the pipes to see if they were cool enough to touch.

"Not really. No. It's summer, and it's hot enough with no torch involved. And it makes my arms and shoulders ache. And the mask is heavy, and makes me feel like there's not enough air."

"A bit of an obvious question," the young man began, "but why, then?"

"Because of this moment right here. When I lift up the mask and breathe cool air and turn off the torch. And then I look down and see that I've created something. A real something, that you can see and touch. Other than a meal, I haven't made a lot of tangible things in my life. I guess I like it because it's hard. I have to struggle for it. But then, when it's done, I feel good about what I did. I feel gratified. And the fact that it was difficult makes it even better."

She looked up to see the young man nodding firmly. "Everything in life is like that," he said.

"You think so?"

"Everything worth having. Thanks for showing me. I guess I should get out of your hair."

They stepped out of the barn together. Moved toward the gate.

Nelson stopped, though, and pointed down the hill toward the creek. "If you don't mind my asking, miss . . . is that your property down there?"

"Down where?"

"I've noticed the last couple miles—I can see from where I've been walking how there's a nice deep creek flowing down that hill. I wanted to see if there're fish in it, but I figured it's all private property. Do you happen to know if there's any good fishing down there?"

"I have no idea," she said. "It's my property. But I've never been down there."

"Never been down there?" He sounded genuinely shocked. "How is that possible? How can you own a piece of land you haven't seen?"

"I've only been here not two months. And I wasn't in such great physical shape when I moved in. I'm working up to things slowly. It's a steep hill. I guess I wasn't relishing having to hike back up."

"Well, in my humble opinion, miss, you need to know if there's good fishing on your own property. If you've got a year-round stream on your farm, you have to've seen it with your own eyes. Walk down there with me. If you have trouble coming back up, you can grab a strap on my pack, and I'll tow you up like I was a draft horse. Sound fair enough?"

"Sure," Roseanna said. "That sounds fair enough."

"I think that's probably true what you said about my parents," Nelson said.

They sat in the shade on one bank of the stream, in a spot where the water looked surprisingly deep, watching the ghostly shapes of three or four silvery fish dart back and forth under the surface of a slow pool.

"And other people who're like them," he said when she didn't respond. "I guess you were speaking more generally. So . . . hey. Not to overplay my hand here, miss, but I have a collapsible

171

fishing rod in my pack. Mind if I try my hand at getting one of those?"

"Not at all," she said. "Take your best shot."

"I think I just got incredibly scared," Roseanna said, after telling him the story of Alice's sudden stroke.

It was probably an hour later. They were still sitting in the shade, their backs up against the narrow trunks of their respective trees. He still had not caught anything.

He didn't answer, so she added, "It's hard for me to admit that, but it's true."

"We're all going to die," Nelson said, leaning forward over his knees and staring down the end of his fishing pole. "So it doesn't pay to go through life fearing death. Mind you, I realize as I say so . . . it's one of those things that says easy and does hard."

"It's not that. I don't mean I'm afraid of dying. Well, I am, of course. Most people are. But that's not the main thing."

"What's the main thing?" he asked.

They sat in silence for a moment.

This is how it is, she now realized, when you're fishing. Most of the time is spent fishing, not catching. It's not the most scintillating process. So you'd best be prepared to pass the time some other way. Good conversation if you're not alone. Worthwhile thoughts if you are.

172

"You know how . . . ," she began, and then stalled briefly. "A person goes to the doctor. They think everything's fine. Just some minor complaint. Doctor comes in with the X-rays or whatever and says, 'Bad news. You only have a year to live.' That person's life changes completely in that moment. All of a sudden they realize they're about to be out of time. They start thinking about how they want to live while they still can."

He waited briefly for her to go on. But she was hoping she wouldn't need to.

"But that didn't happen to you. Did it?"

"No. But why should it have to? I'm going to die. We all are. And we all know it. We like to think it's eons in the future, but we could walk out in front of a truck tomorrow. Hell, today. And we all know that, too. But we waste our precious time. Why? Why do we live like we're not going to die?"

He mulled that over for a moment or two, flicking the end of the fishing rod up and down to try to tempt the trout, who were definitively not biting.

"You would be asking the wrong person, miss," he said. "I know less than nothing about human nature. I feel like I've spent my whole life staring at the people around me and thinking, 'What am I missing?'"

"I know the feeling."

"So you got scared that you weren't going to live enough before you died."

"Exactly."

"Then I'd say you did the right thing, miss. Running away from home and all."

And with that he reeled in his line, apparently giving up.

"You're the only one who thinks so. So far, anyway."

"Well, you should listen to *me*, Miss Rosie. Because I'm very wise." His face broke into a self-deprecating smirk. "Actually I'm not. But I'm agreeing with you. So why not think so? I give up for this afternoon, miss. They're in there all right, but they're just not biting." As he spoke, he carefully removed the bait from his hook. Tiny, bright red salmon eggs that he gingerly returned to a small glass jar. He collapsed the rod again, taking it apart section by section. "So, listen. I'm probably pressing my luck with this. But I'm going to ask anyway. Never hurts to ask, and you can always tell me to go to hell. Sundown and sunrise is the time I'm most likely to catch one. And it's a little late in the afternoon to be moving on by foot when I don't know what's ahead of me—what's within walking distance, and whether or not I'll be able to hitch a ride. Any chance you'd let me pitch my tent here for tonight? I'll wade across the creek and go behind that stand of trees. You won't see me from the house. And I'll be as quiet as a whisper. I promise."

"You're more than welcome," she said, surprising herself. Because under normal circumstances, she knew, she did not make people feel more than welcome. Or even barely welcome. It was probably because he was polite, and he agreed with her thinking about running away from home.

He tipped his hat to her as an unspoken thank-you.

"Want me to tow you up that steep hill like I promised?"

"No," she said. "Thank you. I want to get up there all by myself."

And she did, without even pausing to rest. She puffed and panted, but didn't stop moving her feet to do so. She had been here two months, she realized, and she was getting in shape. It pleased her in a way she could not remember having been pleased in the past.

Willa hauled the young man up to the house by his hand the following morning. Roseanna couldn't miss noticing because the little girl was shouting, "Rosie! Rosie! Rosie!" quite stridently, as if something were on fire.

Roseanna dashed out onto the porch to see nothing on fire, and Willa dragging the semiwilling ex-Army man up onto her porch.

"He's *Nelson*," Willa said, as if this were a sobering and highly relevant fact.

"Yes, I know," Roseanna said. "We've met."

"Oh," Willa said. She sounded disappointed. Apparently the scoop factor in discovering a new person on the property had been important to her. "You have to *feed* him."

"No, that's not the case," Nelson said, his face reddening. "You don't have to feed me, miss. Willa, remember? You weren't going to say that."

"Oh," Willa replied. "I *wasn't* going to say that. I was thinking it was the other way around."

Then the little girl ran off to join her mother, who was watching carefully from a distance. Nelson looked at Roseanna and she at him, and his face flushed even redder.

"So," Roseanna said. "Can I offer you some breakfast?"

The young man looked down at the wooden boards under his sturdy boots. "I'm not destitute," he said. "I have a little money on me. I set out prepared to take care of my own self and not sponge off anybody. Just, after I had my breakfast yesterday morning, this road took me out in the middle of nowhere. Does no good to have money for food if no one is selling any."

"Do come in," she said. "I was just about to make some scrambled eggs and toast."

He stepped into her living room, doffing his hat

and holding it respectfully in front of his belly with both hands.

"I was hoping to catch one of those nice big trout to solve the problem," he said as she began to gather the ingredients for their breakfast.

"But how would you have cooked it?"

"I have a little camp stove. That's not the trouble. Trouble is, they're not biting. At first I thought it was the wrong time of day, and they just weren't in a feeding sort of a mood. But I've tried an awful lot of times of day. Now I think they just won't go for my artificial bait. They seem to be natives. You know. As opposed to stock fish—the fish that get poured into streams by the thousands so the sport fishermen have something to catch. The stock fish'll take just any old thing. They feed them on some kind of pellets at the hatcheries. Sometimes the natives only want bugs or worms. That's all that looks familiar to them." He leaned his back against her kitchen wall and watched her work. "This is good of you," he added.

"It's not a problem. We can't send you out on the road half-starved."

She specifically mentioned the road because she already sensed that he felt comfortable in this place, and that his wanting to stay here was not out of the question. Though exactly *how* she sensed such a thing, she could not have said.

He seemed to pick up on the hint.

"This is an amazing place you have here," he said. "You're lucky."

"I agree that I am," she said, breaking the first of seven eggs into a bowl.

"It has a special feel to it. I woke up this morning and put some coffee on the camp stove and sat cross-legged staring out over the hills for the longest time. It was just as the sun was coming up. It was a tad misty down in that valley. And I watched the sky turn colors, and I just felt like . . . like there's something akin to heaven here. It's just so natural and so quiet."

"Natural it is," Roseanna said. "But it's only quiet until Willa wakes up."

He smiled, but it was a sad little thing. He knew he was about to need to go. She could see it in his eyes. He didn't want to go. She could see that, too.

"Wish we had a fresh trout to go with those eggs. Ever had trout and eggs for breakfast?"

"Can't say as I have, no."

"Well, but . . . you know how a fish tastes when it's fresh out of the water."

"I don't know that I do. I'm sure I've had some fish that's fresher than others. But I lived in the city all my life . . ."

"You never had a fish fresh out of the water? Like, not twenty minutes from his last swim?"

"I have not."

"Well, it's official, then," he said. And the lost

puppy look disappeared from his eyes, replaced by a surging enthusiasm. "You need to taste that. And I'm here to make sure you do."

"But you couldn't get one to bite."

"I'll dig some worms. But don't worry. I won't leave holes all over your property. I'll dig right in the creek itself. In the shallow places. And the flowing water'll fill the holes right back in. But I'll get you a fish. And then we'll have the best breakfast you ever had. Or lunch, or dinner. Depending on when I catch one. But don't you worry. I'll catch one. I don't care if it takes days."

Roseanna offered no reply. She couldn't help noticing that he wasn't asking her, the property owner, if *she* cared if it took days.

But he was so fresh faced and enthusiastic, so earnest in his desire to share this experience with her, that she couldn't bring herself to dash his youthful hopes on the matter.

Just as he left her house, his belly full of breakfast, Nelson turned and looked straight into Roseanna's eyes.

"You need to tell more people that story," he said.

"What story is that?"

"About that friend of yours who died. Who thought she had time to live later. But she didn't. I'm sorry, but I can't think of her name now."

"Alice," Roseanna said. Quietly.

"Right. You need to tell more people that story about Alice."

"Why do I need to do that?"

"Because they're not happy, miss. Haven't you noticed that? Because hardly anybody is happy."

Chapter Eleven

Thank You for Not Biting

A couple of weeks and several trout-and-egg breakfasts passed, and no one new came along to whom Roseanna could tell the story of Alice and her miscalculation. The young ex-Army man did not move on, and she did not force the issue.

Then one day Roseanna looked out her window and noticed that a couple had pulled their beat-up compact car off the road in front of her fence. They were standing by her gate, taking pictures of the sculptures with a cardboard-covered disposable camera.

She walked out of the house and toward the gate to greet them, waving as she did so, to telegraph that the impending encounter would be a friendly one.

They waved giddily in return.

They were middle aged. Maybe a couple of years younger than Roseanna. The man had bushy dark hair partly smashed by a silly-looking boater hat. The woman was blonde, though probably not naturally, and more than a little bit stout. Beyond that their faces were effectively hidden behind dark sunglasses.

"Those animals are just so much *fun,*" the

woman squealed. She was naturally loud, which had become Roseanna's least favorite quality in a person.

"I'm glad you like them," Roseanna said, covering over her distaste for the sake of an opportunity to tell The Story.

The man strode up to her with the camera in his left hand, his right hand thrust out to shake hers. "Dave," he said. "And this is my wife, Melanie."

"You live around here?" she asked him.

"Oh, no. Never been around here before."

"What brings you through here?"

"We're on a sort of a road trip," Melanie said. Which was unfortunate, because, being Melanie, she said it too stridently. And too loudly. "Only we're not sure where to. We're teachers, and we have the summer off school, and we're trying to decide where to go all summer, or whether to even go back at all. If we find a really great place we might just take early retirement. But that's probably more than you wanted to know."

While she spoke, Roseanna noticed their dog. A short-haired, nondescript-looking brown dog, of medium size, sniffing around on the broken yellow line in the middle of the road.

"I never mind hearing people's stories," she said. "I have stories I like to tell, too. But before I do, I think you'd better get your dog out of the road. I realize there's not a ton of traffic coming through here. But that's a blind curve right there."

She pointed toward the piece of road that curled sharply around CPR Hill. "And the locals take this road at top speed because they figure they know it like their own living room. They might never think of the possibility that somebody's dog could be standing right in the middle of it."

Melanie and Dave turned their heads to look at the dog. But they said nothing. And they made no move to call the dog to them.

"Seriously," Roseanna said. "It could be dangerous for him."

"That's not our dog," Dave said.

"No, we've never seen him," Melanie said too loudly. "Or we hadn't, before we got out of the car. We figured he was yours."

"Hmm," Roseanna said. "Don't go away."

She stepped through the gate and began walking in the dog's direction. He noticed. For a moment he seemed painfully torn. He stood with his back arched. He tucked his tail between his hind legs, but still wagged it hesitantly. He seemed to want to meet Roseanna and to run from her in equal measure.

She extended a hand to him, and he reached a tentative muzzle out to sniff the hand.

Just then a speeding car tore around the blind curve. Without thinking, Roseanna reached out and grabbed the dog—who was heavier than he looked. She pulled him up into her arms and against her chest, realizing as she did that he might bite. She had no way of knowing for a fact that he wouldn't bite.

She jumped back a few steps, and the car swerved around her, fishtailing in the dirt, horn blaring. Then it sped on.

She looked into the face of the dog, which was only inches from her own. The dog looked back.

"Thank you for not biting me," she said.

Then she struggled to carry him back to the gate. Because if she set him down, she was afraid he would run off. And, if he did, the next time he got in trouble there would be nobody there to save him.

"That was close!" Melanie said.

"Yes. Too close."

"He doesn't look like a stray," Dave added. "He looks like somebody's dog. He's plump enough, and clean. But no collar."

"Yes, I'm guessing someone will be looking for him. I'm going to put him in my barn for a few minutes, so he can't get into any more trouble. And then I'll see if I can't find out who owns him. But first, if you two will hold still for it, I'd like to tell you a story."

"That settles it!" Melanie said, slapping her husband, Dave, hard on the knee. "We're retiring!"

They sat cross-legged in the grass behind Roseanna's barn, staring out over the hills and valleys, the forests and streams. Dave nodded, his boater hat bouncing up and down with the force of his assent.

"I think you're right, babe," he said. "I really see your point."

"Oh, that is just so *sad!*" Melanie fairly shrieked. The word "sad" came out so loud that Roseanna was tempted to press a palm to her Melanie-side ear. "I never thought of that. Not once. Why, Dave and I tossed out a million ideas on why we should or shouldn't retire. We even listed all the pros and cons on a sheet of paper. You know, with a line right down the middle—that whole thing. And not at any point did it occur to us that one of us could fall dead, and then it would be too late. We just never once thought of it!"

"People don't like to think about things like that," Roseanna said. Quietly. In case it was possible to set a good example, volume-wise.

They sat in silence for a few moments. Roseanna noticed that she could see a scrap of Nelson's tent down the hill and through the trees.

"We never even considered it!" Melanie shouted.

It startled Roseanna, who decided she'd had enough.

"Well," she said, levering herself to her feet and dusting off the seat of her pants, "I'm going to take that dog into town."

Both Melanie and Dave looked up at Roseanna as if she'd said she was going to take the poor beast out behind the shed, give him a blindfold and a last cigarette, and stand him up in front of a firing squad.

"What are you going to *do* with him?" Melanie asked.

"I guess . . . put an ad in the paper? You know. Found. Dog. Brown, nondescript. Medium build. That sort of thing."

"Why even take him along for that?" Dave added. "I doubt you can get him to write a check for the ad."

Then he waited, as if expecting someone to laugh. No one did.

"I was thinking they'd want to take his picture," Roseanna said. "I mean . . . don't they?"

"I don't think so," Dave said. "I never saw a lost and found ad for a dog with a picture to go along."

"Just don't take him to the pound and dump him there," Melanie said. "Please. You know what they do to dogs at those places."

"But isn't that where his owner will be most likely to find him?"

"If it was me," Dave said, "and I lost my dog, I'd look in the classified ads in the local paper first thing."

"Whatever," Roseanna said. "Between the dog and me I'm sure we'll figure something out."

Roseanna stepped into the newspaper office in Walkerville with the dog in her arms. She set him down on the carpet. The woman behind the front-office desk had a round face and big hair. Curly and big. She looked up at Roseanna, though not directly into her eyes. And she frowned. Noticeably frowned.

It had occurred to Roseanna that a dog might not be welcome in the building. And yet the woman wasn't looking at the dog. She didn't seem to have noticed him yet. She was staring at Roseanna—at a spot somewhere in the vicinity of her nose, the way people do when they don't enjoy eye contact.

"My name is Roseanna Chaldecott," Roseanna said.

The woman lifted a half-eaten candy bar, still mostly shrouded in its wrapper, and took the tiniest bite with her front teeth only. It showed off her prominent overbite and made her look like a bunny rabbit. Then she set the candy down and wiped her lips with what looked like a clean tissue. She frowned again.

"I know who you are," she said.

"Now how would you know that?"

Roseanna walked to the desk and perched on the edge of an uncomfortable chair. The dog, having no special reason to stay with her, sat leaning against the door, hunched over, with his head down and his shoulders protruding like a vulture.

"Small town," she said. "You bought Macy

Peterson's old place. You have all that junk where it can be seen from the road."

"You must be thinking of somebody else."

"No." The woman scratched behind her ear with the eraser end of a pencil. "I'm thinking of you. All those metal shapes."

"That's not junk," Roseanna said, her gorge rising. "That's art. It *was* junk. But now it's art."

"Make it into any shape you want," the woman said. "It still is what it is."

Roseanna took a deep breath and chose to ignore the rudeness. She opened her mouth to request the ad she wished to place, but the woman interrupted her.

"No dogs allowed in here."

"But I need to place a 'found' ad. And he's what I found."

"There you go again."

"I don't follow."

"A thing is exactly what it is, no matter how you try to twist it."

"Let me start over," Roseanna said. "I think we got off on the wrong foot. I'd like to place a classified ad."

"Fine," the woman said, and nibbled another minibite of her candy bar. Then she held both hands in the air above her keyboard, poised. "Shoot."

"Found. Chudley area. Medium-sized brown dog. Nondescript looking. Short haired. Friendly enough. Doesn't look like a stray. Well fed, but no collar."

She paused. The woman stopped typing and hovered again.

"Is that it?"

"Well. My phone number."

"That's usually best." The woman picked up her pencil and tapped the eraser against the monitor a number of times. She seemed to be counting words. Or maybe even characters. "Sixty-two fifty."

"Sixty-two fifty?"

"Sixty-two fifty."

"I thought newspapers placed found ads without charge. You know. Because advertising something you found is a good Samaritan thing to do."

"I wouldn't know anything about that."

"He's not even my dog."

"You want the ad, or don't you?"

"No. Not that one. But I still need to find his owner. So let's start over."

The woman sighed. She held her finger down on the delete key for a couple of seconds. Then she re-poised. "Okay, shoot."

"Found. Dog. Chudley. And the phone number."

"Thirty-two dollars."

"It's about one-tenth as long!"

"That's our minimum. Thirty-two dollars."

"Fine," Roseanna said.

She sighed, and began to dig around in her

purse. She glanced over her shoulder at the dog, who was still leaning nervously against the door. She shot him a look that said he was entirely to blame for all of this. He returned a look that said he accepted all that guilt and more.

"You could have left the dog in the car," the woman said.

"I thought you'd want to take his picture."

"Why would I want to do that?"

"So his owner can recognize him?"

"Do you really want to know what an ad with a photo would cost you?"

"No," Roseanna said. "Never mind."

She dictated her phone number to the woman and counted out thirty-two dollars in cash onto the desk.

"Okay," the woman said, still not looking directly at Roseanna's face. "This will run a week from Thursday."

"*A week from Thursday?* Is that a joke? What am I supposed to do with him in the meantime?"

"That would not be my department."

"Why will it take so long?"

"The deadline for this Thursday's paper is passed."

"Why does it have to run on a Thursday?"

The woman stole a direct glance at Roseanna, but just a quick one. And somewhat sideways, if such a thing were possible. "This is a weekly paper. I thought you knew that."

"And this is the only paper that serves this area."

"It is."

"And it's a weekly."

"Correct."

Roseanna sighed again and pulled to her feet.

Her plan had been to ask the whereabouts of the nearest animal shelter. But now she couldn't. Because a week from Thursday was too long. By then a shelter might already have done what shelters do to unwanted dogs.

She stood over the unwanted dog and stared down at him, which seemed to intensify his anxiety.

"Okay," she said. "I guess I have to take you home with me."

"I've never seen that dog," the woman said to Roseanna's back. "I don't think he lives around here."

"You couldn't possibly know every dog in the county."

"Couldn't I?"

"Well, anyway, even if you did know every dog in the county, he could be a dog someone just brought home."

"You haven't lived here for long, so let me tell you what happens. People don't want a dog, so they drive it way out into the country and put it out of the car. It's like that old thing where your father takes your dog to the pound, but he says he took it to live on a farm where it can chase rabbits all day long. People convince themselves it's some kind of a dream life for a dog out here, but mostly they starve or get run over on the highways."

Roseanna took her eyes off the dog and looked back over her shoulder at the irritating woman. "You're just a treat in every sense of the word, aren't you?"

The woman glowered at Roseanna in return. "You know, a handful of the locals are looking into whether there's an ordinance against your junk."

"They can look the other way as they drive by."

"You're missing the point. It's mostly the extra traffic they don't like. Though some are into the principle of the thing because they don't find them scenic."

"I feel sorry for people like you," Roseanna said. "You look at whimsical animal sculptures and see junk. You look at this perfectly nice dog and see something that somebody threw away like garbage. Now why would someone throw away a perfectly nice dog like this?"

Roseanna bent down to grab the dog up into her arms. He half stood in nervous anticipation, then urinated all over his own front legs and the newspaper-office carpet.

"That might be a clue right there," the woman said.

• • •

Roseanna held the dog with the sheer force of her will, staring at him where he sat on the curb and repeating the word "stay" in the most authoritative voice she could muster.

In between stays she bought a local—weekly!—newspaper out of an automated rack, separated out its double pages, and used them to cover the passenger seat of her Maserati.

"Okay," she said to the dog when the paper seemed thick enough. "You can get in now."

The dog hopped into her car as if he understood English perfectly. Clearly he was used to being somebody's dog.

Based on his confidence level, Roseanna thought, *maybe not somebody very nice.*

Roseanna sat down in the driver's seat and watched for a moment as the dog padded around on the crinkling paper, which seemed an impediment to his sitting or lying down. Eventually he settled, seemingly against his nature.

They set off toward home together.

Roseanna looked over at the dog, and he looked back. His eyes seemed to hold a better understanding of the situation than a dog should by all rights possess.

"Okay," she said. "I get it. We all have something like that in our lives. Something we look back on with a wince. That we know was not our finest moment. I can forgive that if the newspaper people can. But if you think you're coming into my house, you have another think coming. You'll live outside until your owner calls. If it's rainy and cold, you can stay in the barn."

The dog stared into Roseanna's face as if translating her message into Dog one word at a time.

Roseanna knew, as the words came out of her mouth, that the dog's owner was not going to call. Much as she had wanted to resist the rude woman's assessment that the dog had been dumped, it struck Roseanna's intuitive gut as a likely scenario.

"Damn," she said suddenly, making a U-turn in the deserted road. "I forgot to buy dog food while I was in town."

When she arrived home, Roseanna had a talk with the dog before letting him jump out of the car.

"Now, you have to stay on the property," she said. "No more of this sniffing around in the middle of the road. I'm not going to tie you up, because that's just plain mean. So you'll have to be on the honor system."

Good going, Roseanna, she thought to herself. *Like a dog understands the honor system.*

"Maybe I'll make it the little girl's job to keep tabs on you," Roseanna said.

She stepped out of the car and opened the

passenger door for the dog, who jumped down. Roseanna balled up the newspapers and began to walk them over to the outside trash cans.

There she ran smack-dab into Melanie. More or less literally.

"Oh, you're still here," Roseanna said, hoping it would be enough of a hint. Then, just to be sure, she added, "I didn't think you'd still be here."

"Yeah, I hope you don't mind!" Melanie squealed. But then she talked over any chance Roseanna might have had to express her objections. "We met that nice young man, David Nelson. He's teaching Dave to fish. Dave's always wanted to learn how to fish, but we live in the city, you know? As soon as Dave catches his first fish, we'll be moving along."

Great, Roseanna thought. *It only took Nelson three days to catch one, and he seemed to already know quite a bit about the task.*

"I was just thinking it's getting late in the afternoon," Roseanna said, trying to be more polite than the situation warranted. "You know. When you move on, you want a little daylight to get wherever you're going."

"Oh, we already set up our tent down there. On the other side of the trees, where the other guy's been camping."

"You have a tent?"

"Yes, this is a camping trip for us, didn't we

tell you? We figured if you didn't mind the young man's tent down there, you wouldn't mind ours. We're not where you could see us or hear us from the house."

Then Melanie trotted off down the hill toward the stream before Roseanna could offer any objection.

I could probably hear you from Myanmar, Roseanna thought as she watched the woman's back grow smaller.

She looked down at the dog, who looked back at her with some visible measure of distress.

"Sure," she said. "No problem. Everybody just make yourself at home."

The dog turned his head away in shame.

Roseanna asked him, "You think if I placed a newspaper found ad for those people anybody would call?"

The dog wagged nervously, as if it pained him not to be able to answer.

Roseanna gave up, sighed, and walked back into her house.

Chapter Twelve

Nice Life You Got Here . . . Be a Shame if Something Happened to It

Roseanna was chopping firewood with a splitting maul—no small task even in her improved physical condition—when the old man came puttering up on his motor scooter, trailed by a cloud of brownish smoke. He pulled off into the dirt when he saw her metal zoo. He set the kickstand on the tiny bike, which was loaded up with fully packed saddlebags, and cut the noisy engine.

He didn't seem to have noticed her yet.

He walked to the fence and pulled off his helmet with what looked like a great deal of effort, exposing a mostly bare scalp. He leaned on her fence.

In time he sat down carefully in the dirt, his elbows braced on his own knees, and stared some more.

Roseanna left her work and walked to where the old man sat. He jumped when he saw her. Tried to struggle to his feet but failed quite miserably and fell back onto his rump again.

"Sorry," he said. "Hope you don't mind. I was just looking."

"Not at all," she said. "That's what they're for. I made them for looking."

She opened her mouth to start more of a real conversation with him. Something that could lead to the story of Alice. Then she closed her mouth again. Because it struck her that a few of the people to whom she'd told that story still had not moved on.

Granted, most had. She'd had three iron-zoo-related conversations just that week with people or couples who had politely loaded into their cars and gone home to their own lives afterward. Still, the surprising number of people who hadn't—three, to be exact—had left a mark on her psyche. It made her want to be more cautious.

"I wonder if I can trouble you for a glass of water," he said. "I hate to be a bother. But it's been such a long ride since the last time I saw anyplace to stop and eat or drink."

"Of course," Roseanna said, realizing that the poor old man was overheated and weak. "Come up and sit on the porch in the shade, and I'll get you something."

"I'm sorry. I didn't catch that. My hearing's not the best."

"Come up and sit on the porch in the shade, and I'll get you something," she said again, much closer and louder this time.

"Well," he said. "You're very kind."

"I think I made a calculation error," he said. Then he took several long gulps of the water.

She placed a bowl of corn chips between them and sat with him.

"Not really calculations," he added. "I think that's the wrong word. It wasn't mathematics I was working on. What I miscalculated was my own ability. I'll be eighty years old in a couple of weeks, but I'm as healthy as a mule. So I thought I'd be fine riding that little scooter in the long haul. But I think I was giving myself too much credit."

"How long a trip did you plan?" she asked, being sure to keep her voice strong.

He cut his eyes away. "That's hard to say," he muttered under his breath.

Roseanna decided not to press him, as he clearly did not wish to be pressed.

"Oh," he said suddenly. "I haven't introduced myself. My apologies. Martin Mayhew."

"Rosie Chaldecott," Roseanna said. "What made you decide on such a small motor scooter?"

"I wouldn't really say I decided on it. More like it decided on me."

That hardly explained the situation. But Roseanna realized she was famous for such dodges herself. And, for that and other reasons, it was against her nature to pry.

Meanwhile he had finished his water. And between the two of them, the bottom of the corn chip bowl was no longer fully covered.

Roseanna realized she had developed a strong

sense for that moment when people knew it was time to leave her property but badly wanted not to. It struck her as a strange talent to haul through life.

"Have you eaten?" she asked. Because part of her wanted to hurry him back on his bike and make sure he left, while another, stronger, part of her wanted to do so with no guilt whatsoever.

Martin cut his eyes away.

"It's kind of you to ask," he said. "But I've troubled you enough."

They crunched in silence for a moment more. Then Roseanna reached into the corn chip bowl and found nothing but a sprinkling of leftover salt.

"That doesn't really answer the question, though. It's your own business, so I'm certainly not insisting you answer. But there's nothing rude about saying you're hungry, if that's what you're afraid of."

"I had coffee and a pastry at a gas station this morning. It was a poor choice, though, because it's nothing that'll stick with you, if you know what I mean. Just sugar and flour. When it runs out, it runs out on you hard. And what with these days getting so warm and all, I ended up feeling a bit woozy. So it was mighty kind of you to take me into the shade and offer some water and a little snack. I'm indebted to you for that."

"I don't have a lot of food in the house,"

Roseanna said. "I was supposed to drive into Walkerville later this afternoon and do some shopping. And I haven't yet. But I could make peanut butter sandwiches. And I have some milk. At least we could get some protein and some calories into you before you move on."

Roseanna watched his refusals crumble. She could see it in his eyes. Once the food in question had been described, he could no longer push it away by suggesting it was too much trouble on her part.

"A peanut butter sandwich and a glass of milk would be manna from heaven, Rosie. You are very kind."

As they walked into the house together, it struck her that all this kindness to strangers might have been a contributing factor in their not tending to leave.

"Tell me again how you happened to come by that tiny little scooter?" Roseanna asked, loudly, as they sat back from their finished meal. "I think I didn't quite understand your answer about that."

"It was my wife's."

"Was?"

"My wife passed away last month."

"Oh, I'm so sorry."

"She had cancer. Suffered with it for the longest time. And our finances suffered right along with her. But I guess that's getting a little personal,

201

and, anyway, you don't want to hear my troubles."

"Nonsense," Roseanna said. "I'm beginning to think that's the reason we're all down here on this planet together. To try to make things a little easier for each other. Why else would we interact with people at all? You don't have to tell me anything you don't want to, but if you feel like talking about it, I don't mind."

"We had insurance," Martin said.

Then he stared at his empty plate for a surprising length of time in silence. She sensed he was teetering on the edge of a decision about disclosure—to clam up entirely or let it all out. She could see the moment—a brief instant before he spoke again—when he opted for the latter.

"That is, she had insurance. I have Medicare, but my wife was a good bit younger—sixty-four to my eighty—and it didn't come quite soon enough to help her. I don't know if Medicare would have been better than the insurance we had for her. Looking back, seems just about anything would have been."

He scowled at his mostly empty milk glass as if it were an errant insurance provider. Then he plunged on.

"We both worked all our lives and put money away for a rainy day. Kept our policies in good standing and all that stuff. You know. All the things they tell you to do to take good care. But it's a funny thing about insurance companies.

They love to take your money when you're healthy, but then when you get sick, they don't pay nearly as much as you were set to expect. In fact, they almost always manage to pay you less than you paid 'em in premiums all those years. But then I guess if they didn't, they wouldn't still be in business and doing fine. They disallowed a bunch of charges and only paid eighty percent, and the twenty percent was enough to bury just about anybody. I lost the house and I had to sell my car. That scooter is most of what I've got left. That and a little pension. Emphasis on the word 'little.' "

Roseanna said nothing for a time, because she had no idea what to say.

"I really don't think well of insurance companies at this point in my life," Martin added.

"Can't say as I blame you."

"Starting to seem like a racket to me. A little bit of one, anyway. Like when people used to have to pay protection to the mob, otherwise something terrible would happen to their business. I guess the difference is that the insurance companies don't literally cause the bad thing to happen. But they ask so much money, and you don't have a lot of choice, because you want to protect that nice life you built. I paid the high premiums so I wouldn't lose the house. And I lost it anyway. So they might as well have been the mob."

He downed the rest of his milk and frowned.

"I'm sorry," he said. "I still think that was rude of me. You don't want to hear *that much* about my troubles."

"I don't see why not," Roseanna said. "I've got nothing but time. Besides. I have a story I wanted to tell you, too, so long as we're talking about the losses that changed the direction of our lives."

"So," Roseanna asked—hesitantly—as they stepped out onto the porch together. "Now that you've lost the house, where will you live?"

"Haven't quite figured that out yet."

"Is your pension enough to cover a place? A rented apartment, maybe?"

"Not anywhere near where I lived."

"Which was . . . ?"

They paused in the shade of the porch, surrounded by that feeling. His having to go but not wanting to go. What was it about this place that drew people like a magnet, then held them?

"Newark. Not that you can't live cheaply in Newark. I mean, compared to New York City. But really, my monthly pension is very small. I'd have to move to someplace like Arkansas or Kentucky. Somewhere the cost of living is just entirely different. And even so, if I pay rent, I won't be able to afford much else. I guess I thought if I lived on the road . . . you know . . . camping at night and such . . . maybe I'd have enough for incidentals and food. And maybe I'd find a cheap enough place to settle. But I don't know. It's grueling on my old bones, being on that bike all day long. I'm beginning to think it was a lousy idea."

Based on her interactions with the last two parties she had taken the time to get to know, it almost sounded as though he already planned to stay. But he didn't. He was thinking no such thing; she could tell. Because the possibility of such a plan had not occurred to him, would not occur to him all on its own. He had felt it too much of an imposition to trouble her for a sandwich so he wouldn't faint from heat and hunger and fall off his motor scooter.

Still, she began to wonder if she should offer. One night, maybe.

She shook the idea away again. It always started with one night. It never ended there.

They walked down the steps together and moved off toward the gate.

A little shriek of laughter caught their ears and turned them around. Melanie was down by the creek, near the tents. As usual, she was being too loud.

"Neighbors?" Martin asked.

"No, that's my property down there."

"And people *camp* on it?"

So there it was. The idea that he might stay had just jumped into his head. She could see it in his eyes. Hear it in the tone of his voice.

And out of all four of the drifters—six if you counted Patty and Willa, seven if you counted the dog—who could possibly need accommodation more than this poor eighty-year-old widower?

It wouldn't be so bad, she thought. It might be a good thing for her purposes. She could invite him to pitch his tent for one night. Then in the morning she could tell them all that it had been fun, but it was time for them to move along. She could kill all four birds with one stone. Just have the big talk once and clear the premises.

"Yes," she said. "There are people camping down there by my creek. If you'd like to set up down there for one night and then drive on in the morning, I suppose I wouldn't mind. It's just one night, and, after all, what's one more?"

In the morning, after a bracing cup of strong coffee, Roseanna walked downhill to the creek. The plan had been to take off her shoes, roll up her pant legs, and wade across to the tents.

She didn't. It looked deep and fast, and the stones at the bottom had been worn shiny and smooth, which she assumed would make them slippery. The last thing she wanted was to take a fall in running water. Or anywhere else, for that matter.

"Good morning!" she called, cupping her hands around her mouth.

Nothing.

"Good morning!" she called again.

A few seconds later Nelson came hurrying out of the woods.

"Sorry, miss," he said. "I was off using the little boys' room."

"I'd like to have us all together for a talk," Roseanna said.

His face fell, and she could not miss his disappointment no matter how hard she tried.

"Here on this side of the creek would be nice," she added, "since you all seem to be better at wading the thing than I expect I would be."

"I'll get everybody together," he said, his understanding of her meeting agenda sadly clear in his voice.

"So what's this all about?" Melanie asked, rubbing her eyes more dramatically than necessary. "I was still sleeping."

Yes, on my property and only with my permission, Roseanna thought. She could have said so. Almost did. But she decided against it. So long as they were all on their way out, what was the point of getting snippy?

"Sorry if I got anybody up before they were ready," she told the four of them. Then she immediately regretted having said it. The idea that she should apologize to any of them, but especially the unwelcome Melanie and Dave, seemed laughable.

"I was awake," Martin said politely. "I'll be out

of your way before you know it, Rosie. Thanks for letting me rest up a bit."

"And thank you, Martin, for helping me slide into the topic of this little meeting. Martin's been here just the one night, as you all know. But for the rest of you, it's been a couple of weeks. It was never really supposed to be that way. It's not something we talked out in advance. I know you all like it here, and maybe it even seems like some kind of heaven to you. It does to me, too. But one of the reasons I moved here was for solitude. My version of heaven involves a lot of silence and alone time."

"Say no more, miss," Nelson interjected. "I'll pack my things."

"Well, gosh darn it," Melanie said. "We were so hoping to stay the summer! Then we could go home and tell the principal and the school board we're retiring, and then we could make a new winter plan from there. But this . . . this is just . . . inconvenient."

Roseanna did not look at Melanie as the woman gave her aggravating and fairly rude monologue. Instead she watched Nelson attempt to contain his own agitation. In the end, it could not be contained.

"But the lady didn't *invite* you to stay the summer!" he barked at Melanie. "And it's not polite to just invite yourself." Then his face reddened. He glanced quickly at Roseanna, then cut his eyes away. "Well, I guess I'm not much better, am I, miss? You didn't invite me to stay for weeks, either. But at least I'm willing to leave without complaints when you ask me to."

"You just stay out of this," Melanie barked back. "This is not even your property."

"No, but it's hers. And she just told you it's time to clear off."

"Now listen, you . . ."

Roseanna jumped into the pause, verbally speaking. "See, this is exactly what I'm trying to avoid."

"You don't worry about a thing, miss," Nelson said with almost exaggerated respect. "You just give us a few minutes to pack up our stuff, and we'll be out of your hair. *All of us,*" he growled, turning a withering look on Melanie.

She narrowed her eyes at him in return, but said nothing.

Roseanna sipped at a second cup of good coffee and watched them slog up the hill toward her house. More importantly, toward the road. Nelson seemed to be carrying both his own and Martin's belongings. They all looked a bit downtrodden, like weary and wounded soldiers returning from a battle that had been decisively lost.

For a moment Roseanna felt guilty, but she shook the feeling away again. She had every right to ask them to go. She had been more than hospitable. And in just a few minutes she would have her lovely heaven. She would have this beautiful, natural, quiet place all to herself to enjoy in silence.

The thought was interrupted by the shriek of the five-year-old, reminding her that she had been counting incorrectly. There were still two squatters who had not been asked to leave. One and a half, at any rate.

She stepped out onto the porch and watched Willa chase the brown dog around in a wide circle. The dog seemed to enjoy the game. He looked back over his shoulder at the girl to be sure she was still chasing. His tongue hung out sideways, his mouth held wide open, making him look as though he were grinning broadly. His tail wagged furiously as he ran.

Roseanna saw Patty standing by their tiny shack of a guesthouse, watching her daughter. Supervising the play. She stepped down off her porch and walked to the young woman.

"He seems like a nice dog," Patty said.

Roseanna ignored the dog-related small talk. "It's been a few weeks since you told me you were going to approach your parents about a loan," she said.

Patty's face fell. Roseanna seemed to be having that effect on everybody this morning.

"They said no."

"I'm sorry to hear that."

"But I figured you'd changed your mind about wanting us to go. Because all these other people are staying now. I figured you must've decided you liked the company after all."

"Hardly," Roseanna said.

"Why are they here, then?"

"They're not. Not anymore. They've broken down their tents and packed up their stuff, and they're on their way up the hill right now. Headed for parts unknown."

"Oh," Patty said. "Why were they here so long?"

"Now *that's* a good question. I've been asking myself that a lot lately. I guess I'm not very good at confrontation."

Patty laughed out loud, an embarrassing pig-snort of a sound. "You? But you're an attorney."

"True. I guess I'm good at other people's confrontations. Turns out I'm not so good at my own."

"Miss, miss!" Nelson's voice called out. "We have some trouble!"

Roseanna turned to see him running toward her. He crossed the play circle formed by the dog and Willa. The dog skittered out of his path.

"Martin collapsed coming up the hill. He has a high fever, I think. I don't have a thermometer or anything, but his forehead's all clammy and hot. And he says he's been having body aches. I think he might be coming down with the flu."

211

"Oh dear," Roseanna said. "Maybe we need to bring him into the house."

"I'm not sure about getting him the rest of the way up the hill, miss. The only way he's making it is if I carry him. And he's not small. He's bigger than I am. But I guess I could try."

Roseanna sighed deeply. "Let's go see what's what."

Martin was sitting up in the grass, Roseanna noted as they headed down the hill. But it looked as though that was only the case because Dave was supporting the old man.

When she reached him, Martin looked up at Roseanna with a look of utter shame and humiliation.

"Oh, I feel just terrible about this, Rosie. I guess I must have caught some kind of bug. No wonder I've been all dizzy and tired. I swear I'm a solid old guy when I'm feeling well. I'm just not sure quite how to get up to the road in the state I'm in."

Roseanna held a palm to his forehead, the way she'd done with her son when he was little. Martin definitely had a fever.

"We need to get you up to the house," she said.

"No, ma'am. I won't hear of it. You deserve your privacy, and anyway, if I'm in your house I'll get you sick, too, and I won't be having any of that."

"I could take him back down the hill and set up his tent again," Nelson said.

"He shouldn't be living in a tent if he has the flu."

"Don't see why not, Rosie," Martin said. "It's warm enough. And I have my little sling cot."

Roseanna stood a moment. Thinking, yet not thinking. Just waiting for the details to settle in. For some kind of plan to emerge. A direction, at least.

"Let's try it for now," she said after a time. "Nelson, will you keep a good eye on him? And if you're concerned at all, you have to come tell me. If things take a bad turn, let me know right away."

"You bet, miss."

It was a worry. Martin was almost eighty. An eighty-year-old can die from the flu. It had been a contributing factor in the death of Roseanna's own mother. She could take him to a hospital, if Nelson could carry him up the hill. Still, the hospital would likely just give him some kind of medication and release him back into Roseanna's care. Since he had nowhere else to go.

"Okay, then," she said, and began the grueling walk back up to her house.

On the way she offered a quick prayer that nobody would die on her property any time soon.

Then she amended "any time soon" to "ever."

It was a good four days before she realized that Melanie and Dave had not left her property, either. Apparently they had simply kept their heads down instead. Melanie had even managed to be quiet.

But one day Roseanna glanced out the window and noticed Dave fetching something out of their battered compact car.

She slipped out of the house and stood on the path he would have to take to circle the house and head back down the hill.

When he saw her there, he stopped in his tracks and offered a sheepish grin. He tipped his silly boater hat back on his head and scratched his scalp through all that bushy hair.

"Right," he said. "Sorry about that, Rosie. But Melanie figured since the other two didn't have to go yet . . . But anyway, don't worry. As soon as Martin's back on his feet we'll all be out of your hair."

Roseanna said nothing as he hurried by.

If she had said something, it likely would have been something like "I used to think it was just that easy. Now I'm not so sure."

THREE MONTHS AFTER
THE MOVE

Chapter Thirteen

Not a Horse in Any Sense of the Word

Lance, who was not a breakfast person, had been out of the house for ten or fifteen minutes on a walk. He called it a "morning constitutional." Roseanna had no idea where he'd gotten that term. Not from her.

Roseanna, who was most definitely a breakfast person, was enjoying her breakfast when he stuck his head back through the door.

"Okay," he said. "I'm a little surprised you didn't tell me about the horse."

"What horse?"

"Um . . . yours?"

"I don't have a horse," she said, her mouth still full of toast.

"Not that I begged you for one or anything. But here we were counting who all gets to live here, and . . ."

"I don't have a horse," she said again, wondering how to make her answer any clearer than that.

"Oh, I get it," Lance said. The early morning sun lit his head and shoulders from behind like a halo. "You concede that he's a horse, but you don't exactly have him. He has you."

"There's no horse," Roseanna said, marveling at

217

the disconnect. "Nobody has anybody in any way that involves a horse. There is simply no horse."

"Then what do you call that four-legged animal in your barn?"

Roseanna sighed audibly and rose from the couch, leaving her food behind. Which was irritating, to put it mildly. She knew when she got to the barn this would all be revealed as some kind of joke or misunderstanding. And then she would be mad about her food getting cold. Which she was already, to some degree. It was something of an anger preview.

She followed Lance through the barely cool morning, ignoring a couple of lookie-loos leaning on her fence and snapping pictures of the metal zoo. There were plenty of them these days, since that damned article had run. Roseanna no longer felt inclined to engage them in conversation. There were too many. And besides, what had it gotten her in the past? Just an open worm can. A swirl of problems she knew she'd be happier without.

Together she and Lance stuck their heads into the barn.

An animal undeniably equine swung his head around and looked at Roseanna—with mild curiosity—over the roof of her Maserati. With perhaps a trace of good humor mixed in, though that might have been her imagination. What did Roseanna know about horses, after all?

He was white, or nearly white. Maybe gray,

or maybe a white horse who had spent too much time since his last bath rolling in the dirt. It was hard to tell if his longish, raggedy coat was stained by mud or was just a muddy color in places. His back was slightly swayed, his big head Roman-nosed and stubborn looking. He might even have been part donkey or mule, she thought, looking at his huge and ungainly ears, which swung back and forth, following sounds.

To say he was not the most beautiful horse would have been laughably understating the case.

Roseanna noticed that her son was staring at her. Also that her mouth was hanging open.

"You seriously don't know this horse?" Lance asked.

"I never saw that beast before in my life."

The beast lazily swished his tail. Swatting flies, maybe.

"So what do you suppose he's doing in your barn?"

"Maybe a practical joke on somebody's part? Anybody who knows me would know the last thing I want is a horse. Or any other animal, for that matter."

A flash of bright pink sailed by Roseanna at about waist level. It took her a moment to realize it was Willa at a dead run.

"Earnest!" Willa shouted, hugging the horse around one hairy front leg. "Earnest! You came back!"

"You know this horse?" Roseanna asked.

She walked closer to the little girl, which unfortunately involved moving closer to the outsized beast. But if a five-year-old could survive it . . .

"Of course," Willa said. "It's *Earnest*. Everybody knows *Earnest*."

"I don't."

"Well, everybody *else* does," Willa said with an air of condescension. She was still hugging one of Earnest's hairy legs.

"Do you know why Earnest is here?"

"He lives here."

"Beg to differ," Roseanna said.

"I don't know what that means."

"Let me try this another way. Does your mom know Earnest?"

"Of course. *Everybody* does. I *told* you."

"Will you please be a helpful girl and run get her for me?"

Willa sighed, and regretfully let go of the hairy beast's hairy leg. "All *right*," she said on a great out breath of sigh. It clearly was not all right.

She stomped out of the barn. Dramatically.

Roseanna took a few steps back and stood beside her son.

"He's not staying," she said. "If that's what you were thinking."

"I wasn't thinking anything," Lance said. "I didn't say a word."

• • •

"Oh, look," Patty said, stepping into the barn. "It's Earnest."

"That much we've established," Roseanna said. "Any idea what Earnest is doing here?"

"I'm not sure." Patty moved close to the beast, who reached out and bumped her with his bony Roman nose. "The week before Macy died, she gave him to Archie Miller, down the road. I guess he ran away and came back."

"Okay," Roseanna said. "That's progress. At least now we know how to return him to his owner. Would you happen to have this Archie Miller's address?"

"Not really. But it's not hard to find. Just go a mile or two down the road toward Walkerville. His name is on the mailbox. You don't have a trailer, so I guess you'll have to walk him back down there. But go slow, and give him a drink of water first. He's old."

"How old?"

"Thirty-seven or thirty-eight."

"Is that old for a horse?"

"Very."

"How long do horses live?"

"Maybe thirty years if you're lucky."

"Okay. Thanks. I think."

Roseanna watched Patty take her daughter's hand and lead the little girl reluctantly out of the barn. Clearly the sight of Earnest on his way home was going to be a problem for the kid.

She looked at Lance and he at her.

"Long walk," she said. "Too bad I don't have a horse trailer."

"Maybe we could get a phone listing. Call this Archie guy. Maybe he has a trailer. It's his horse. Let him come get him."

They walked out of the barn together and into the glare of morning sun. As if thinking—or in this case dreading—with one mind, they stood together looking up at CPR Hill.

"I'll go," Lance said, digging his phone out of his jeans pocket.

"Thanks."

But he had only managed to get three or four steps away before she changed her mind.

"Lance, wait," she called to him. And ran to catch up. "I'll go with you. The idea was to spend time together. Right?"

"I think that's what I read in the instructions," Lance said.

Just as they crested the hill together, Lance broke the silence. He was puffing lightly. Roseanna was practically wheezing. Although it did get marginally easier every time she climbed this monolith. Could she actually be getting into some kind of physical shape?

"Why don't you just get a landline?" he asked.

"It's funny," she said. But then for a few seconds

she didn't say why or how it was so funny. "For the first few weeks I literally forgot there still *was* such a thing. In people's houses, I mean. And then when it dawned on me . . . well, it just reminded me how awful it is when someone can jangle a loud bell in your home whenever they want you to pay attention to them. What a system, right? You can tell it was invented by people who'd never imagined a better way. I can climb this hill if it's an emergency. And if it's not, well . . . incommunicado has been working very well for me."

They sat cross-legged in the dirt, surveying Roseanna's personal heaven.

Lance dialed directory assistance.

"In Chudley, New York. Last name Miller," he said, robotically. Talking to robots made real humans more robotic. Roseanna had noticed that. "Oh. Wait." He lowered the phone and pressed it against his shoulder to mute it. "Is Archie short for something?"

"Archibald."

Lance laughed. Lightly and spontaneously, as if he really enjoyed these little jokes between them. Except there had been none.

"Wait," he said again, this time directly to Roseanna. "You're serious?"

"You never heard of the name Archibald?"

"No. And I hope I never do again." Then, into the phone, "First name Archibald." A pause. "It's connecting me," he said.

Roseanna waited. And waited. And waited. There was another eagle, or hawk—or whatever she had seen on her first day in this place—riding thermals over the valley. It gave her something to watch while she waited.

Lance shook his head, clicked off the call, and slid the phone back into his pocket.

"No luck. No answer, no voicemail, no machine."

"Oh," Roseanna said, and watched the hawk-eagle glide out of sight behind a golden hill.

"I guess we're back to the manual plan. Put a rope around his neck and lead him home."

"Seems that way."

"I'll go," Lance said, sounding sacrificing and brave.

"No. We both will. I'll come along. Same as I told you before. We're getting to know each other. Hard to do that if you're leading a horse down the road and I'm sitting at home." They stood, Roseanna struggling a bit with balance. She dusted off the seat of her pants. "See, now you're getting to experience it for your own self, what I keep trying to tell you. I don't ask for a dog, or a horse, or a kid, or a squatter. They just appear. They just find me."

"We'll get this one back where he goes."

"I certainly hope so," Roseanna said.

They walked along the road together, the three of them. Lance walked on the inside, one foot in the traffic lane. "Traffic" in this case was an exaggeration. Only two cars had come by in twenty minutes of walking. Roseanna walked on the shoulder. Earnest, a stiff rope looped loosely around the base of his neck, more or less straddled the white line, his hooves clopping rhythmically on the tarmac.

Roseanna didn't think that rope would do much to hold the horse if he decided to take off. Then again, an unscheduled nap seemed more Earnest's wheelhouse than an unexpected burst of energy.

The morning had grown uncomfortably hot. Roseanna had begun to feel oppressed by it, and it was dampening her mood even further.

"Good thing we remembered to give him a drink before we left," she said to Lance. "Too bad we forgot to give ourselves one."

"It's probably not too much farther. Maybe old Archibald will give us a lift home. Seems the least he can do after we bring his horse back."

"Oh yeah. Absolutely. Clearly a valuable animal. Surely a reward is in order."

"People love their animals even if they're not valuable."

"Not sure who could love this beast."

"Hey," Lance said. "Watch that. He's walking right beside you."

Roseanna stopped suddenly on the gravelly dirt of the road shoulder. Earnest noticed, and stopped as well. Lance hit the end of the rope, which stopped him.

"Are you suggesting this animal speaks English?" she asked.

"Not really. Not exactly. But if somebody said something mean about you in a foreign language, I bet you'd know it wasn't a compliment."

"Fine. Sorry, Earnest."

They walked again. Clop. Clop. Clop.

"Can I ask you a personal question?" Lance said.

"I think that's the whole point of all this."

"Was there something between you and Alice?"

Roseanna stopped walking again. This time Lance noticed.

"You mean like . . . ?"

"You don't have to—"

"No. There *so* wasn't. No, we were friends. There was nothing . . . why would you even ask that?"

"You just seemed so close to her."

"I adored her. But not like that."

"I'm sorry."

They clopped in silence for a moment. Well, Earnest clopped.

"And I'm sorry if I made it sound like that would be a terrible thing," she said. "I didn't mean it that way. It just so . . . wasn't like that."

"It's not your fault," Lance said. "It's me. I do that. Look at the world through gay-colored glasses. That's what Neal says, anyway."

"Neal?"

"Blank."

"Blank?"

" 'My partner's name is Blank.' "

"Oh. Right. I did say that. Didn't I?"

"And maybe partly because I never saw her with anybody. And I never really knew why you and Dad split up."

"You didn't? I'm sorry."

"I could have asked. I was probably afraid to ask."

"I divorced your father because he's emotionally immature and has rage issues."

"Oh. Well. I knew *that*. But I figured it out on my own."

"I think that's it," Roseanna said, pointing to a dusty white mailbox twenty or so paces down the road. "Doesn't that say Miller?"

A car pulled up from behind them, a fairly new Mercedes coupe. The passenger window powered down. Roseanna found herself looking into the face of a woman about her own age. A stranger. Someone she had not seen around these parts before. Then again, that was just about everybody.

"You have Earnest!" the woman piped in a squeaky tone. "Thank goodness."

"Wow," Lance said quietly in Roseanna's ear. "The kid was right. Everybody *does* know him."

"We don't have him for long," Roseanna said.

"We're bringing him back to his owner right now."

"You can't very well do that," the woman said, as though the reason should have been obvious.

"Why can't we?"

"Archie passed away."

They all stood in the road in silence for a moment. Except for the woman in the car, who sat in silence.

"How long ago?" Lance asked.

"They found him three days ago. He might have died the day before that. Heart attack is what they think. His kids and grandkids came yesterday to clear out most of his stuff. But he hadn't had Earnest long. Took him in after their last family visit, so I guess they didn't know. Millie Fairfield went by last night to see if Earnest was okay, and he was nowhere to be found. I guess he got tired of nobody feeding him. You should probably give him a flake of hay and a drink of water before you take him home. It's hot out today, and he's very old. Thirty-seven, I think. Maybe even thirty-eight."

"So I hear."

"I'm so glad he has you. Everybody will be so relieved."

Roseanna opened her mouth to challenge the supposition that Earnest "had her." But it was too late. The window powered up and the car drove on.

• • •

Lance drank deeply from a steady stream of water put forth by the late Archie Miller's hose. He bent forward at the waist to keep the rest of him dry. Then he seemed to think better of the plan, and turned the hose directly on himself, letting the water pour down over his head and drench him.

"Is there a bucket around here for the horse, do you think?" she asked him.

"I don't know. I could go look."

Roseanna poured hose water over her own head while she waited, and watched Earnest assault a flake of hay that they had thrown directly on the ground in front of him.

Then, much to Roseanna's alarm, the horse lifted his head and moved decisively in her direction. He marched in way too close, crowding her. Nearly stepping on her feet. He reached out with his whiskery muzzle for . . . it took her a moment to realize for what. He wanted water, and was more than willing to take it directly from the hose.

She turned the arc of it in his direction, and he opened his mouth, peeling back his upper lip to show ancient yellowed teeth. He drank the water in what looked like a series of bites, spraying Roseanna with blasts of water that ricocheted off his massive pink tongue.

"No bucket." Lance's voice from behind her. "But I see you two worked it out on your own."

"We can't just leave him here to die," Lance said.

They were sitting shoulder to shoulder in the shade of a maple tree, watching Earnest eat.

"No," she said. "We can't."

"Maybe we can find somebody who wants him."

"Seriously? A horse who looks like that? Who's eight years older than horses even tend to live, if you're lucky?"

"I don't know what we're supposed to do, then."

"Oh yeah you do. We have to take him home with us. He's Macy's horse. He lives there. I have a barn. I have squatters coming out of my ears, so what's one more? At least this one won't complain to me about eggs. But I'll tell you one thing. We're coming back with the pickup and loading up all that hay from Archie's shed and taking it home with us. Wherever Archie is now, hay is the last thing he needs."

"Okay. Well, when he's done eating . . . if he's ever done eating . . . we'll go."

They sat in silence in the heat for a moment longer.

Then Lance said, "Are you worried about what Jerry said?"

The words twisted deeply into her stomach, spoiling everything. Tanking the mood she had thought to be thoroughly tanked already.

"I *wasn't*. I was fine a second ago. Because I

was managing not to think about it. But you had to go and ruin that, now didn't you?"

They were more than halfway home when Earnest did the very thing Roseanna had assumed he was too old to do. He pulled away from Lance, making a sudden turn that dragged the rope right through her son's hands.

"Ow," Lance said, looking at his rope-burned palms.

Roseanna expected the horse to run away now that he was free. Instead he stopped in the shade of an evergreen tree, dropped his head, and let out something that sounded like a cross between a sigh and a snort. It left his nostrils looking mildly runny.

"You okay, honey?" Roseanna asked her son.

"I will be, I guess. But that really stings."

"Let me see if I can get him back on the road."

Roseanna approached the beast cautiously. He watched her with wary eyes but did not move. She bent down. Picked up his rope. Pulled slowly and carefully, making sure her pressure didn't tighten the rope too much around Earnest's neck.

Earnest did not move.

"Well, now what do we do?" Lance asked, appearing at her shoulder.

"I'm not sure. Let me think." She didn't think, exactly. Her mind felt strangely blank. But a moment later she came out with a plan anyway.

"How about if you walk the rest of the way home and get Patty and Willa? I'll wait here with the horse. They know him, so maybe they know how to get him moving."

Lance had been gone a minute or two, leaving Roseanna standing foolishly—holding a rope that was clearly useless for containing the horse—when Earnest collapsed. Or that seemed to be what he did, anyway. He sank to his knees with a deep grunt, then let the rest of his body fall to the ground with a second pained sigh.

Oh dear, Roseanna thought. *Maybe this is it for him. He's old. Maybe he's just . . . dying.*

She moved closer to the beast, who lay with his neck curled around in an arc, his muzzle tucked over his front legs. She sat. If this was Earnest's final moment on earth, then Roseanna knew she was the last person the horse would ever see. The least she could do was make this moment a fairly good one for the poor old guy.

She reached one hand out, hesitantly. Patted the flat, bony area between the horse's eyes.

"I'm sorry for what I said about you," she began, feeling foolish because she was talking to a horse. "Of course somebody loved you. Macy loved you, probably. Maybe even Archie did in those last few months. Willa still does. I should watch what I say, because you're just old. You just look the way you do because you're old. I'm going to be old myself pretty soon here, and I hope a few people will still love me even if I don't look so great."

Earnest raised his head and considered Roseanna for a few seconds. His eyes looked clear, and he seemed to be taking in everything. He did not look like a horse in his last moment on earth. He looked as though he was quite curious to know what she was so concerned about.

Then he set his head down on his front hooves again and sighed.

Lance showed up in the pickup truck a few minutes later, with Patty and Willa in the passenger seat.

He stopped the truck right in the middle of the road, and they all three jumped out and stood over Roseanna and the horse.

"I think this might be it for him," Roseanna said.

Part of her didn't want to say it in front of Willa. It was a tough reality. But the little girl would have to find out sooner or later.

"Why do you say that?" Patty asked.

"Well . . . look at him. He just collapsed."

"He's lying down. Horses lie down all the time."

"They do?"

"Yeah. They do."

"I thought they slept standing up."

233

"They do. A lot of the time."

"So when do they lie down?"

"When they feel like it."

"Got it," Roseanna said.

She had mixed feelings about the development. She certainly was not thoughtless enough to want poor Earnest to die. Then again, there was something neat and fitting about the horse ending his life right then and there, just after both his sequential owners had ended theirs. Now Roseanna would have to be his owner. She would have to take in one more four-legged squatter.

"Willa and I will stay here with him," Patty said. "You guys go on ahead. He'll get up and go home with us when he's ready."

By the time Roseanna and her son arrived home with the first pickup truck load of Archie's hay, Patty, Willa, and Earnest were walking slowly through her gate. Willa was sitting astride Earnest, holding a double handful of his scraggly mane.

Roseanna slowed and rolled down the window.

"So he's okay," Roseanna said. "That didn't take him long."

"He was just tired of walking," Patty replied. "He was just trying to tell you he needed to take a break. He's old."

"I seem to recall hearing that somewhere," Roseanna said, before rolling up her window and driving by.

As she did, she noted yet another gaggle of lookers at the fence.

"How about *you* go talk to them?" she asked Lance.

"Why me?"

"I'm done with them."

"I thought you liked that meeting-of-the-minds thing."

"I guess I thought I did, too." She pulled up beside the barn and parked. "But it was based on the assumption that it would only be a brief meeting."

"Got it," Lance said, and jumped out of the truck.

"Do make it clear that we're full up," she called after him. "No room at the inn."

"Count on me," Lance called back.

Chapter Fourteen

When Your Wiper Blades Meet Somebody Else's Intestines

"Mom," Lance said, and shook Roseanna gently by the shoulder.

She sat up in bed and blinked at him in silence, still effectively asleep.

"I'll be gone all day, Mom. I just wanted you to know."

"Where are you going?"

"I have to go back to the city and get some of my stuff."

"Oh. That's right." She threw the covers back and swung her legs over the side of the bed. Pressed her feet to the hardwood floor. It was not even barely cool. It didn't cool off much these summer nights. "You were going to do that yesterday."

"Right. But then we had . . ." He allowed what seemed like a purposeful pause.

For a second or two, Roseanna literally did not know where he was going with that sentence. She'd forgotten.

". . . Earnest," he added, as if speaking to a kindergartner.

"Oh, damn." She squeezed her eyes shut.

"I'd forgotten about Earnest. I wish you hadn't reminded me."

"I made coffee," Lance said.

There was a hopefulness in his voice that Roseanna could not quite parse out. It seemed bigger than any issue currently before them.

"Okay. I'll get up and have some with you before you go."

She rose and followed him into the kitchen in her nightgown. A robe would have been too heavy and warm.

"Actually," he said, still walking and faced away, "I was hoping you'd come along for the ride."

Roseanna stopped walking.

Lance reached the coffeemaker and poured two servings for them in the chipped cobalt-blue mugs. When he turned back to hand one to her, he seemed surprised that she was not right behind him. And also a bit perplexed by whatever he saw in her face.

"What's wrong?" he asked, walking the coffee to her.

She took hold of it. Let the smell rise into her nostrils. Something cold had solidified in her lower intestines. It was a sickening feeling, and she wanted it to go away. But she didn't even know how to begin to get in to where it was hiding.

"Go with you?" she asked. As if he had asked her to go bungee jumping. From a plane, maybe.

"Yeah. You know. For the ride."

"To the city?"

"Yeah."

"Why would I want to do that?"

"Because ... ," he paused, cuing her to remember on her own. She remembered nothing. "Because the idea was for us to spend time together. Remember?"

"Right. Right."

"It's almost a four-hour drive each way. It would give us so much time to talk."

"Oh, honey. We'll have every minute of every day to talk. As soon as you get back here."

He was looking closely at her face, so she turned it away. She took her mug of coffee to the couch and sat, staring at the woodstove as though there were a lovely fire crackling in it and she couldn't take her eyes off it.

A moment later she felt him sit down beside her.

"What's the issue here, Mom? Afraid of motor vehicles suddenly? Worried the farm will be taken over by squatters the minute you walk out?"

"Of course not."

"What, then?"

"It's just ... the city. I just don't want it anymore."

"Well, you don't have to have it, Mom. I'm just suggesting you come for the ride. We'll be in and out of the city in two hours."

"Which is two hours more of the city experience than I'm willing to face."

A long silence. In time she risked a glance over at his face. He looked peeved. Problematically so, as if Roseanna had unexpectedly sprouted another dog.

"You don't have to get all angry and silent," she said. "It's not about you."

"Right. It never is. It never was."

"Oh, come on, Lance. I just have a . . . sort of a . . . thing about the city now."

"You were willing to go back and get *your own* stuff."

"Oh, no I wasn't."

"So how did it all get here? Bought its own bus ticket?"

"Nita brought the immediate stuff. The kind of stuff you're going to fetch right now. Then I had a professional service pack up everything else and ship it out here. It's mostly on pallets in the barn."

They sipped their coffee in silence for a time. Utter silence. Normally there would have been commotion outside the windows by this time of the morning. But whatever the squatters were up to, they were doing it quietly. It made Roseanna feel as if she and her son were the only two inhabitants of a planet that might or might not have been Earth.

"That makes no sense," he said after a time, clearly irritated.

"It doesn't. Yet there it is."

"You lived in the city for more than fifty years."

"Therein seems to lie the problem."

"But you can just . . . I mean, you don't like it anymore. Fine. Whatever. You can put up with it for a chance to spend some time with me."

"I wish I could, sweetie. But . . ." She paused. Poked around in that frozen wasteland of her gut. It was fear. Abject panic. There was no explaining it, but no denying its existence, either. "It's like a PTSD sort of a thing. I don't know how to explain it any better than that. Until I drove out with the intention of staying out, I had no idea how much I'd been hating it. I held it down for too long. Put it away so I could live there. But now it's out and I can't put it back away. It's too big."

Lance rose and dumped the rest of his coffee down the sink drain.

"Fine," he said. "Whatever."

He strode toward the door.

"Can you please not leave mad?"

He paused briefly, one hand on the knob.

"Can you please make me the priority for a change?"

He gave her a space to speak, but not a very big one. Her hesitation seemed to tell him everything he was waiting to hear.

"Right, I didn't think so. Well, I like the city. And if nothing's changed with you, and I'm still not that important, maybe I'll just stay there. Maybe I won't come back at all."

Then came an even briefer pause—her split second to rescue the moment. And possibly their entire relationship. She fumbled it again through hesitation.

Lance slammed the door hard on his way out.

It took Roseanna nearly an hour to realize she would have to go into the barn and bring Earnest a flake of hay. Having not been a horse owner the previous morning made that chore something short of her established habit.

She found the mangy-looking beast in the barn where she had left him, standing far too close to her Maserati for her liking. The place now held the distinct and pungent odor of horse manure.

She walked close to Earnest with the flake of hay, allowing him to get a good look—and sniff—at her offering. Then she walked into a far corner of the barn, away from her beloved car, and dropped the hay on the dirt floor. Earnest moved in to devour it, bumping Roseanna with his bony shoulder and nearly stepping on her foot.

On her way out of the barn she looked at her car and noticed something odd. One of the windshield wipers was standing up, away from the windshield. As if someone had been washing her car windows before suddenly abandoning the task.

She moved closer.

Just as she was reaching out to set the wiper arm back in place, she noticed another alarming development. There was no wiper blade on the arm. Someone had pulled it off and taken it. She checked the other wiper arm, which was in its proper place against the windshield. But it had no rubber blade, either. Roseanna lifted it slightly, as if the blade might be hiding underneath somehow. She noticed a small nick in the windshield where the bare metal clip had apparently snapped back into place and struck the glass.

Roseanna felt a redness and heat building up around her ears.

She stomped out of the barn and made her way to the gate, where she rang the bell loudly and consistently. It's what she did when she wanted all of her squatters to come in for a meeting, pronto.

"I want to know who took them," Roseanna said. "And I want to know why."

They all stood in the barn together. Roseanna. Patty and Willa. Martin. Nelson David. Melanie, though her husband, Dave, was not in attendance. Off property, apparently, which made Roseanna suspect him.

"They're worth hardly anything," she continued, more rage in her voice than she meant to betray. "Maybe one of you just needed a pair for your own car, though I'm not even sure how interchangeable they are. But that's not even the issue," she added, as though correcting herself. "Here I am opening this place up to you and not outright chasing you off, and one of you has the gall to *steal* from me? Granted, it's not a big-ticket item, but it's a damn nuisance, because there's not exactly a Maserati dealership on the next block, if you catch my drift. And if I can't trust you with those smaller items, how can I trust you with anything that's actually valuable? Am I going to walk into the barn next and find my car gone? And why does the phrase 'No good deed goes unpunished' keep coming to mind? I expect all of you to at least have the good sense to limit your thieving to those who haven't shown you a significant kindness."

Roseanna felt the little girl tugging at her sleeve. She brushed her away again.

"Please don't, Willa," she hissed. "I'm trying to make a point here."

"But—"

"Later, honey."

"But . . . is this your wiper thingy?"

Roseanna looked down.

On Willa's miniature palm lay a small scrap of rubber. Maybe an inch and a half or two inches in length. One end was blunt and clean, the other raggedy. Chewed-looking.

Roseanna took it from the girl and eyed it more closely. It was indeed a piece of a wiper blade. But not a very large piece.

Her squatters crowded in more closely to see.

They all stared at it for a moment. Then they looked up. Looked around at each other. Patty turned her head and looked at Earnest. A second later all eyes fell on the mangy beast.

Earnest whipped his long neck around and stared back at them, with a look in his eyes that seemed to say, "What?"

Roseanna sat cross-legged in the distinctly uncomfortable dirt at the summit of CPR Hill. While Lance's line rang—probably enough times to put her in voicemail territory—she looked out over her property, and the Maserati. She had parked it outside the barn for obvious reasons.

When she first heard his voice, she thought for a split second it was him. The words "This is Lance" sounded like his live voice. The "I'm not here right now—leave a message" made her heart fall down into the pit of her stomach. Quite a bit lower than she thought a heart could go.

"Hi, honey," she said. "I'm just . . . I just need to . . . Oh, crap. Bad start. Lance, you were absolutely right and I was absolutely wrong. And it's been brought to my attention that in the past I haven't been the best at admitting such things. So . . . just to show you I really am changing, I'm admitting fault, even though I realize I'm admitting it into a recording device. I do have this weird paranoia about having to go back there.

But I should have just done it. No matter how bad it felt. I should've just pushed through it. For you."

She squeezed her eyes shut.

"Now I'm sitting up here on top of CPR Hill with my eyes closed and picturing myself riding in your car with you, talking the whole way. And it's such a beautiful thing in my head. So that's how I know I really effed things up. I'm not just saying it so you'll come back, either, even though I hope you will. It's just been such a crappy morning. You leaving mad, and now I feel terrible about it, and then the horse ate my windshield wipers, and when I'm done apologizing to you I have to go apologize to everybody I accused of stealing them, which is damn near everybody who lives here. And I thought if I could talk to you, I might feel better. But I guess not. That's not to make you feel guilty. It's my own fault."

She paused, and opened her eyes, wondering if she had time to wrap up her message before the recording cut her off.

"Well, I'll tell you the rest in person when I talk to you. If I ever get to talk to you again. Love—"

But before she could say the word "you," she heard the second beep. The one that says you're done, whether you thought you were done or not.

That was the most important part of the whole thing, she thought. *Why the hell didn't I say it first thing out of the gate?*

She bumped into Patty on her walk back to the house.

"I was wondering if I could borrow your phone," Patty said.

"Yeah. Sure. Where's Willa?"

"She's with Martin. They're stacking firewood."

"Damn it! How many times do I have to tell that man I don't want him doing all that strenuous work on my property? He's eighty."

But she reached the phone out to Patty all the same.

"Thanks," Patty said, and took it from her. "He seems to be in pretty good shape. For a guy his age, anyway."

"Yeah. Right. Everybody always seems fine. Until the moment they drop dead."

A pause. Roseanna looked into Patty's eyes and realized she needed to tone herself down a bit. Not only was her mood toxic to others, it wasn't doing her much good, either.

"Well. Anyway," Roseanna continued, attempting a more friendly tone. "You go make your phone call. I need to go back and apologize to everybody for this morning."

"Oh," Patty said, and seemed to brighten a bit. "I think they would like that."

"I'm sure they will," Roseanna said. "The only one who won't enjoy it is me. So, tell me something. Is this a normal thing? For a horse to eat rubber? I mean, I know a billy goat will eat anything, but a horse?"

"Mostly they don't," Patty said. "No. Earnest is unusual."

It seemed like enough of an understatement to draw a comment from Roseanna, but she was too tired and depressed to bother.

It was twenty minutes and four apologies later when Patty came to the door to bring Roseanna back her phone.

"Thank you," Roseanna said.

Then she was ready to close the door, but Patty didn't seem to want to move out of the way.

"Don't you want to know what the vet said?" Patty asked.

"What vet?"

"The vet I just called."

"I didn't know you were even calling a vet."

"Oh. Did I forget to mention that?"

"Apparently so." Roseanna waited a beat or two, then sighed. "Well, I guess you'd better come in and tell me all about it."

Patty stepped inside and walked around her living room, looking at Roseanna's scant belongings. Maybe comparing every single one of them to what Macy had kept in that same location. Then again, maybe not. You never know what someone else is thinking.

"So why did you call a vet?" Roseanna asked

when she grew tired of waiting for the information to be volunteered.

"To make sure Earnest'll be okay."

"And will he be?"

"We don't really know. The vet said if he chewed up the rubber pretty good, it might go through him without any trouble. But if he swallowed it in big pieces, well . . . it could get twisted up in there and then stop food from going through it, and the next thing you know he could have a bowel obstruction. And that would be very bad. The only thing you can do about a bowel obstruction in a horse . . . well, you can try pumping him with mineral oil, but that either works or it doesn't."

Everything either works or it doesn't, Roseanna thought. She didn't say so.

"If that doesn't work," Patty continued, apparently sure Roseanna wanted every single veterinary detail, "then the only thing left would be surgery. But it's really expensive, and besides, the vet's not going to do surgery on a thirty-eight-year-old horse. He probably wouldn't survive it, and even if he did, it just wouldn't be fair to the poor old guy. And if he swallowed any of the metal clips that hold that rubber blade in place, then it's game over for Earnest."

Roseanna plunked down onto the couch and waited in silence. After all that detail, she felt strangely sure there must be more.

"So what do we do?" she asked, when no more was forthcoming.

"We're supposed to listen for gut sounds."

"I hope you know what that means. Because I don't."

"Yeah, I can show you. Come on."

Then Patty was at the door, and then out the door. Before Roseanna could gather herself up to say how much she didn't want to go, Patty was halfway to the barn. So Roseanna just gave up. It was easier that way.

She sighed deeply, and followed.

Earnest looked up at them with soft and soulful eyes as they stepped into the barn. She'd never seen that look from him before. Roseanna wondered if horses manipulate people with such gazes. She also wondered why she hadn't put the horse out of the barn and kept the car in.

"You just put your ear to his side," Patty said. "Like this." She demonstrated. Earnest swung his neck around and nibbled on her hair. "Oh yeah. I can hear it. That's good. It sounds kind of gurgle-y. Want to try it?"

"Not even a little bit."

They stood in silence for a moment, looking at the horse, who looked back.

"I'm having trouble," Roseanna said, "understanding how something as small as a windshield wiper blade could take down something as big as that horse."

"Horses have very finicky digestions. They can't throw up."

"What do you mean they can't throw up?"

"It means just what it sounds like it means."

"Why can't they throw up?"

"I have no idea," Patty said. "You'll have to take that up with God."

Roseanna mulled that over for a moment but could find no suitable rejoinder. "So we just listen to his intestines every day?"

"Yeah, and hopefully in the next day or two we'll see that it went through him okay."

"You do realize I won't be the one picking through his manure looking for partially digested wiper blades."

"Oh, I doubt he'll digest them."

"The main point is the same."

"Yeah," Patty said. "I didn't figure you *would* be the one."

They turned to walk out of the barn together. Roseanna's eyes fell onto her tarped belongings in the corner of the barn. Furniture. Important paperwork. Albums of family photos. Everything that didn't fit in her new house.

"Wait," she said, and Patty stopped walking. "You know how you guys are always saying you'll do anything at all to get to stay here? Well, I have an assignment. Build that beast a stall if he survives. You can all put your heads together on how to do it. Just get it done, okay? I don't care what it looks like. But if he survives the wiper blades, he's not going to survive eating my furniture. Because I'll kill him."

"Okay," Patty said. "We'll work something out."

They walked out into the sun together. Roseanna squinted and shielded her eyes with one hand.

"Why did Macy name that beast Earnest, anyway? Earnest like the man's name? Or like the quality of being earnest?"

"The quality, I think."

"Because he's just about the least earnest being I've ever met."

"She might've been trying to give him something to work up to," Patty said.

Roseanna was in bed asleep when the knock came at her door, startling her and making her heart pound.

She put on her robe and made her way through the living room in the perfect darkness. There was no moon, or it hadn't risen yet. Roseanna was not sure which.

"Who's there?"

"It's me. Lance."

Roseanna sighed away her fear and opened the door. They stared at each other as best two people can in the pitch dark of a moonless night.

"I only said *maybe* I wouldn't come back," Lance said, his voice sheepish and almost painfully sweet.

"Come in, sweetie. Come in." He did, with two heavy-looking duffel bags.

"I'm so happy to see you I could almost cry."

"Why almost?"

"Well, you know me."

"Yeah, Mom. All too well. *The horse ate your windshield wipers?*"

"It's kind of a long story. Well, actually no. It's not. It's pretty short. In fact, that was all of it right there."

"The metal parts, too? Or just the rubber?"

"Just the rubber."

"Glad to hear it. For Earnest's sake."

"The last part of the message was 'I love you.' The recording cut me off."

"Yeah, Mom," Lance said. He draped an arm around her shoulder and pulled her close, kissing her temple. "I kind of figured that's where you were going with that."

Chapter Fifteen

Equine Gastrointestinal Tracts and Other Happy Subjects

They sat on the couch in the barely light morning, Roseanna and her son. They sipped good coffee. Lance fiddled with his phone, staring at the screen and tapping it with his thumbs as if typing.

"What can you do on that phone without reception?" she asked him.

Lance laughed. "Close to nothing," he said.

There came a knock at the door, which seemed odd before seven a.m.

Lance jumped up to answer it, which also seemed odd to Roseanna, but in a more pleasant way. He had already come to treat the place as though he lived here.

"I was just typing out an email that I'll send later," he said over his shoulder on the way to the door.

He swung the door wide. On Roseanna's porch stood Patty, looking tight and slightly worried. Willa hung off her mom's hand, uncharacteristically silent.

"I have a question," Patty said, coming in without having been invited.

Perhaps there's a limit to this treating the place

as if you live here, Roseanna thought. *Maybe it cuts off at blood family.* But she didn't say so, because first she wanted to hear the turn of events that had Patty so concerned. In case this was entirely the wrong moment for such a pronouncement.

"Okay," Roseanna said. "What's the question?"

"If I had to get the vet out here this morning for Earnest . . ."

She paused. But Roseanna had no idea what she was supposed to interject into that pause.

"That's not really a question," she said when she'd grown weary of waiting.

"Right. I'm worried about Earnest. I'm thinking the vet might need to come out and pump him through with mineral oil. Keep it from turning into a bad colic situation. Because a horse can go real fast with a colic situation. Even a young one."

Roseanna opened her mouth to note that no question had yet been placed on the table.

Patty beat her to it. "Right. I know. Still not a question. I was hoping you might have picked up on the question by now."

Lance stood idly by with his hands loosely in his shorts pockets. She caught his eye in case he had any relevant thoughts he might be inclined to share. He didn't seem to.

"Sorry," Roseanna said. "Still on my first cup of coffee."

"Well, it's more than I could afford myself," Patty replied. Still not a question. But they were moving closer. "And, you know. He's not even my horse. Trouble is, whose horse is he? I'm not sure you consider him yours, either. Horse needs an owner on the day the vet has to be called, and I don't think this horse has what he needs to get the right care."

"You want to know if I'll pay for it," Roseanna said, feeling ever so much clearer.

"Yeah," Patty said. "Exactly that."

"How much does a thing like that cost?"

"Couldn't say for a fact. Vet's not cheap, though."

Roseanna sat back, took a long sip of coffee. Sighed deeply. "Go ahead and give him a call. I don't wish any harm on poor old Earnest. He has to be somebody's horse today, so I guess he's mine."

Willa looked up into her mother's face. "Did she say yes, Mommy?"

"Yes, honey. She said yes."

Willa broke away from her mother and ran to where Roseanna sat on the couch. She hugged Roseanna tightly around the knees, laying her head sideways on Roseanna's lap.

Then she popped up quite suddenly.

"You have to give my mom your phone," Willa said. "And you have to come walk Earnest around and around while we go up the hill to call."

255

"Why do I have to walk him around and around?" Roseanna asked the little girl.

"Because that's how you do it when a horse has the colic."

"Why do I have to walk the horse around?" Roseanna asked Patty just before they all parted ways at the barn door.

"Because that's what you do when a horse has colic."

"At least you and your daughter have your stories straight."

Patty smiled a wry smile and took the offered phone from Roseanna. Roseanna watched for a moment as Patty and her daughter walked off, hand in hand, the dog wagging happily behind.

Then she turned her attention to her son.

"What's that dog's name?" Lance asked.

"He doesn't have a name."

"Why would you not give him a name? You have to call him something."

"I do call him something. I call him the dog. I only have one dog, so that works out fine."

"You only have one horse, but he has a name."

"Yeah, well, he came with that. If he had shown up on his own with no one to tell me his name, I'd likely call him the horse."

"I bet Willa has a name for the dog."

That's probably true, she thought. She would have to look into that. But in the meantime, she would have to turn her attention back to poor sick Earnest.

"You know how to walk a horse around?" she asked Lance.

"We walked him down to Archie's place and half the way back. I'm guessing it goes a little something like that."

They stepped into the barn together.

Nelson was leading Earnest in a big circle around the inside of the barn, using a makeshift halter that had been formed from knotted rope.

"Oh, good," he said. "The swing shift is here." He held the rope out to Roseanna, who stared at it the way she might at a nonpoisonous—but nonetheless creepy—snake. "Don't let him stop and lie down," Nelson added. "Keep him moving."

"How do I stop him from lying down?"

An image filled her mind. Earnest falling to his knees at the side of the road, grunting, then allowing his body to collapse onto the dirt. This was a thousand pounds of unpredictable animal. What was she expected to do? Catch him and set him on his feet again?

"Bring his head up and hope his body follows," Nelson said. "It's hard for him to lie down if you don't give him his head. Try to keep his attention. That helps."

"Can't you stay and—"

"It's okay, Mom," Lance said, and took the rope. "We can do this."

Roseanna was not at all sure she agreed, but she liked the sound of that "we" coming from her son. So she made no objection when Nelson hurried out of the barn.

She looked at Lance and Lance at her. Then they began walking that same slow circle they had seen Nelson walk with the horse.

At first they didn't speak. Roseanna felt a dark cloud sitting on her being, as though weighing down her head from above. She had felt it for a while, she realized. Almost a day, maybe. It was not horse related, though the fact that the horse was old and now sick did not help one bit. Trouble was, it was *something*-related—everything was—but Roseanna had no idea what that something might be. She had quite purposefully avoided poking it or asking it any questions.

Earnest stopped, swung his head around, and bumped his round and shaggy belly with his muzzle.

Well, that's what you get for eating windshield wiper blades, Roseanna was tempted to tell the beast. She didn't, because the situation was too grave for that type of comment. Lance brought the horse's head back around, and they moved forward again. Roseanna felt inordinately proud of her son and wondered how he felt able to perform a task so entirely foreign to anything he had encountered in his life to date.

"I may not know you as well as some sons

know their mothers," he said, startling her. "But I know when you're bothered by something."

"Right," Roseanna said. It wasn't enough to say, and she knew it.

"I can't imagine it's all worry about the horse. Because you only met him day before yesterday. And because he's a horse. And you're . . . you know . . . you. No disrespect intended."

"None taken," she said, and sighed.

Then they walked two full laps around the barn without any more words being spoken.

Somewhere about halfway through the second lap Roseanna identified the dark cloud. Not because she had been trying. Quite the opposite. She had been trying to push it back down into a place where she couldn't possibly see it clearly, and so would not be overly troubled by it. But then it popped up and stared into her face with that pesky attitude of having won a victory over her. Though maybe she was reading that last part in.

"Since we had that conversation . . . ," she began. Then she trailed off.

"Which one?"

"The one about Alice."

"Oh. Damn. Did I really stick my foot in it about that? I'm sorry, Mom. Can we pretend I never asked?"

"No. We can't. Because it got me thinking. And now I'm thinking Alice might have been gay, and

I never even knew it. Or maybe I even knew it, but I just never paid any attention to it. I never really met anybody she was involved with. There were only a few—at least, that I knew of. And they didn't last long, and somehow she always seemed to tell me about them later, after it was over. And now that I look back on it, I'm realizing she only spoke about these people in the most general terms."

"Would that be a bad thing if she had been?"

"Yes," Roseanna said. With surprising sureness.

They walked three more laps without talking.

"So," Roseanna said, unable to stand the silence any longer, "is it true that gay people have that 'gaydar' extra sense, and can guess when someone else is?"

"That's what they say."

"I'm not asking what *they* say, I'm asking what *you* say."

A pause.

Then Lance said, "I can usually tell."

"Alice?"

"Pretty much. Yeah."

They walked a couple more silent laps.

"That's the other reason I asked that question," Lance added.

Another silent lap around the barn.

"So why is that a bad thing?" Lance asked. "You didn't think it was bad when it was me. Is me, I mean."

"Two reasons I can think of right now. First of all, I can't believe the two very closest people in my life didn't feel they could confide in me about a thing like that."

"It's not that, Mom."

Earnest stopped. Grunted. Tried to go down to his knees, but Lance pulled his head back up and got the horse walking again. She wondered if her son's rope-burned palms still stung.

"What is it, then?"

"It's not that we didn't think we could talk to you about *that*."

"It's that you didn't think you could talk to me about much of anything."

She waited. And they walked. And he never directly answered. But his silence spoke volumes.

"So much better!" she said, her voice steeped in her trademark sharp sarcasm. "I feel relieved now. I'm so glad we had this little talk."

She expected him to say something comforting. She glanced over at his face, but he seemed to have gone somewhere else in his head.

"What's the other thing?" he asked after a time.

"What other thing?"

"You said there were two things you could think of. Two reasons why it bothered you. The Alice thing."

"Oh. Right. What if she loved me?"

"Well, we know she loved you, Mom. You loved her, right?"

"Of course I did. But you know what I mean. What if the reason she never had a long, happy relationship . . . What if I was the reason she made work her whole world? Always at the office instead of off somewhere having a happy life with someone?"

"I guess that's possible," he said.

"Not a good answer."

"I thought you wanted me to tell you the truth."

"Now when did you ever know me to want to hear the truth?"

"Point taken," Lance said. "What would it really have changed, though, anyway? Even if you're right? Maybe she loved you *even more* than you loved her. I don't know. But if so, what would you have done differently if you'd known?"

Roseanna stopped dead and allowed the Lance and Earnest train to go off without her. She watched Lance keep the old horse's attention. Watched him discourage the beast from bending around to focus on his own ancient belly.

When they came around again Roseanna said, "I would have been kinder."

"Were you unkind to her?"

"No. Never. But I would have been kinder. If I'd known."

She looked up to see Patty and Willa standing in the bright morning light in the open barn doorway, the dog wagging at their feet. Behind them, Roseanna saw lookers milling at the fence. Four of them.

"We can take over now," Patty said. "If you like."

"That would be very nice," Roseanna said. "I'm hungry for breakfast. Is the vet coming out?"

"Yes. He'll be here in less than an hour."

Patty walked closer, holding her daughter's hand, and gave Roseanna back her phone. Then she took the lead rope from Lance.

Roseanna looked down into the face of the little girl, who looked back. Willa's concern seemed to fall away, and her face lit up from the simple experience of seeing Roseanna again. Roseanna wondered how that must feel to be so utterly in the moment. So open to whatever life chose to bring you next. So willing to drop whatever had been weighing on you.

"Does the dog have a name?" Roseanna asked the little girl.

Willa rolled her eyes. "He's *your* dog."

"Yes, but I didn't think he had one. I was wondering what you thought."

"I think he has one."

"And what do you think it is?"

"Buzzy."

"Buzzy?"

"Right."

"Why is his name Buzzy?"

"I don't know," Willa said, and grabbed the

loose end of Earnest's lead rope, below where her mother held it. "Just is."

The mother and daughter began walking the circle with the horse.

As they came around and passed her again, Patty said, "She knows. She just forgot. The first time we saw the dog he was jumping up and biting at a bee."

"Got it," Roseanna said. "Did he ever get the bee?"

"No, he's not good at that."

"Just as well."

As she walked out of the barn with her son, she glanced over at him, guessing that he would return an "I told you so" look.

As it turned out, she had guessed correctly.

She turned toward the road to look, but the zoo-goers at the fence had driven away. Roseanna breathed a sigh of relief.

Lance stuck his head through the door as Roseanna was washing up the breakfast dishes.

"You want to come see this?" he asked. "Since it's happening on your dime?"

"A horse having his stomach pumped? I think that's a clear no."

"It's not exactly that."

"How do they get the oil into him?"

"There's a tube going in through his nostril."

"Doesn't he mind that?"

"He's been sedated. He doesn't mind much of anything."

"Well, you let me know how it goes. When it's time to write a check, that will be when I step up to the plate." Then, just as his head pulled out of the doorway again, she called after him. "Lance? Is Earnest going to be okay?"

His head poked back in. They looked at each other for a long moment, each probably thinking the same thing. That it was interesting to note that she cared.

Neither said so out loud.

"We don't know yet," Lance said. "But I'll keep you posted."

Three hours and almost six hundred dollars later, Roseanna sat in the barn with her son. They stared at the horse together. Someone had to stare at the horse, and it was Roseanna and Lance's shift.

"I know I never did before," Lance said, breaking a long silence. "But can I tell you my thoughts on something? Almost like giving you advice? Which feels a tad dangerous, you being you and all. But still. I have some rather strong feelings on the subject, and with your permission I'd like to take my chances."

Roseanna didn't answer. While she was not answering, she inwardly winced, thinking her posthumous friendship with Alice was about to take another beating.

Lance seemed to hear her silence as assent. He plunged in.

"I think you should offer to settle with Jerry."

"I already did."

"I think you should offer him more. Enough that he goes away."

"To make him go away, I'd have to give him more than I can afford. I'd have to give him money I really need. Or will need. In my lifetime."

"I think you should do it anyway."

They sat in silence for a time. Roseanna stared at Earnest and noted that his head was still a bit low and saggy from the sedative. Which, according to the vet, should have worn off by then. Or maybe the poor guy was just having a rough day.

"I'm not going to roll over for Jerry. I'm not going to roll over for anybody."

"So instead you're going to give him this new life you've found. You're going to give away any chance at serenity to fight him."

"I'm going to do no such thing."

"There's no way around it, Mom. You'll have to come back to the city for court appearances. Meet with your lawyers regularly. Be deposed. It's exactly the opposite of what you say you want. You want to live in peace and be left alone. You need to decide if you're serious about it or not. How much it means to you. Because part of what Jerry wants is to screw you out of that. And what if you ruin your life for a year or more over this, and you lose, and he gets the money anyway? You said you were willing to keep chickens and eat their eggs and grow vegetables and get by on very little. Did you really mean that? So tell me what matters more. Money? Being right? Or being happy and living a peaceful life?"

Another long silence.

Then Roseanna said, "Let's talk about horses and their gastrointestinal tracts. It's a happier subject."

"Right," Lance said. Obviously disappointed. "Got it."

"There's a reason why you never used to give me advice."

"Yeah," he said. "I do see that."

Chapter Sixteen

Go Fish

Roseanna squatted on her haunches in a corner of the barn and watched Lance weld. It was his second lesson, and his first chance to add an animal to the iron zoo. Though, frankly, Roseanna had no idea what variety of animal this was supposed to be. Lance's first effort had moved beyond fanciful and into a territory more like unintelligible. But he was trying, and she didn't care to rain on his parade.

From the opposite corner of the barn, Roseanna could hear the rhythmic thunk, thunk, thunk of the posthole digger. Nelson was digging a hole in the barn floor into which he could cement a post. The post would then form the corner of Earnest's new stall.

Meanwhile, Earnest, who was still noticeably alive, nibbled hay from a hay net hanging on the wall. He was temporarily roped off into that corner to keep him away from Roseanna's car.

Lance turned off the welding torch and lifted the big mask on his helmet.

"Well, that pretty much sucks," he said, indicating the . . . whatever it was supposed to be. That thing he'd been attempting to weld.

"It takes practice," Roseanna said.

Lance reached out a heavily gloved hand and lifted the freshly welded section of his creation into an upright position. The weld did not hold, and it fell to the hard dirt floor with a clang, spooking Earnest slightly.

"I don't even want to try again right now," Lance said, clearly discouraged. "I'm hungry. I just want to eat lunch and forget all about it."

"We'll try again tomorrow."

"I don't know."

"It takes practice," Roseanna said again.

"It might be time to accept that I'm just no good at doing things with my hands like this."

"That's an awfully sweeping pronouncement," she said with an exaggerated frown.

"Look at it this way, though, Mom. Let's say I try again and again and eventually I learn how to be a decent welder. Can you even tell what this is? That I'm trying to make?"

"Hmm," Roseanna said, and tilted her head. In case that slightly shifted perception was all she needed. But in truth, she could not even venture a guess. "It's a . . . help me out here."

"A penguin."

"A penguin? Really?"

"I give up." Lance lifted off his welder's helmet and set it on the dirt floor. "We need to face facts here. I'm not the creative type."

"You used to like to play musical instruments."

"But you're forgetting that I was always terrible."

"You were a kid. You just needed practice."

"I took flute for *six years*."

"Oh," Roseanna said. "Did you?" She could not remember how long her son had attempted to learn to play the flute. She remembered quite well that his flute music was always painful to the ears. "Well, we all have different things we're good at."

Lance did not answer.

They sat on the dirt floor for a few moments, knowing lunch was next on the agenda, but not hurrying off to fix it.

"You know," she said, glancing at his discouraged expression, "you can bring a guest around here if you like."

"A guest?"

"Yes. You know. Blank."

"Blank?"

"I'm sorry. It's terrible. I'm terrible at this. I already forgot your . . . partner's name."

"Oh. Neal."

"Yes. Neal. It must be hard for you two. This separation. He can come around here on the weekends or whatever. I realize my couch is not a suitable accommodation for two. Hell, it's not even all that suitable for one. But there's always the motel in Walkerville."

Lance frowned.

Roseanna watched him pull off the huge welding

gloves one by one and slap them down onto the barn's dirt floor.

"Here's the thing about that."

Then for an awkward length of time he did not go on to explain the thing.

"I guess the whole idea of this is that we confide in each other," he said, restarting himself. With some effort, from the look of it. "Right? Tell each other things that are hard for us, or that we'd rather keep to ourselves. So here goes. Neal and I are . . . I don't want to say 'having problems.' Because if you asked me what the problems are, I wouldn't even know what to say. It's more like things are just not clicking very well right now. I don't know how to explain it any better than that."

"You don't need to explain it," Roseanna said. "I've been in relationships. I know they're complicated. And hard."

"I think the reason I didn't tell you this sooner . . . When you asked me to stay here, and I said yes, I wanted you to think it was all about us. About having a better relationship between us. And mostly it was. But then the more I thought about it, the more it felt like this huge relief to take a vacation from Neal. And then when I went up the hill and called him and talked to him about it, I got this strong feeling that he felt the same way. I just don't want you to be offended by that. I don't want to devalue the fact that I was willing to do this."

"Don't worry about stuff like that," she said,

patting him on the knee. "If you get too tangled up in subtext, you'll just freeze up and go back to not sharing anything. We've spent enough of our lives in that place, wouldn't you say? Now come on in the house. I'll make us some lunch and you can tell me more about it."

He levered himself to his feet and reached a hand down to Roseanna. Lifted her up.

They walked to the open barn door together, squinting into the daylight. There they ran smack-dab into a total stranger.

He was a young man, maybe in his twenties, with neatly combed hair. Wearing a leather jacket that looked far too hot for the weather.

"Oh, here you all are," he said. "I've been knocking at the house."

"Can I help you?" Roseanna asked him.

"Roseanna Chaldecott?"

"Yes."

He handed her a plain manila envelope. It was unmarked, and sealed shut. He didn't say anything to indicate why he was giving it to her or what was in it. Then again, he really didn't need to. Roseanna had been an attorney for too many years to fail to recognize this scenario.

"I'm being served," she said to the back of the young man, who had already turned away and was striding toward his car.

"Right you are," he said over his shoulder. Still moving. "Only, past tense. You have been served."

• • •

Roseanna sat on the couch, leaning forward, her elbows braced on her knees. She eyed the cards on the coffee table trunk in front of her, then laid another card down with a sharp slap.

Lance twitched slightly. He was lying on his back on her living room floor, one arm draped over his eyes. It was the hottest part of the day, and the house was the only livable space in which to ride out the heat.

"I know you're thinking about what to do," he said. "Because you always play solitaire when you're thinking. You said it yourself. And the louder you slap the cards down, the harder you're thinking."

Roseanna didn't answer. While she was not answering, she learned something about herself. She had been playing the game with no thoughts in her head whatsoever. Not one. It was not true that she played solitaire when she was thinking. She played it when it was important not to think.

Lance sat up on the floor, probably to see why she was not answering. He leaned over to look at her cards.

"Play your red nine on that black ten," he said.

"Right. I know. I was just thinking."

But that wasn't true. She wasn't thinking. She was trying to avoid it.

"So what are you going to do?"

"Well, I have to fight it. I just have to. It's my

life savings. It's everything I've worked for all these years. And I need it to live on for the rest of my life, so I can't just let Jerry take it."

She braved a glance at his face. He looked disappointed. Unless she was reading that in.

"You own the Maserati free and clear, don't you?"

"Of course I do. You know I always pay cash for my cars."

"Couldn't you live pretty comfortably just on the proceeds of that?"

"Depends on what you mean by 'comfortably.' But yes. I could live on it until Social Security kicked in. If I scrimped. But then I'd have to sell it."

"I see," Lance said. "So it's not really about whether you'd survive and be okay. It's more about a radical change to your financial status. You'd be a woman who really genuinely owns a used pickup truck and no other vehicle. No more bumper sticker on the truck that says, 'My Other Car Is a Maserati.'"

"Excuse me," Roseanna said. "Can't you see I'm trying to play cards here?"

She slapped the red nine down on the black ten.

Lance lay back down again and draped his arm over his eyes.

A few minutes of silence passed.

"What do you *do* around here?" he asked. The words seemed to burst out of him as if they had been contained under pressure. "It's just so *boring*. How do you make all this time go by?"

"You adjust," she said. "You get over that urge to check your phone every couple of seconds. It's a mind-set, and you break it. Sometimes I get more bored than usual. So I get up and do something. Cook something, or do a chore around the place. Or weld a new animal to add to the zoo. Other times I just sit with the boredom. If you even want to call it that. We could just as easily call it serenity and not put the negative connotation on it. It's not the worst thing in the world, doing nothing. You just have to get used to it."

"Maybe I'll go down the hill and see if Nelson is around and if he'll teach me to fish."

"The heat of the day will be the worst time to catch one."

"I expect the lessons will take a bit of time, though," he said, pulling to his feet. Towering over Roseanna. "I'm a rank beginner, after all."

He crossed to the door in three long strides.

"Alice would want me to fight," Roseanna said. Before he could turn the knob and let himself out. Before he could get away.

He looked back at her. Stared into her face for a moment, which caused her to shift her gaze down to avoid his.

"Alice would have wanted you to stay with the firm to begin with."

"Now there you go again. We've been through

this. Yes, if she was alive, maybe. But she made a huge mistake. And if she has any form of consciousness now, she'll feel differently. She will have learned. I told you that. We went into this at some length already."

"When did you tell me that?"

Roseanna blinked too much and tried to straighten out her thinking. Or lack of same.

"Oh, that's right. That wasn't you. That was Nita."

"You're trying to have it both ways," Lance said. Taking that tone she hated. As if he were the parent and she were some errant child. "You say if she were here now she would feel differently—want you to leave the firm and have some retirement-style living while you still can. But then you say she'd want you to fight the lawsuit. If she were here, and saw her mistake, how do you know she wouldn't tell you to forget Jerry and the money and just enjoy your life? Death either changed her or it didn't."

He paused. Screwed up his forehead.

"This is a really weird conversation," he added.

"Go learn how to fish."

He shook his head. But then, after a moment of silence, he did.

It was still dark the next morning when Roseanna noticed that Lance was awake. She'd been sitting on the edge of her bed, head in hands. When she

276

lifted her gaze from her own palms she saw him sitting up on the couch, looking in at her through the open doorway.

"You okay?" he asked, sounding for just a moment like the young boy she remembered so well.

"I didn't sleep," she said. But the words barely made it to him. They came out rusty, like unoiled metal joints. As though she hadn't used her voice in a month.

"I'm sorry," he said, and came to her bedroom doorway. "What did you say?"

"I said I didn't sleep at all."

He didn't reply. Just hung in the doorway for a few moments. Then he crossed the small room and sat on the edge of the bed with her, draping an arm around her shoulder.

"The Jerry thing, right?"

"More or less. But it's more that I was thinking about my part of it."

"You mean like . . . seeing his side of the argument?"

"More like my part of how I'm handling it. I think you're right. I think you were right all along, and you tried to tell me. And it's not so much that I didn't agree, or that I didn't see your point. It was more that I refused to look. Which is a very bad quality in a person."

He opened his mouth to speak, but she plunged ahead.

"I want to have plenty of money because it's part of how I see myself. Sure, I can *say* that I'll keep some laying hens and grow vegetables. And it's all very romantic to say so. But it's hard to make an adjustment like that. And I don't want to do it. So what does that say about me?"

For a moment, he didn't answer. Almost as though he was waiting to be sure it was his turn. That more emotion was not about to spill from her.

Then he said, "It's not so ignoble as you make it out to be. Everybody is afraid of stuff like that."

"They are?"

"Of course they are. All big changes are scary. And it's scary to think of being without money. It doesn't even have to be an ego thing, but it would be pretty human and normal if there was some of that mixed in. We need money to survive, and to solve basic problems. And, you know . . . they tend to come up. It's hard to be without it, especially if you're used to having plenty. Cut yourself a little slack."

They sat in silence for a moment or two. Roseanna was enjoying the sensation of his huge arm holding her snugly.

"I'm not sure what I'd do if you weren't here with me during all of this," she said.

The arm disappeared and Lance stood, towering over her.

"Well," he said, "that might cross the sappy

line even for the new us. So, look. I didn't mean it was terrible if you chose to take on a big legal fight. I'm just saying it's a good chance to figure out your own priorities. I know you know what I mean."

Roseanna nodded. She knew what he meant.

"I know my priorities now," she said. "I figured them out in the night. I'll make us some coffee. And breakfast. And then when it's office hours, I'll slog up that nasty hill and call my attorneys. And I'll give them a new figure to offer Jerry."

"Why don't you let me go up the hill, Mom? You haven't slept."

"Shouldn't I talk to them myself?"

"I don't know. Do you have to? Isn't the only thing that's changed just the bottom-line number? If you were still working in your office right now, on somebody else's case, wouldn't you just have Nita call and give the attorney the new number?"

"Probably not," she said, pulling to her feet and walking the short distance into the kitchen. "I'd probably make the call myself, out of respect to the client. But in this case I'm the client. And I really don't relish hiking up that hill after a night of no sleep. So I'll take you up on it."

She pulled a small pad of paper out of a kitchen drawer. The one she used to make shopping lists before driving into Walkerville. She scribbled a number on the paper. One it pained her to write.

Literally. It created a pain in her belly and chest that felt like trapped gas.

"Here," she said, folding the paper and sliding it across the counter toward her son. "Tell him to tell Jerry I'll go this high if it will make the whole thing go away."

Lance had only been gone for fifteen or twenty minutes when Roseanna began watching out the window for him. Which was silly. Because it would take him longer than that just to reach the top of CPR Hill.

In the better part of an hour she grew tired of the waiting and checking, and walked to the barn to look in on Earnest and feed him his breakfast.

"So, you survived," she said to the horse as she tipped a flake of hay into his new plastic feeder, which Nelson had installed just the previous day.

Earnest nodded his head briskly, which almost looked like a response to the question but was more likely a response to the hay.

Roseanna stepped out of the barn.

In the bright morning sunlight she saw that Lance had returned. He was lying on his back in the dirt, roughhousing with the dog. Buzzy was straddling Lance's chest, tail wagging furiously, and Lance was half hugging the dog, half wrestling with him. There was something touching about it. It almost made Roseanna feel that she wanted to cry.

She moved closer, and Lance lifted the dog off himself and sat up.

Roseanna sat in the dirt with her son, overcome with a tangle of emotions she had not begun to identify.

She squinted to look into his face, but the sun was too directly behind him. So she didn't see his expression clearly. But from the energy that hung around his huge frame, Roseanna sensed that he had no good news to share.

"I'm sorry, Lance," she said. "I am so, so sorry."

"For . . . what?"

"I should have gotten you a dog."

A silence, during which Buzzy came back and licked the air in the direction of Lance's face.

"Yeah," he said. "You should have. But thanks for saying that, anyway. I appreciate it."

"It didn't go well with the attorney, did it?"

"No."

"He was able to get Jerry on the phone?"

"Yeah."

"And Jerry didn't accept my counteroffer?"

"No."

Another silence.

Roseanna felt the summer sun bake her neck and warm her scalp right through her hair. "How much does he want to settle the thing?"

"A little more than twice what you offered."

"Twice my *second* offer? Twice what we offered him *just now?*"

"I'm afraid so." Silence. "Could you give him that much and still keep this place?"

"No," Roseanna said. And left it at that.

"Right," Lance said. "It's a high number. I didn't really think so."

Chapter Seventeen

Selective Evictions

Roseanna slipped on the loose dirt of the steep hill and almost went down hard on one knee. But she caught herself, calmed the startled feeling in her belly, and climbed on.

A moment later she arrived at the top of CPR Hill and gazed, panting, over her beloved property.

Lance and the dog were playing Willa's dog game. Lance chased the dog around in a wide arc, then turned and ran and allowed the dog to chase him in return. Nelson trotted and cantered around the barn area like a show horse, Willa on his shoulders. Roseanna briefly wondered why the little girl didn't ride the *actual* horse. Probably because no one could coax Earnest into a trot or a canter, not even under threat of nuclear annihilation. Earnest was willing enough, but he was one slow carnival ride.

Melanie was washing her clothes in the creek while Dave lay shirtless, sunning himself in the grass.

It was more than time for those two to go, Roseanna thought. They were definitely the squatters she liked least. The rest were charming, and, much as she hated to admit it, she had positive feelings for them. But Melanie and Dave were just pests. Maybe she would have Lance evict them.

At her fence, she saw a couple of strangers leaning, snapping pictures of the animals. The zoo-goers were thinning out a bit since the publication of that article. Still, Roseanna was not surprised to see a few stragglers now and then.

She sat down hard in the dirt and pulled her attention back to the task at hand. She had bigger fish to fry, she thought, and the words made her painfully hungry for a trout breakfast.

She hit the stored number for her attorney's office, then quickly tapped to end the call before it could ring.

The idea had been to call and say that a counter-suit against Jerry would be an appropriate next move. It might even have been nice if Franklin, her attorney, could have helped her brainstorm the direction of the suit. But she couldn't just call and say, "I want to sue Jerry but I don't know what for." How could he proceed on such instructions? How could the call not end in embarrassment over its own prematurity?

Still, when you've worked with someone as long as she'd worked with Jerry, there's always something. Some unfairness. Some skeleton in some closet.

But her mind felt blank.

She sat cross-legged at the top of the hill,

surveying her kingdom from on high, until the morning sun began to burn.

She stared one last time at her phone, then slipped it into her shirt pocket with a deep sigh.

She began the long slog back to the house.

"Why the long face, miss?" Nelson asked, Willa still on his shoulders.

She was crossing the dirt area between the barn and the house, and stopped to talk to him even though she didn't feel like talking to anyone at all. A blanket of depression had fallen on her.

It's amazing when you stop to consider it, she thought, *that I was able to hold it at bay for so long.*

"Just some . . . trouble, but nothing you need to worry about, Nelson. Thank you all the same."

He *would* need to worry about it, actually, if she lost this place. It would be relevant to his situation. But lawsuits take time, and he was due to be moving on to his own place sometime soon anyway. She chose to let it be her problem alone. For the moment, at least.

She turned away and began the slow, shuffling walk back to her house.

"I just hope you'd say if there's anything I can do, miss. Any of us. Well, not so sure about Melanie and Dave. They seem to be in it mostly for themselves. But any one of the rest of us, why, we'd lay down our lives for you."

Roseanna stopped and turned back to him, drawn by the earnestness she heard in his voice.

"What a sweet thing to say, Nelson."

"I mean it completely, Miss Rosie. Somebody gives you a bad time, you come tell me. They'll have to take it up with me. You need to do something you can't do, I'll do it for you if I can. You need to get hold of something you don't have, I'll get it for you if I can."

"You're a lovely young man," she said.

Willa responded by patting Nelson on the head as if he were a good dog.

Problem was, in this case, Roseanna knew he couldn't. But it made her feel better all the same. At least she wasn't in this mess alone.

She smiled at him, probably a little sadly, she thought. Then she walked into the house.

Lance looked up at her from the couch and smiled. He was reading a copy of the *New York Times*, which was spread all over her coffee-table trunk.

"Where did you get a newspaper?"

"Drove into Walkerville. I brought pastries."

"How lovely. I wondered where you were when I woke up."

"Did you call Franklin?"

"No."

His eyes drilled into hers for a moment. Then she looked away.

He never asked, so she volunteered.

"I couldn't get my thoughts together on what to

say to him. What's the point of saying I want to file a countersuit if I don't have all the elements of it together? I would've had to slog up the hill and call him again anyway when I got my thinking straight on it. And in the meantime, he would have thought me disorganized."

"You have *got* to get a landline," Lance said.

Roseanna shook her head and headed for the kitchen in search of pastries. "We've been through this, honey."

"Mom," he said. "Mom." On the second "Mom" she felt his hand on her shoulder, which made her jump. She didn't realize he'd crossed the room after her. "Get a phone installed. Then take the little phone line and unplug it so it won't ring. When you need to make a phone call, plug it in. Make your call from the comfort of your own home. If you're expecting a callback from Franklin, keep it plugged in for an hour or two. Then disable it after he's called. It's utterly within your control."

Roseanna said nothing for a moment.

She took a bite of a Danish that turned out to be filled with cream cheese and apricot. It was all she could do to keep her eyes from rolling back in her head. It was that good.

She chewed thoughtfully, still not answering.

"Well?" Lance asked. "Your thoughts?"

"I'm humiliated because I didn't think of that myself. I'm going to finish this amazing Danish, and then I'm going to order a phone."

But as she said it, her eyes moved to the window in the direction of the daunting CPR Hill. She'd have to climb it again to make the call to a phone company. And she couldn't. Well . . . physically, she could. Not easily, but she could if she had to. Psychologically, not so much. Not twice in one morning. She just couldn't bring herself to do it.

Lance seemed to be following her eyes and her thinking. There was something to be said for the company of those who know you well.

"Allow me," he said, and moved toward the door.

"Thank you."

Then, just before he was able to get through the door, his cell phone in his hand, Roseanna used his name to stop him.

"Lance. While you're out there, I wonder if you'd do me one other favor."

"What's that?"

"Tell Melanie and Dave they're evicted."

"I'd be delighted," Lance said. "I never liked those two, anyway."

Lance had been gone for twenty minutes or so when the knock came.

She crossed the room and opened the door to see Martin standing on her porch, looking more than a little bit humble. The hat he wore to keep his scalp from burning in the sun—a fabric hiker's hat—was clutched against his belly as he briefly lifted his eyes to hers.

He didn't look good. He looked sweaty and red and as though he might be ready to drop from exhaustion.

"Morning, Rosie," he said. A quiet mumble.

"Are you okay, Martin?"

"Eh? I'm sorry, what was the question?"

She had momentarily forgotten how deaf he was. She moved closer, and raised her voice.

"I asked if you're okay."

"Yes, ma'am. Why do you ask?"

"You look tired."

"Just a long, hot slog up the hill is all. Mind if I come in for a quick chat? I promise I won't take up much of your time."

Roseanna stepped back from the doorway, and Martin came in. He settled on the couch with his hat over one knee, showing his nervousness by leaning forward, as if protecting his own soft underbelly.

"So Melanie and Dave are gone," he said.

Roseanna sat close to him on the couch. The better to be heard when she spoke.

"That was fast."

"Saw 'em hauling their stuff up the hill. They didn't seem to be in the best of moods."

"I can imagine. Did they take their chickens with them?"

"No, they left 'em behind. I guess they belong to Nelson now."

"He'll like that."

"He will indeed. I asked 'em if they were headed out of their own accord. Melanie and Dave, I mean. They said no, it wasn't their idea. They said your son told 'em in no uncertain terms that they were evicted, effective immediately. So that's why I wanted to come talk to you, Rosie. Before things went any further."

He paused. Stole a quick look at her face.

"I don't want you to think—" she interjected.

He cut her off.

"No, you don't have to say anything, Rosie. It's your place and you can have anybody here you want and nobody you don't. That's just a simple fact of the world, and anybody who can't understand it wasn't brought up right. And I didn't come here to argue for myself, though another month or two would have helped a lot. I came here to ask you to please let Nelson stay on a little longer. Extenuating circumstances, that's what that boy's got. But maybe you already know all about the situation."

Roseanna blinked a few times, trying to organize and gather what she knew. Nothing with Nelson's name on it came to mind.

"I guess I don't," she said.

"He's in love."

Roseanna felt her eyes go wide. "In love? With . . . ?"

"Well, who else, Rosie? There's only one young lady his age around here, right?"

"Oh. Patty."

"Yes, ma'am. Patty."

"She's not exactly his age. Is she? Isn't she a little older?"

"Four or five years, I think. But he doesn't mind if she doesn't."

"Does she care for him in return?"

"Well, she might. These things take time, don't you know. She seems open to him, and she appears to like him more as time goes by. She's a bit cautious, but probably only because she has that little daughter to care for. It helps that Nelson adores the girl. But these things need to develop in their own good time, and it doesn't work to rush 'em. You remember how it feels to be young and in love, don't you, Rosie?"

"Barely," she said, fidgeting slightly on the couch.

"Sometimes the object of your affection needs to get to know you. And you need time to work your magic, and in the meantime, you need the chance to keep bumping into her. You need that access. So I was just hoping you'd have some mercy on the poor boy and let him stay around a bit. Until he wins her over, or not. Whatever fate would have for their situation."

Roseanna sat back on the couch and mulled over this new information.

"I wasn't planning to ask either you or Nelson to leave," she said.

In her peripheral vision, Roseanna saw him sit up quite a bit straighter.

"You weren't?"

"Not right away, no. I was thinking more like when the snows come."

Or when I have to leave because Jerry owns and/or sells the place, she thought. *Whichever comes first.*

"Well, of course when the snows come," Martin said, pushing to his feet and slapping his hat against one thigh as if to dust it off. Which made no sense, as it could not have gotten dustier since he entered her house. "It's really summer accommodations here, now isn't it? Well, I must say that's a huge relief, Rosie. See, that little pension I was telling you about? It goes in my bank account on direct deposit. And since I've been here, I've been able to let it. Just let it sit there and collect up, I mean. So when I leave at the end of the autumn, I'll have me a little pot of savings. That'll help quite a lot."

They walked to the door together.

"You sure you're okay, my friend?" Roseanna asked him.

His face still looked sweaty and flushed red. The rest on the couch hadn't changed those conditions as much as she figured it should have done.

Martin stood at the door, hat in hand, while Roseanna watched his expression entirely change.

As if he were melting from the inside out.

"I might be having a little chest cold, but nothing I can't handle. I'm your friend, Rosie?"

"Well . . . yes. Of course you are."

"I had no idea. I thought we were just a bunch of pests to you. A small collection of thorns in your side. Why did you want Melanie and Dave to go and not us, if you don't mind my asking? Or was that Lance's idea?"

"No, it was my idea. I asked him to put them off the property."

"Because . . . ?"

"They weren't my friends."

"Got it," Martin said.

"They didn't understand that simple fact of the world," she added. "About how I can have anybody here I want and not anybody I don't. So they weren't brought up right. I only want people here who were brought up right."

They stepped out onto the porch together. Roseanna peered off in the direction of CPR Hill, hoping to see Lance on his way back.

Not yet.

Meanwhile, Roseanna realized she had more resentment to vent on the Melanie and Dave score.

"They were the only ones who never asked for permission to stay here," she said, shielding her eyes from the sun and watching the path to and from the hill. "Or that I never at least offered my permission to. Not even for one night. Nelson, he asked me if he could stay one night, and then we extended it so he could catch a fish and cook it for me."

Roseanna stepped off the porch as she spoke. Walked down the stairs and into the dirt to peer around the barn, still hoping to see Lance on his way back.

"And with you, I offered you one night, and then we extended it a few days because you had that bad flu. And then, yes, things got a bit out of hand. But not because of any lack of politeness or respect on your or Nelson's part. But Melanie and Dave—"

Roseanna heard a distinct thump, something falling on the porch boards. It stopped her in mid-sentence. She whirled around to see that Martin had collapsed smack onto his face on the porch and was lying sprawled and—from the look of it—not fully conscious.

She looked around desperately, hoping to see someone who could help. Nelson would have been a good bet.

She saw only Willa playing with the dog.

"Willa!" she screamed, and Willa jumped. "Willa, run get your mom. Quick, okay, honey? Tell her I need her to take my phone and run it up the hill and make a call. It's an emergency, okay, honey? So run fast."

As the little girl skittered out of sight, Buzzy in

close pursuit, Roseanna reflected on the importance of a landline.

You just never knew when you'd find yourself in a situation where it could save somebody's life.

"Oh, honey," Roseanna said, looking up to see Lance jog into the hospital waiting room. "You're here."

"I came as soon as I could. I got stuck up on CPR Hill after Patty told me. I ran up to make the call instead of her, and by the time I got back to the house I'd just missed you and the ambulance."

She struggled to her feet, and he wrapped her in his big arms. They just stood that way for a time, her head against his chest. Roseanna was wondering how people coped with moments like this when they lived in a heaven all to themselves.

Then again, in a private heaven there's no one to have a sudden coronary and be rushed to the hospital. Yet somehow that didn't strike her as a good enough argument. Life always held some surprise that made you wish you had two strong arms and a solid chest for support.

"What happened to him?" Lance asked quietly, leaning down to speak close to her ear.

"Coronary event."

"Is he going to be okay?"

"So far as I know, we don't have the odds on

that yet. If we do, nobody's bothered to tell them to me."

He let her go, and they sat side by side in two uncomfortable plastic seats.

"I guess it's not so important now," Lance said, "in light of more pressing developments . . . but the phone company will come do an installation between nine and noon tomorrow."

"It's important. Believe me. It's more important than I even knew. You don't know what a phone is worth until somebody has a heart attack on your porch, and you can't even call 9-1-1 without jogging up a massive hill first. Especially when you know it's a long ride to the nearest hospital. Kind of a desperate feeling."

An awkward silence fell.

"He seems like such a nice old guy," Lance said. "But I don't really know him well."

"Neither do I," Roseanna said.

She saw his eyebrows lift slightly in her peripheral vision. But he chose not to comment.

"I mean . . . I know him," she said, wrestling with a chokehold of possible words and their meanings. "I guess I meant I don't know him as well as I should. I could've taken more time to get to know these people. So long as I'm letting them stay."

"Not in your nature," he said.

Roseanna sat with the sting of that for a few beats before he said more.

"That came out colder than I meant it to."

"It's okay."

"Is it?"

"Yes and no. But don't blame yourself."

For what might have been three or four minutes they only stared at the patterned linoleum together.

"Maybe I should just throw myself on his mercy," Roseanna said suddenly.

She looked up at Lance to see him staring at her, his brow knitted.

"What does that even mean?"

"Oh. Sorry. I guess I changed subjects on you. I meant Jerry. Shows you where my mind keeps going. Maybe I should throw myself on Jerry's mercy instead of trying to fight him and losing. You think he has any?"

"Hmm," Lance said. Then he seemed to go inside himself for a few seconds. "Yeah. Maybe. But it's not *a lot* of mercy. It's a thin little sliver of who he is, if I'm guessing correctly, so if you're going to throw yourself at it, you'd better hit that tiny sucker just right. If you know what I mean."

They fell silent again. Roseanna watched nurses bustling by.

Then she said, "I've been such an idiot."

"Why do you say that?"

"I've been acting like heaven is a place with no people in it, so there'll be no one to bother me. Like that's what's really important in life—no minor irritations. But then there's no one to delight me, either. And what did it take to force me to figure that out—that's what bothers me the most. All of a sudden one of the pests I really did like might be about to get yanked out of my world, and so now it seems perfectly reasonable to think heaven on earth is probably a place with shrieking children and running dogs and a horse who eats the rubber blades off your windshield wipers. Now I get it, but it's too late, because I'm about to lose it all to Jerry just as I finally figured out what's best about it. Hell, if all I wanted was to avoid minor inconveniences I never would've considered children—well, child—and so I wouldn't have you. And then where would I be?"

She paused briefly in the tangle of thoughts, realizing she was babbling. Realizing that a genuine sense of grief was forcing the rush of badly organized words.

Lance opened his mouth to answer, but he never got the chance.

A doctor walked briskly up and stood over them. A young man in his thirties, in green scrubs.

"If you'd like to come in and see your father now," he said to Roseanna, "just for a few minutes, that would be okay."

"Rosie," Martin said. Thin. Weak.

Roseanna had to lean over his bed to hear him.

But then, she would have had to lean in close anyway before she spoke. So *he* would hear *her*.

He looked pale and half-asleep. Maybe on pain medication, or maybe fighting for his life. More likely both.

"I've gone and messed it all up now, haven't I, Rosie?"

"Don't be silly, love," she said, close to his ear. "You can't help what happened."

"But here I am trying to be no trouble to you at all. And you end up having to rush me to the hospital and sit here waiting like you're my next of kin. What a thing to have happen. You should go home, Rosie."

"I don't mind staying a little longer."

She pulled up a chair and sat, grasping one of his ancient hands.

The heart monitor caught her eye, and she watched it for a time, the line of Martin's status as a living being looking ragged and weak. She tried to pull her eyes away, but it didn't work. It tapped into a horror in her gut that ran deeper than the moment she was currently living. She did her best not to dwell on why.

"We'll get you home soon," she said.

He seemed to smile. Or to try to smile, in any case. It didn't quite pan out. It seemed to involve more effort than the poor old guy could currently spare.

Roseanna sat, watching his face, and realized

that the promise she had just made to him would be impossible to keep. Assuming he left the hospital in one piece, it made no sense to think he could return to living in a tent, wading the creek every day, and slogging up and down that steep hill. And yet her property was the only home he currently had.

As if reading her mind, he said, "Not so sure, Rosie. Not as sure as you are. But it's okay. Either way it's okay. I like the world with all its faults. It was an honor to have a place in it. But going where Nan went is an appealing option, too. Whatever fate has for me will be all right."

Roseanna felt herself begin to cry, which was rare for her. Had she even cried openly when Alice died? She wasn't sure. She didn't trust her own memory. Then again, if she hadn't, she was crying in great part for Alice now.

Martin gave her hand a squeeze.

"You're a caring person, Rosie. You try to pretend like you're not, but I see right through you. I can smell it the way a bloodhound picks up a scent trail."

He opened his mouth to say more, but his sleepiness and lack of energy seemed to torpedo the effort. His eyes flickered.

"I'm going to go away and let you get some rest," she said.

He opened his mouth but no words came out. He did manage a weak nod.

ONE MONTH BEFORE
THE MOVE

Chapter Eighteen

Lifelines and Badly Timed Snubs

Roseanna leaned forward in the hard plastic chair, her upper body hovering almost over the hospital bed. Her whole torso felt rigid, like concrete. The less she moved it, the less she felt able to.

It took her many seconds to realize she was not breathing.

She gasped in a double lungful of air, and it made a big sound.

Alice noticed.

It would have been hard for Roseanna to explain how she knew that Alice noticed. Because, as far as she could tell, only Alice's eyes were functional. She seemed to be able to shift them from one direction to another. And it was painfully clear from the look Roseanna saw in them that her friend was able to take everything in. She was awake and aware. She was *in there*.

But to be "in there," in Alice's current predicament, represented a massive dilemma.

Roseanna shifted her eyes up to the monitor beside Alice's bed. It traced a line that represented her best friend's life. But it did so weakly, as though fresh out of enthusiasm. Still, machines are not capable of enthusiasm, or lack of same. They simply perform a function, without adding their own attitude—and the knowledge of that led Roseanna to understand that Alice's life was dangerously weak.

Again, Alice noticed.

Roseanna forced her gaze away from the lifeline on the screen.

She looked directly into Alice's eyes and saw fear of a variety she had never witnessed before. And the fact that those panicked eyes appeared in a face devoid of expression made it all the more alarming.

Alice did not raise her eyebrows in fear. She did not wrinkle her forehead. Her facial muscles did not contract. Her face was a soft mask of what appeared to be relaxation, but in reality was an inability to force her face to respond to signals.

Still, the eyes said it all.

"You know I'd do anything for you," Roseanna said out loud.

Alice's eyes softened just the tiniest bit. Maybe five percent of the fear fell away. Unfortunately, it seemed clear that they both understood the subtext of that statement.

I'd help you in any way I possibly could, but there's not a damn thing I can do, and we both know it.

Roseanna glanced at those eyes again, then looked away.

It should have been a comfort, that Alice was alert. That she was demonstrably *in there.*

It wasn't.

Her friend was trapped. Imprisoned in a body that had been an ally just an hour earlier. Now it was nothing but a tightly fitting cage, a cause for the abject alarm brought on by claustrophobia. It had suddenly, unexpectedly, turned on its owner.

I have to help her get out, Roseanna thought, a panicky rush of words in her brain that added up to nothing even vaguely actionable.

That's when she was struck with the worst thought of all. The one she had been holding at bay.

There's only one way to get out of your body.

A movement caught Roseanna's eye, and she looked up to see Jerry standing in the doorway, looking lost. Looking as though someone had recently wakened him from a sound sleep and shaken him hard before standing him up in that doorway and forcing him to say something coherent.

"I came as soon as I heard," he said. It sounded breathless.

Roseanna looked down at Alice's eyes and saw that the presence of their partner Jerry was not helping. With nothing to guide her but that window onto the inside of her friend, Roseanna made a snap judgment that things had been better for Alice before he arrived.

"This is not a good time," she said to him, her fear causing it to come out more harshly than she had intended.

"Excuse me?"

"Could you just wait out in the waiting room?"

"But *you're* here."

"I won't be for long. She needs to rest."

Then Roseanna connected with Alice's eyes again and told her, without words or overt expressions, that her last statement of intention had been a lie. She was not leaving.

When she looked up again, Jerry was gone.

It might have been a minute later, or five.

The line on the monitor gave up. It was simply too weak to continue. It collapsed into a flat line, and Roseanna imagined a great sigh as it did so. A big sound of relief in being allowed to surrender, to set down something that had been so desperately strenuous to carry.

Then she realized the sound was real, and had come from her own chest.

And there was another noise in the room. Some sort of buzzing alarm. The monitor was screaming, but Roseanna felt so distant in her shock that it was simply a background noise, as if she were wearing earplugs, or had fallen mostly asleep.

The room filled with bodies.

Nurses rushed in. A man in scrubs who could

have been an orderly or a doctor ran by her chair.

She slid herself and the chair back to offer them more room.

One of them, a female nurse, turned to Roseanna and shouted words quite loudly, but Roseanna could barely make them out. The woman seemed too far away, as if viewed through the wrong end of a telescope, and the meaning of her words remained veiled, as if spoken in a foreign language.

Roseanna shook her head hard to bring in more clarity. Only then did she realize that she had heard the nurse's instructions. They had just taken a strange amount of time to sift down into her awareness.

She had been told to leave.

She hunkered down more tightly in her chair.

Alice wanted her to stay, so she would stay.

Roseanna rose from her chair and craned her neck to see beyond the swarming bodies. It worked. She got one last glimpse of Alice's eyes. They were wide open. But they were not the same. They had joined the rest of her face, the rest of her physical being. They were slack, and contained nothing.

Alice matched with herself now, all over. The jarring disconnect between her eyes and the rest of her body was gone.

That's when Roseanna knew it didn't matter if she walked out of the room or not.

"I get it," she said, out loud but under her breath. She paused briefly at the doorway, still feeling as though she were walking in a dream. "There was just no other way out."

Jerry was there when she stumbled into the waiting room.

He looked up. Met her eyes. She watched him realize what was what, understand the gravity of exactly what was happening to all of them.

He had wanted to downplay it. His face had said so. Who wouldn't want to minimize this? Now he was no longer able.

"How is she?" he asked.

Roseanna shook her head.

Jerry turned away and left without further comment.

THREE MONTHS AND A COUPLE OF WEEKS AFTER THE MOVE

Chapter Nineteen

Metal Martin

Roseanna stumbled out of bed in the morning to find all the inhabitants of the property in her living room.

Lance and Nelson were sitting on the couch together, talking quietly. Willa was pacing around the house, looking closely at everything Roseanna owned. Her mother held both the little girl's hands in her own and guided her from location to location as though that might be the only way to keep their host's belongings intact.

"Are we having some sort of meeting?" Roseanna asked, her voice still thick with sleep.

"We're working out details of a hospital visit," Lance said. "They were hoping to ride with us."

"One of us has to stay here for the phone installation," she said, and made a sharp turn toward the coffee machine.

"Oh," Lance said. "Right."

Silence. It was a dark silence, freighted with dark thoughts and expectations. It made Roseanna shiver briefly. Made her wish she could shrug it off like a too-warm coat. Before it suffocated her.

"I was going to go there myself on Martin's scooter," Nelson said. "But then Patty and Willa wanted to go see him, too, and besides, it's almost out of gas."

"Fine. Whatever. Let me just get some coffee and breakfast into myself, and then I'll drive you all out there. Lance can stay home for the phone guy. We can bring that gas can that's in the barn and carry some gas home for the scooter."

"Actually . . . ," Lance said. "You might need to sign for it."

"For . . . what?"

"The phone. The new installation."

"Oh. Okay. Fine. I'll stay. You all go."

"I'd like that," Lance said. "I didn't get to see him yesterday. I feel kind of bad that you all know him and I hardly do."

He didn't go on to add that he might soon be out of chances. Then again, he didn't need to. It was part and parcel of the dark thoughts and expectations that filled the room and made everyone's shoulders sag. Every one of them, with the possible exception of Willa, knew it was there, whether any one of them formed it into words or not.

No one did.

The moment the phone guy stepped out the door again, Roseanna stood nervously over her new telephone and called Lance's cell.

She expected him to pick up, because reception was good at the hospital, and he always had the phone in his pocket.

He did not pick up.

Instead she heard his outgoing message, and knew better than to be fooled into thinking it was the live Lance.

"Oh," she told the recording after it beeped. "You're not there. I thought you would be. Well. I just called to tell you my new phone number."

For a moment she almost read it off to him from the paperwork the phone installation guy had left. Then she realized that was twentieth-century thinking. It would read out on his cell phone.

"But you have it now, because I called. I'm going to jump into my car and join you there. Call me back if you get this, though I might not be in a reception area if I'm on the road. Bye."

She replaced the receiver to hang up the call, something she hadn't done in quite some time. Then she grabbed her car keys off the little table by the front door.

Before she could even pat Buzzy's head and cross her own front porch, she saw Lance's car come through the gate, trailed by clouds of dust.

And she knew.

She walked in the direction of the car, and Lance drove in the direction of her. When they met, his window powered down.

"That was awfully fast," she said.

313

No one spoke in reply.

Roseanna scanned the crestfallen faces in the car and sighed.

"Did you at least get to say goodbye?" she asked.

Lance shook his head. "He passed in the night. The hospital tried to call us. But . . . you know."

"Right," Roseanna said, knowing there would be a tragic message on her cell phone next time she drove into town. Or maybe she could now access her voicemail from the landline. Then again, at a time like that, who cared? "I do know."

"They wanted us to tell them who his next of kin was," Nelson said, leaning over Lance to be heard out the driver's window. "We told them we don't think he had one. He never mentioned anybody to me. You?"

"No," Roseanna said, strangely aware of the ground under her feet, and the warm air of mid-morning on her face. Notably alive. "I think if he had a next of kin, he would have gone to them and asked to be taken in."

"Anyway," Nelson said, "I'm going to go see if he has a wallet in his tent. If he does, I'll drive it over to the hospital. I can use the scooter."

"Take the pickup," Roseanna said.

Nelson said nothing, but his face changed. He looked surprisingly comforted, as if buoyed by that tiny concession—a privilege normally only extended to family and close friends.

. . .

"So you were the last one to talk to him," Lance said.

It was after lunch. They were several minutes into their nap ritual, lying on the rug together, waiting out the hottest part of the day. Most definitely not sleeping. In Roseanna's case at least, not even trying.

"How did he seem?" Lance added.

"Calm. Accepting. He told me the world was a good place in spite of its flaws, but going where his wife went would also be good. He didn't seem to have a strong preference."

Lance didn't answer for a few moments.

"Hard to imagine," he said in time. "But you hear about that. I guess when people get closer to the end they don't fear death so much. They get into some kind of acceptance about it."

"Some, I guess," she said. Hoping to leave it at that.

"Were you the last person to see Alice?"

Roseanna squeezed her eyes shut.

"I was." It came out barely stronger than a whisper.

She waited, but he never asked the question. It just hung there in the air, unspoken. Which seemed to create an even greater pressure, though it made no logical sense that it should.

"No," Roseanna said. "To answer your question. The one you didn't ask. Thank you for not asking, but I'll answer it anyway. It wasn't that way with Alice. She looked scared to death. Though that's a bad choice of phrasing, I guess."

"Sorry to bring it up, then."

"She wasn't eighty," Roseanna said. "That might make a difference right there. She wanted more time."

"Don't we all?"

"Martin didn't. But I think it's because he was old and he missed his wife."

She expected her son to respond. Explore the subject more deeply. He never did. In time she heard the soft patterns of his sleep-breathing.

A few minutes later she dozed off herself.

It was two mornings later when Lance suggested he might want to make a trip back home. To the city.

"Just for a day or two. Three, tops," he said over breakfast. "But I don't want to leave you here at a bad time."

"Why would it be a bad time?"

"Well, you know."

"Not really. Hence the question."

"The thing with Martin and all."

"I'm okay. Go. It's fine."

"You sure?" he asked, mouth stuffed with toast. The two words were barely intelligible.

Just for a moment she almost called him on it, the way she would have when he was a boy. *Don't talk with your mouth full.* That sort of motherly jab. She stopped herself. He wasn't a boy. A time comes in the life of a mother and son when that kind of mothering crosses the line into critical behavior. At age thirty he could eat and talk in any way he saw fit.

"I'm sure," she said. "If Martin was okay with it, I can deal with it, too. It was a much bigger thing for him than it was for me."

"I know it's brought the Alice thing up again," he said. This time empty mouthed and fully intelligible.

"I suppose. But it's not like I'm alone here. I've got Patty and Willa and Nelson. And a phone if I need to call you. Or you need to call me."

"True," he said. "Okay. I'll leave right after breakfast."

Not two minutes after he left, Roseanna wandered out to the barn to give Earnest his morning feeding.

She found the horse already munching contentedly from his hay bag, and Nelson crouched on the dirt floor in the opposite corner of the barn. The latter was welding.

It was a talent Roseanna had not even known he possessed.

He looked up and saw her there. Turned off the welding torch. Lifted the visor of his mask.

"I fed him already, miss," he called to her.

317

Roseanna crossed the barn to Nelson and sat close by his side. He lifted off his heavy welder's mask—well, it was her mask, actually—and set it beside him on the hard dirt.

"I didn't know you welded," she said.

"I didn't. Till yesterday."

"Winging it?"

"Not really. Not entirely. I didn't want to maim myself or burn down the barn. I took a lesson."

"From?"

"Patty's friend. That same guy who taught you."

They sat in silence for a moment while she visually examined his creation-in-progress. It didn't seem to be shaping up into an animal. It looked more human. A stick-figure man with pipes for arms and legs. Pipe elbows for joints. And a sphere of rusty metal, currently separate from the rest, on which Nelson seemed to have been welding some lengths of chain.

"So what are you making?" she asked him.

"Is it okay if it's a surprise?"

"Yes, of course."

For nearly a minute, a literal sixty seconds, there was no sound except the birds outside the open barn door, and Earnest's absurdly loud chewing.

Then Nelson said, "I have an idea to run by you."

"Okay."

"It's just an idea. No pressure. You can hate it and I won't take offense. I'll just drop it if you want me to. But it never hurts to ask, right?"

"I think it's time to tell me the idea."

He shook off one of the huge welding gloves and scratched his stubbly chin. "I was thinking I could use Martin's scooter now. I just know he wouldn't mind. I was thinking I could ride it back and forth into Walkerville. You know."

"Not sure I do," she said when he failed to elaborate.

"Work a job."

"Oh. Well. You don't have to run that by me."

"That actually wasn't the heart of the idea yet."

"Got it. Go on."

"When I'm working, my life could go a couple of ways. There's the obvious way. Find a place of my own. And then some less obvious ideas that could work out for both of us."

"This is an awful lot of prefacing," Roseanna said.

He averted his eyes. Stared down at the dirt, his face reddening.

"Sorry. Right. I was thinking I could maybe build something. Here. On your property. Not to live in forever. But maybe to live in for a set number of years. Two or three, maybe, and then after that I can go off on my own, and the guesthouse'll belong to you. And it'll be an improvement to your property."

"And who would buy the building materials?"

"I would. With my job."

"I'm not sure you're being realistic about how much it costs to build."

"You might be thinking of something fancier than I am. I was thinking more like one outbuilding that could go right up against Patty and Willa's little place. Just a big room. When it's done I could open a doorway between the two. And their little house would be a bedroom for a more reasonable-size place. It's a good size for a bedroom, what they've got. It's just not a good size for a whole house."

Roseanna sat a moment, wondering if she should ask the obvious question. Though, based on her recent conversation with Martin, it might have gone without asking. Still, she decided it was best asked. Most things are.

"And then who would live in it for those two or three years? Patty or you?"

She watched his face redden further. She'd known Nelson was a blusher, but this was extreme even for him. Apparently he'd had nothing to blush this deeply about before now.

"If I'm lucky, miss, maybe . . . both of us? Plus Willa, of course."

"Well, it's not a bad idea—" she began.

Nelson cut her off.

"No, never mind, miss. Forget I ever mentioned it. You don't like the idea. I can tell."

He shot to his feet, brushing his hands off on his dusty jeans.

"I like it fine, Nelson. There's just an unrelated problem."

He held still a moment. As if he could find the problem on his own. As if he might simply fish it out of the air over her head. Then he squatted on his haunches and looked into her face.

"I told you, Miss Rosie, if you have a problem, I'll tear up the world to solve it for you."

"You can't solve this one."

He leaned his elbows on his thighs and laced his fingers together in front of him. Like a polite student, paying attention at his desk.

"Tell me and we'll see."

"It's hard to talk about."

"You can tell me anything."

"I might lose this place."

Nelson sat down hard on the barn floor. Smacked onto his butt with an audible thump.

"I thought you owned this place free and clear."

"I do. But I'm having some legal trouble with a former partner. He's suing me. And if he gets everything he's demanding, I probably won't be able to keep this property."

A moment's silence, during which she did not dare look up at his face. But soon not looking at his face became something akin to not thinking of a white elephant. The more you try not to do it, the more you're doing it in spite of yourself.

She quickly looked away again, burned by the absolute devastation in his eyes.

"That can't happen, miss."

"It could."

"It's wrong, though. It's a thing that shouldn't happen. We can't let that happen, miss."

"That's a nice thought," she said, feeling motherly in that moment. As though she could nurture him through this shock. But also as though he needed a gentle lesson in "adulting." "But sometimes things happen that shouldn't happen. And sometimes there's not a damn thing we can do to stop them. But it's not definite yet. We'll just have to wait and see."

It was about an hour before sundown when Roseanna realized how much she missed Lance. It hit her in a way she could not have imagined and had not seen coming.

He had only been with her for a double handful of days, and yet it had changed everything. She'd already grown accustomed to having him around to such a degree that it made his subtraction painful.

She brushed her teeth, watching her own eyes in the tiny, scarred bathroom mirror, and thought about change. Thought about how afraid everyone is of change, and how sure they feel that their adaptation to change cannot, will not, happen. Then something new comes along, and a couple of weeks later it feels as though life has been exactly that way since the beginning of recorded time.

Then she spit, rinsed, and wondered how she had ever lived without him for so many of his adult years.

She decided to call him.

She scooped her cell phone off the coffee-table trunk and stepped out into the slightly cool late afternoon. The last of the sun threw long shadows of her barn and other outbuildings as she trudged toward CPR Hill. She walked along through the loose, dry dirt thinking almost nothing until she was on the other side of her barn and almost to the road.

There she stopped, looked at the phone in her hand, and laughed.

"Old habits," she said out loud, and turned to walk back to her house. In which lived an actual hardwired telephone.

Halfway there she stopped walking unexpectedly and stood frozen.

There was a new addition to the metal zoo. But it wasn't an animal. Nelson had apparently finished his creation and set it in place, and it stole Roseanna's ability to breathe. She actually had to concentrate on filling her lungs with air again. It took a few seconds.

The pipe man Nelson had created had no face. Just a rusty iron sphere of a head. But the sphere had a ring of hair over where its ears might have been, had it had any. Nelson had welded lengths of fine chain to create a version of the long and unruly hair of a mostly bald man. On top of that sat a fabric hiker's hat. But not just any hat. Martin's hat. At the end of the pipe man's legs sat Martin's red high-top sneakers. He wore Martin's khakis and favorite yellow shirt, and at the end of his pipe arms Roseanna saw the old man's leather work gloves. They were somehow affixed to a pipe splitting maul, which the figure held raised. On the ground beneath the statue sat a piece of uncut firewood—a full round that had been cut from the trunk of a fallen tree.

Roseanna sat down hard in the dirt and just stared at it. For how long, she could not have said.

In time Buzzy came around and licked the air in the direction of her face. A moment later Willa landed against her back and wrapped her arms around Roseanna's shoulders.

"Do you like it?" Willa asked, too loudly, into Roseanna's ear.

"Very much," Roseanna said.

"It's *Martin*."

"Yes. I see that."

"He's chopping wood."

"He is."

"He was always chopping wood."

"Much of the time he was, yes."

"And you were always telling him to stop it."

"Well, I won't tell him that anymore."

"Good," Willa said.

Then she kissed Roseanna hard on the back of the head and disappeared back into her tiny home.

She called Lance, and it felt strangely momentous. It was the first time she had ever sat on the couch, in the comfort of her own house, on her new property, and made a telephone call. Then she remembered she had called him once already, the morning they learned that Martin had died. But she had not been seated comfortably that morning, so she decided to consider this a first all the same.

Unfortunately, Lance didn't pick up, which made her feel painfully hollow inside.

"Lance," she said to his voicemail.

Then she opened her mouth and listened to nothing come out. For an embarrassing length of time. The strain of knowing her inability to speak was being recorded only made the situation stickier.

Finally she forced out, "That has got to be the longest silence in the history of voicemail."

Then a—blessedly—much briefer lag.

"Problem is, I guess . . . I'm not a hundred percent clear on why I'm calling. Just to say I miss you. Which seems strange, because we've spent so much time without each other since you grew up. But now that I've gotten to know you again . . . oh, never mind. Never mind what I was about to tell you. I know exactly what you would say. You'd say, 'Mom, that crosses the corny line even for the new us.' Or 'mushy,' or whatever that word was you used. Anyway, I'm going to bed, but I just wanted to say thank you."

Then she quickly hung up the phone.

She stepped out onto her porch and sat on the edge of the boards, feet dangling and swinging. Buzzy saw her and came wiggling up onto the porch to sit by her side. She massaged the muscles under the short fur of his neck and shoulders and stared at the new statue.

The setting sun turned its clothes, especially the yellow shirt, a brilliant orange. Clothes that would slowly deteriorate in the weather, she realized. But maybe it didn't matter. Maybe everything deteriorates in time, and maybe that doesn't make it any less worth having while it lasts.

She sat until it was too dark to see, watching the new iron Martin chop wood. He didn't, of course. The pipe splitting maul never moved. It would remain forever poised in the upstroke, never to slam down on that round of tree trunk.

But the intention was there.

Chapter Twenty

Meteor Showers and Star-Crossed Lovers

Lance arrived home the following night, quite some time after Roseanna had fallen asleep. He still didn't have his own key, so he had to knock and wake her up.

More to the point, when she stumbled to the door to let him in, he did not come in. Rather, he insisted she come out.

"What time is it?" she asked, blinking too much.

"It's after midnight."

"Why would I want to go outside after midnight?"

"You have to trust me. Do this for me. Please, Mom?"

Roseanna sighed deeply. When he put it that way, she really had little choice. But the situation was making her grumpy.

"Fine. Let me go get some clothes on. And a jacket."

"Just a light jacket. It's really lovely out."

He was leading her across the dirt and into the big grassy field behind the barn—literally holding her hand and towing her—when she spoke up in her own defense.

"If the point of this is just to enjoy a lovely night outside," she said, "couldn't we do it tomorrow night? I could drink a cup of coffee in the evening and stay up late. So much better than getting yanked out of sleep."

"Sorry," he said. "Has to be tonight."

He stopped suddenly. Roseanna glanced down to see what looked like a blanket spread out on the dry grass.

"Get comfy," Lance said.

"And then you're going to take this blanket back *into the house?*"

Roseanna tried to ask the question in a manner that didn't drip with disapproval. She failed.

"It's not a blanket. It's one of those painter's drop cloths from the barn."

"Oh. Okay. Good."

Being out of complaints, or pretty much any other comments clear enough to express, she stretched out on her back. Lance settled beside her in the dark, his hands laced behind his head. Together they looked up at the stars for a minute or more.

Roseanna started a conversation because she didn't want to insult her son by falling back asleep. And it would have been easy to do so.

"There really are a lot of stars out here, aren't there?"

"Well . . ." He sounded so very awake. Perky, even. "There are a lot of stars, period. Everywhere. We just see them better out here. So far from the city lights and all."

"You know that's what I meant."

"You used to do that to me all the time when I was a kid."

"I wanted you to learn to express yourself clearly. Even if I don't always."

She took them in for a moment, all those stars. Clear and bright, and clustered so close together. And there were millions of them. She felt as though she could raise her hands and frame off a little section, like a photographer composing a shot, and there would be hundreds just within the frame of her hands.

"Is that what we came out here to see? How many stars there are without the city lights?"

"No. There's more."

She fell silent for another moment, waiting. Looking. But still she could not find the "more."

"How was your trip to the city?"

"It was . . ." Then he paused. And in that pause she felt something tight. Something he was holding onto. Something he probably would rather not say. ". . . okay."

"How are things with you and Neal?"

"You remembered his name!"

"I did. Finally."

"They're good. Actually."

"Really?"

"Yeah, really. I think absence is making our hearts grow fonder."

Before Roseanna could open her mouth to answer, something caught her eye. A bright but very distant flash of light in the sky. It fell in a soft arc through the millions of stars, trailing a bright tail, which faded into nothing again.

"Did you see that?" she asked Lance.

"Yes. A meteor. That's the 'more.' There's a meteor shower tonight. Well, for a bunch of nights in a row, but tonight between midnight and four is supposed to be the best viewing."

Roseanna hoped he didn't plan on extending the viewing session until four, but she didn't say so. She was glad to be here with him, and glad to see the meteor she had just seen. It was her first "shooting star" experience. Having grown up in the city, she had seen them in movies but not in the real world.

"So, you see," she said, "there's something to be said for living out in the country, where you get a clear view of a dark night sky."

"There's also something to be said for living in the city, where you get phone reception and internet and TV so you know when there's a meteor shower coming. Otherwise how would you know what night to look up?"

She considered that for a moment.

Then a huge mass appeared between her face

and the stars, startling her. She jumped, and screamed, and the mass spooked away in such a motion as to clearly reveal itself as Earnest.

The animal stood a moment in the dark, as if regaining his composure. A moment later he stretched his long neck down and began to graze in the dry grass a few feet from Roseanna's elbow.

"What's he doing out here?" she asked Lance, who had been gone for a couple of days and was unlikely to know.

"He's been flipping the latch on his stall door."

"How did you know that? You've been gone."

"He was already doing it before I left. But Nelson was there to catch him. He was going to try a solution. Taking a stick and pushing it into the latch where a lock would go. I'm guessing it didn't work. Knowing Earnest, he probably has a stick in his belly right now. I hope he chewed it well."

"You and me both," Roseanna said. "I can't afford too many more of those vet visits. Especially if . . ."

But she trailed off and never finished the sentence, because it had to do with financial reversals, and she didn't care to talk about such things.

Besides, a tension had sprung up between them. She could feel it rolling her way from Lance's side of the drop cloth blanket. She didn't know

331

why, or what it was, but she knew it wasn't her imagination.

"We have to find a way to keep him in," Roseanna said. Mostly to talk over that tight feeling she was picking up from her son.

"I was thinking just the opposite. Let him out all day to graze. Just bring him in at night. Then he might be more content to stay put in his stall."

"But the place isn't fully fenced. He could just walk away."

To her surprise, Lance laughed.

"Yeah. Right, Mom. You should be so lucky that Earnest walks away from this place. When he left Archie's, where did he go?"

"True," she said.

They lay in silence for a few moments, except for the chirping of crickets, which she had just now consciously noticed, and the contented sounds of Earnest's chewing.

Another meteor streaked through the stars, and they both said some version of "ooh," more or less simultaneously, then fell silent again.

"Okay . . . ," Lance began.

Roseanna felt her stomach tighten. She knew this was it. The something that had been radiating around him, between them. It was coming up now to be spoken.

"I have something I need to confess," he said.

"Go ahead."

"Oh. You're going to be mad. I'm really afraid

you're going to be mad. But as I was driving home I realized you're probably going to hear about it anyway. From somebody else. And then you'll be even madder because I didn't tell you myself."

"You're killing me here, honey. What's the thing?"

"Just remember it was done out of love. It was all me wanting to help. Even if it doesn't quite work out the best possible way, it all came out of my wanting to help."

"Lance . . ."

"I went to see Jerry."

Silence. Briefly. And in that brief silence, two meteors. Almost at the same time.

"Without talking to me first?"

"Right. I know. It sounds bad. And maybe it is. But I had to be able to honestly tell him that you had no idea I was there. Otherwise . . . if he thought you'd sent me to throw myself on his mercy, he wouldn't have liked that. He would have been ticked that you didn't come face him yourself. And I'm a terrible liar, as you know. So I had to be able to truthfully say I was going rogue."

"Right," she said. "Got it."

She wanted to know how it went, but couldn't bring herself to ask. He might answer. And it might be the wrong answer.

"I've been thinking about Jerry ever since we

talked about him last," Lance said, his stress and guilt morphing into words. So many words. "You remember, right? When you asked if I thought he had any mercy you could throw yourself on?"

Another bright streak in the sky, this one huge.

"Whoa!" Roseanna said as it tailed out, leaving an image of itself burned into her retina for several blinks.

"Good one," Lance said.

"Go on with the story. The suspense is killing me."

"Right. So I tried to gather up everything I know about the guy. And I decided his Achilles heel is being a hopeless romantic."

"Jerry's a romantic?"

"Absolutely. Didn't he ever tell you about that girl he loved in college? He thought she was the one, and that they'd be together forever, but then she got killed in a car crash?"

"I heard about it, but not from him."

"I heard it from him. Two years ago, when I came to the firm's Christmas party. He had a few drinks too many and cornered me and told me this story like it'd happened to him the previous week. Like he hadn't even begun to get over it."

"Hmm," she said, still wondering where this was headed.

"So I decided he's just a big softy when it comes to love. Which is why I made the decision

I did. Which I want to remind you was done entirely out of love and wanting to help."

"Oh, honey," Roseanna said. "You know I adore you. But if you don't spit this out . . ."

Still, for a tense moment, he didn't.

"I told him you and Alice had been madly in love ever since you met in college. Don't say anything yet. Let me explain. There's a logic to it. You have to follow the logic. He's furious because you did something he never in a million years would have done. You walked away from something that's the most important thing in the world to him. And he doesn't understand why. He can't understand it. So in his mind it devalues everything he's built with you. Because you had no clear reason to reject it. But by reframing it into this massive grief . . . which it was, so in that sense I'm not misleading him . . . I'm not sure he could understand it in terms of Alice being a great friend. But the tragic loss of a lover . . . well, I figured that would hit him where he lived. He couldn't resist a story like that."

Roseanna scanned the sky for a few seconds, plowing through the many questions that had gathered in her brain. Trying to single out just one.

"I thought you were a terrible liar."

"I did say that, didn't I? But this one panned out. I think because it wasn't all that far from the truth. I mean, you *did* love each other. And you *were* devastated to lose her. To me I guess it seemed more like a little lie you tell to make things feel even more true. It's just framing it a different way so he gets a better picture of what it did to you when she died."

"Doesn't that . . ." Then she paused, still overwhelmed with questions.

"Doesn't it what?"

"Doesn't it make me a complete cad for getting married and having a kid?"

"Or it makes you someone who's afraid to buck convention and is worried what everybody else is going to think. And who can identify with that more than Jerry? Plus it makes the whole thing additionally tragic."

Roseanna opened her mouth, but nothing came out.

She propped herself up on her elbows and looked over at her son. Her eyes had adjusted to the lack of light, so she could see the overall shape of him. But not the look on his face.

"You would make a great attorney," she said.

"I'm going to pretend you never said that to me."

"It's an interesting take on human nature," she added, realizing as she did that she was not angry. She had scanned herself for anger and found none. "Where did you learn so much about human beings?"

"I don't know. I just pay attention to people, I

guess. Oh. I didn't mean that the way it sounded. I'm not saying you don't."

"But I don't. And we both know it."

She lay back down again, and another star fell.

"You don't sound mad," he said.

"Well, you were trying to do something good, I suppose."

"I really was. But then as I was driving home, I realized that Jerry'll probably tell people. You know. What I told him about you and Alice. And maybe that'll get around. And that might bother you. And I should've thought of that before I dove in like an idiot. But . . . did I mention I was only trying to help?"

"Oh, I don't care about that," she said. "Let people think whatever they want. That's the least of my worries."

"I'm surprised to hear you say that. I thought you were a little touchy on the whole Alice-as-gay subject."

"Only because it pointed up all the ways I wasn't a good enough friend to her. But that guilt aside . . . I'm not gay, but damn, honey . . . I could do a lot worse than Alice. Anybody could." A freighted pause. "So, sooner or later I have to ask this next thing." She felt her stomach tighten and grow cold, like ice crystallizing around the question. "What did he say?"

"Just that he needed time to think about it."

"I see."

"I don't think I made it worse, though. I don't know if I made it better. I guess it'll be a while before we know that. But I don't think I made things even worse than they already are. But I look back now and I see that I could have. Made things worse. Just barging in like that without your permission."

He waited for some kind of response from her. But for a moment she had none. She laced her hands behind her head, imitating his position in some kind of show of body language solidarity. And she watched for another shooting star.

When she saw one, she knew everything was going to be okay.

"It's okay," she said. "We'll be fine."

"You think he'll back off the suit? How do you know?"

"No, I don't mean that. I don't mean everything will work out exactly the way I want it to. I can't possibly know that. I mean whatever happens, I'll be okay. People get by in all kinds of situations. All over the world people are getting by on almost nothing. Losing things they think they can't live without. Or at least that they think they can't be happy without. But then it's pretty hard to be happy . . . you know . . . if it's dependent on some material possession not going away. I don't want to live like that. Whatever happens, I'll get by. If you made it better, I'll thank you for the rest of my days. If you made it worse, I'll kick your ass, but then when I'm done kicking your ass, I'll forgive you, because you're my son and you were acting out of love."

She almost rose to her feet. It was a speech that seemed to want to be followed by a dramatic exit. But another meteor streaked through the sky, reminding her that the show was not over. And also that this celestial show was part of how she knew she would always be all right. She would live under the stars, and they could never be taken away.

What seemed only seconds later, Lance jiggled her elbow, and she came awake, not having realized she had fallen asleep.

"We should go back inside now," he said.

Roseanna woke in the morning—a much later section of the morning than usual—to find Lance sitting on the edge of her bed. He held a cup of coffee that he seemed to indicate was intended for her.

She sat up. Woke up as best she could. Took it from him and let the aroma fill her senses.

"So now you're going to wait on me hand and foot because you feel guilty?"

"No," he said. Then his face twisted into that shy little smile she had loved so much when he was a boy. "Well. Yes."

"Tell me again. I know I'm kind of beating this

to death, but tell me again how you knew exactly what to say to him. Where all his soft spots were."

"*All his soft spots?* Get real, Mom. We're lucky he has *one*." He wove his fingers together in front of his knees and rocked slightly. Clearly thinking. "He did say one thing that tipped me off. I didn't go in there with a script or anything. I was feeling him out as we went along. But he kept talking about how Alice was his friend, too. How he knew you two were closer and had known each other longer, but that it was a loss for him, too. He said it about three times before I realized what he was saying. That if he could keep moving forward after her death, so could you. So I guess we put that notion to rest."

Much to her own surprise, Roseanna laughed out loud.

"This is going to make some great watercooler gossip," she said. "I'd like to be a fly on the wall."

"What do you suppose Alice would think if she could hear all this?"

"She'd be laughing her ass off, and you know it as well as—"

A sharp pounding on the door made Roseanna jump. Ridiculously jump. As though she'd been walking through a haunted house when a hand reached out from under a bed and grabbed her ankle. Had she really been that overtly edgy about all this? If so, she had kept it well hidden. Even from herself.

She looked at Lance, who looked back.

"Probably just Nelson," Lance said. "Or Patty."

"They knock. They don't pound."

On the subject of pounding, Roseanna's heart had begun to hammer.

"I'll go see what it is," Lance said, and jumped to his feet.

When he opened the door, all she could see was her son's back. She never saw who stood on the other side of it. She saw him reach into his shorts pocket. And extend something through the door. And take hold of something, though she couldn't make out what it was. She was fully expecting a scary manila envelope, but it looked much bulkier and more three-dimensional than that.

Lance swung the door closed and turned to face her bedroom again. In his right hand he held a florist's box. Not that she could read the name of a florist from her bed. But there's a special shape to a box made to hold long-stemmed roses, and Roseanna knew one when she saw it.

"You have a secret admirer?" he asked.

"If I do, it's a secret from me, too."

She rose, shrugged on a robe. Walked to the coffee-table steamer trunk, where Lance had set the box. There she tore into it and pulled out the card.

Roseanna, it said. And then, simply, *Sorry for your loss.—Jerry.*

She handed the card to Lance, who had been

hovering over her with poorly disguised impatience. If indeed he had been attempting to disguise it at all.

"I'll be damned," he said. "Maybe I really did soften up the old guy."

"Either that or he's about to take me to the cleaners without having to worry about seeming uncaring about my personal losses."

"Oh," Lance said. "Right. Well, it's definitely one or the other."

Chapter Twenty-One

You and Your Big Ideas

When Roseanna stumbled out of bed the following morning she heard the thump of the splitting maul smacking down onto its wooden target. For just a fraction of a second, she assumed Martin was out there splitting firewood.

Then, with a sickening, sinking feeling in her gut, she remembered.

It put her in mind of a brief incident, months earlier. A moment that had played out on a Manhattan avenue. She had seen a glimpse of Alice in a crowd. And then, less than a second later—before the woman could even turn her head to reveal herself to be someone else entirely—Roseanna realized. Realized not only that it wasn't Alice, but that it could not be. That it never could be again. Because her friend Alice did not exist anywhere on this planet, which struck her as a concept so difficult and foreign that it made her head swim.

Roseanna walked to the window of her little home, but could not see who was splitting wood.

She dressed quickly and stepped outside into the mildly warm summer morning. Buzzy walked with her, his whole body wagging into punctuation symbols—commas, open quotation marks, close quotation marks. She reached down and patted his overly enthusiastic head.

As she rounded the corner of the barn she saw Lance, splitting maul raised for another thump. He had earbuds in place, the wires running into his shirt pocket. She could see his head bob rhythmically to the private music.

He looked up suddenly and saw her standing there. He lowered the maul and pulled an earbud out on the right-hand side.

"What are you doing?" she asked him.

"Isn't that rather self-evident?"

"There you go again. I guess I meant *why* are you doing it?"

"Somebody needs to."

"Not really. It's the middle of summer."

"Indeed," he said. "But only for a couple of months." He leaned on the end of the maul handle and offered up a quirky grin. "You do know it's going to be very cold in a few months, right?"

"Yes, I've mastered the basics of weather and the four seasons."

"Aren't you afraid you'll freeze?"

"Not really. I was planning to get a big heater and air conditioner combo that can sit outside. You know. With a duct into the house."

"Hmm," he said. "Sounds expensive."

Then he raised the maul again and whacked, swinging it down hard onto the pie-shaped piece of firewood. It stuck there, so Lance raised maul and wood both, then slammed them both down again. The wood popped open into two smaller pie-shaped pieces, freeing the maul.

Meanwhile Roseanna had time to realize that she had made her heating plan several weeks earlier, when she had assumed there would be plenty of money for whatever improvements she cared to make.

"I'll probably get one even if I'm fairly broke," she said.

"I didn't mean to act like you couldn't. If I thought you needed help buying a heater, I could chip in."

"Thank you."

"So how are you doing with all this?"

"All what?"

Lance leaned on the maul handle again and rolled his eyes.

"Now that's vintage Mom for you. *This.* What's happening to you *right now.* You know. The fact that Jerry has your fate in his hands and is dragging it out, and he hasn't bothered to call yet."

"Oh," Roseanna said. "That."

"Yes, that."

"You keep reminding me of things like that. When you know my strategy is to think about them as little as possible."

"Maybe it's time to tackle your emotions head-on."

"Why on earth would I want to do that?"

"So they get tackled?"

"Oh," she said, disappointed to realize he might have a point.

"What does it feel like when you do think about it? Like right now, when I'm being a huge thorn in your side by not letting you sweep it under the carpet?"

Roseanna sat down a couple of feet away on a full and uncut round of tree trunk. She thought about that a moment before answering. Or perhaps it would be more accurate to say she felt about it.

"Remember when you were a kid—" Then she stopped herself midsentence. "No. Never mind. No way you would remember. This was ages before your time. This is from when *I* was a kid. Your grandpa used to bring me these little airplanes made of balsa wood. Very thin sheets of balsa, with these airplane parts punched out. You had to put them together. They had little plastic propellers, and they worked on a rubber band. A big, long rubber band that ran the whole length of the underside of the plane. You'd wind up the rubber band by hand—by spinning the propeller until it was twisted all the way along. And then if you were an overachiever like I was, and wanted the plane to fly a long way, you just kept winding. And then the rubber band would twist into double knots. Well, not knots, but . . . into this series of little knot-like . . . I'm not doing a

346

good job describing it. I don't know if you can picture this at all."

"I get the general idea," he said. "You feel like that rubber band. See? It doesn't hurt to get in touch with how you feel now and then."

"The hell it doesn't."

They sat in silence for a moment. Then Roseanna decided to take the conversation in a different direction.

"Why can't Nelson chop wood?"

"He took the scooter into Walkerville to buy a gas pump for Patty's car."

"Does he know how to install a gas pump?"

"Apparently."

"That seems odd," she said.

"Seems right in keeping with Nelson to me."

"But if he knows how to fix a car, why didn't he fix hers a long time ago?"

"They couldn't afford the part."

"And now they can?"

"It's possible that I might have floated them a small loan," Lance said, breaking his gaze away from her eyes.

"I'm not saying that wasn't nice of you. But I also can't imagine how they're going to manage to pay you back. They don't work."

"They're about to. Nelson right now, Patty when Willa goes to school in the fall. That's why they want to get her car fixed."

"Got it," Roseanna said, and looked up into the

glaring sunlight for no reason she could name. "So they have some way to get by if I lose this place."

"Actually," Lance said, "No. They want to have a little money so they can help you."

Roseanna considered that for a moment, then released a burst of laughter she had not seen coming.

"I can't see them earning the kind of money that would get me out of this bind."

"Not that kind of help. They just want to be able to help if you're having trouble. Like if you need more grocery money down the road. If you're pinching and just barely scraping by, they want to be able to help you."

"Why would they do that?"

"Because you helped them."

Roseanna began the process of letting that sink in. Allowing the warmth of it to fill her gut. Letting herself actually believe such a thing could be true.

The process was interrupted by the sound of the phone ringing in the house. It was faint, but she could hear it from where she sat.

Her heart leapt into her throat, and she found herself sprinting across the dirt with no memory of having stood up.

As she ran she heard a second ring. And then a third. Louder each time because she was getting closer. Then she was flying up the porch steps, listening to the fourth ring.

She threw the door wide.

"Don't hang up!" she shouted out loud.

She grabbed up the receiver.

"Rosie?" a voice said.

It was a familiar voice. But it was not Jerry. And it was not Franklin, her attorney. And it was a male voice, so definitely not Franklin's secretary, Jill.

Meanwhile Roseanna said nothing. Just panted.

"You sound out of breath," the voice said.

"Who is this?"

"It's Nelson."

"Oh. Nelson."

She stood silent a moment, feeling everything collapse inside. Feeling her suddenly acquired hopes and expectations sink down into her shoes. There is no better way to learn how desperately you hate waiting than to think the waiting is over and then find out you were wrong.

"You okay?" he asked.

"Yeah. I just had to run for the phone."

"Oh. Sorry."

"Where are you calling from?"

"I'm at a pay phone in Walkerville. I just wanted to know if you need anything while I'm in town."

Roseanna saw a movement in her peripheral vision and spun to see Lance walk into her living room through the open doorway.

"Nelson wants to know if we need anything from town," she said.

Then she watched the same falling process happen in him.

"Maybe some juicing oranges," he said. "I miss fresh juice."

"Juicing oranges," she said into the phone.

"Check," Nelson said.

"Oh wait. I don't have a juicer."

"And a juicer," Lance added.

"Is there a place in Walkerville that would sell a juicer?" Roseanna asked Nelson.

"We're about to find out," Nelson said.

"Okay," she said, her depletion painfully obvious in her voice. At least, it was to her own ears. "See you when you get back." Then, quickly, before he could hang up, she added, "Nelson?"

"Yes?"

"Thank you. This was very thoughtful. All of it, I mean. I guess I mean . . . well . . . you're a very thoughtful young man."

"No worries," he said. "See you when I get back."

Then he hung up.

Roseanna looked at the phone receiver in her hand for several seconds. Suddenly, and without knowing she was about to do such a thing, she smashed it down hard onto the counter on which its base sat. It survived the hit. But Roseanna knew it might not survive the next few. And she was far from done. In fact, she was barely getting started.

She turned around to face the couch, and smashed the phone down onto its soft upholstery. Then she fell to her knees and brought it crashing down again. And again. And again. She just kept raising it and bringing it down, the plan being to do so until she had no more breath or energy, and could not go on.

Instead, the receiver disappeared from her grip on the upswing, and her hand hit the couch, empty.

She looked up to see Lance standing over her, holding the phone receiver.

"Mom. Whoa. Really. Whoa. Take a deep breath and settle."

She pulled up straighter on her knees and looked up into his face, panting.

"But it was your idea for me to get in touch with my feelings. You know. Hit things head-on."

"Oh. Yeah. Well . . . on the other hand . . . what the hell do I know?"

"Here's what disappoints me," she said during their midday nap, which only rarely resulted in any actual sleeping. "When we were watching that meteor shower I told you I would be okay no matter what happens. But then that revelation seems to have gotten lost."

"They always do," he said.

"That's not very optimistic."

"I'm not saying you'll never see it again. Just

that it's not very realistic to think you won't go back and forth on this. It's just how emotions are. They rise and fall. Chunks of them fly up when you least expect it. Even if you do get it that you'll manage one way or another, it makes a huge difference to your situation how these next few days go. You wouldn't be human if you weren't stressed out about it."

She rolled over and looked at the side of his face. His eyes were closed, his face perfectly slack. Just for a moment she thought of Alice in the hospital.

She pushed the thought away again.

But before she could, she touched on something in her mind. Something she had not consciously taken in before. A small moment upon which she had never stopped to dwell.

She remembered the look on Jerry's face when she told him to leave Alice's hospital room.

"How do you know all this?" she asked her son.

"Just from living, I guess."

"I've been living a lot longer than you have."

"But I take my feelings head-on. Everything just comes up and out like a bad dinner. I mean, I deal with things to a fault."

They lay quietly for a moment before Roseanna said, "That doesn't sound like a fault to me."

A minute or two later she opened her mouth to say more on the subject, but just then Lance let out a light, gauzy snore.

● ● ●

In time, Roseanna stood up and left her son to nap on his own.

She walked into the kitchen and took notepaper out of one of the drawers. Got her best pen from the little table by the door. She sat on the couch and—using a book as a lap desk—wrote Jerry a note.

Jerry, it began. *I'm sorry I was rude to you that day at the hospital. But Alice was so scared, and I was just trying to protect her from . . .*

She stopped. Wadded up the paper and made a three-point basket into the kitchen trash.

It would not do to include the part about how Alice clearly withered in Jerry's presence. It would not help him want to show legal mercy. Beyond that, it simply would not help anybody or anything. It would do no good in the world. It was a truth best kept to herself.

She began again on a fresh piece of notepaper.

Jerry, she wrote. *I want to apologize to you for that day at the hospital. Not because you're suing me and I don't want you to, but because I just now remembered that I was rude and dismissive, and I know it must have hurt you. I didn't mean it to. And I didn't mean to act like I belonged there and you didn't.*

She stopped again. Based on what Lance had just told Jerry, that was not a believable sentence. If she and Alice had been in love since college, of course she would feel that she had more of a right to be alone with Alice in her last minutes on earth. They weren't all just coworkers, at least, not in the version of events Jerry now believed to be the truth.

She started over, copying everything but that last sentence. Ending with *I didn't mean it to.* Then she started fresh from there.

I was just terrified, and not handling things well. I don't know how to explain it any better than that. No matter what happens with the suit, I hope you'll accept my apology.

Then she signed her name. Folded the paper and slid it into an envelope. Addressed the envelope to the achingly familiar street number of her old firm.

She stuck a stamp on it, which she pulled from the drawer where she kept the stamps she used when paying electricity and water bills.

Then she walked it out to her mailbox at the road while her son slept.

She raised the red mail flag and let the whole thing go.

Chapter Twenty-Two

Ithaca Is Gorges

"We're going on a field trip," Lance said.

It wasn't a question. It left little room for argument, though Roseanna assumed she would mount one anyway.

It was three mornings later. Three days of staring |at a phone that never rang. Seventy-two hours of losing her temper at the tiniest provocation, usually shortly after swearing the situation wasn't making her the tiniest bit nervous. No, of course not. Not in any way.

She leaned back on the couch and stared up at the mountain of him. He was hovering above her. All the better to control the moment, she figured.

"Why would I want to go on a field trip?"

"To get you away from the damned phone."

"But I need to stay by the phone, and that's the point of staying by the phone. I thought you understood this concept."

"But it's wearing you down, Mom. More than I think you even realize. You need to get away and think about something else for a change. Before you crack right down the middle like that ice shelf in the Arctic that everybody thought would stay in one piece forever."

"Not that I don't appreciate being compared to unstable ice," she said, "but what if Jerry or my attorney calls while I'm away? And then I call back but I can't reach them? So I have to spend part of a day not knowing what they called to say. That would definitely crack me. Come to think of it, I don't even have voicemail or an answering machine yet. So I'd never even know if someone called."

"But you have voicemail on your cell phone."

"But it doesn't get reception."

"Not here. But probably on most of our field trip, it will."

"But Franklin might call me at home."

"No. He won't. He'll call you on your cell."

"Now how could you possibly know that?"

"Because I called him this morning while you were in the barn feeding the horse. And I told him we'd be out all day and to call you on your cell."

Roseanna breathed quietly for a few moments, realizing she had lost the battle. They were going on a field trip. It was a desperate feeling to detach from the lifeline of the telephone. As if she were drowning, going down for the last time, and someone had just convinced her to stop grasping at branches to try to save herself.

In another way it felt like a relief to simply let go.

"Fine. Where are we going?"

"It's a surprise," Lance said. "But you might want to bring a bathing suit. Or wear it under your clothes."

"A *bathing suit?*"

"Yes. I figured you would have heard of them."

"I don't have a bathing suit."

"You used to have one that you wore at the health club."

"True. But now I have no health club. So why would I still have the suit?"

Lance sighed deeply. As if Roseanna were a three-year-old who was straining his patience to the breaking point, and for no discernible reason.

"Fine," he said. "Then just wear shorts and a T-shirt."

"I don't own shorts. I look terrible in them."

Another huge, theatrical sigh from her son.

"I'll bring a pair of *my* shorts, then."

"Knock yourself out, honey. But if you think you're getting me into them, you don't know me as well as you keep thinking you do."

"I hope you know better than to drive me any-where near the city," Roseanna said. Then she went back to staring out the window.

They had taken the Maserati, at Roseanna's suggestion. If she was about to lose it, which it seemed she was, it would be a fitting last fling with her beloved car. But Lance was driving. Because she had no idea where they were headed.

"Of course I know that," he said.

Roseanna felt a spot just under her diaphragm relax.

"Thank you," she said simply.

They seemed to be on some kind of back road. Not exactly a country lane, but not the New York State Thruway. They had driven a series of smaller state routes since Lance had spirited her away from her property. The drive was becoming wooded and as remote as home. If not more so.

It should have soothed her. She refused to let it.

She woke up her phone display with her thumb and stared at it for a few seconds, watching the bars of reception rise and fall. Now and then they disappeared entirely. Then one bar would struggle to make itself known.

The phone disappeared from her hand.

"Stop that," Lance said, and tucked the phone into his shirt pocket.

"That was cold."

"You're getting obsessed about this, Mom. I'm not saying it's not understandable. But you have to at least try. All my life I've had to sit back and watch stress eat you alive. And watch you not even try to manage it. Not even try to save yourself from it. Now I at least want you to try."

Roseanna sighed deeply and said nothing.

They drove in silence for a few miles.

"*Now* do I get to know where we're going?" she asked after a time.

"No. It's still a surprise. I'm only going to tell you that it's beautiful and natural. Which we both know soothes you. Granted, that's a bit of a late life surprise, but now that we finally know it, let's squeeze everything we can out of that revelation."

More silent miles.

Roseanna had a question rattling around in her gut, but wasn't sure she could see her way clear to ask it. She almost let it sink back down into the abyss again.

Then it hit her. That was the old Roseanna and Lance. The way she'd done things all his life. That was how he'd grown to age thirty without mentioning whom he'd been seeing. Or even the gender of those he felt most inclined to see.

Sooner or later you have to recognize the old patterns. But even that wasn't enough, she now realized. It wasn't sufficient to simply watch them play out while thinking, *Yes, indeed, that is my pattern,* and then continue to do it that way all the same. No. Sooner or later you had to get up off your sorry butt and do a little better for yourself.

"And what about you?" she asked, startling them both.

"What *about* me?"

"You've been living surrounded by nature for a few weeks. We're both city people born and raised, but it didn't take me more than an hour in the middle of nowhere to know it's where I wanted to be. Where I *needed* to be. But you haven't said much about it. You know. About your opinion of the wilderness experience. At least, wilderness by New York City standards."

"Oh, it's wilderness to me. And then some."

"You seem to be evading the question."

For a strange length of time, Lance didn't answer. He just took one hand off the steering wheel, made a fist, and cleared his throat into it.

Then he said, in a quiet mumble, "I don't think you'll like my answer to that."

"It's not a matter of whether I'll like it or not. You just have to tell me the truth. You don't have to filter it through the net of what you think it will please me to hear. That's how we got in all that trouble in the first place."

"True," he said.

He lifted his sunglasses and rubbed a spot on the bridge of his nose where the pads had left red indentations.

"Well . . . ," he began. Then he stalled for an uncomfortable length of time. "I guess I'd have to say . . . I hate it."

"Where I live, you mean?"

"Yes. I'm sorry. I want to say it's beautiful and peaceful, but really I just . . . I hate it. Granted, it's pretty to look at. But I'm the kind of guy . . . I look at it once, and I say, 'Yeah, yeah, very nice.' And then I've seen it. And I don't have the need to just keep staring at it. I'm a city person,

Mom. I can't help it. I like Wi-Fi and cell phone reception. And the theater, and comedy clubs. I even like all that raucous traffic noise while I'm trying to get to sleep. It's kind of hard not to wake up in the morning feeling like I'm in a bad *Green Acres* remake."

He fell silent. The dense forest rolled past Roseanna's car window while she thought about nothing at all.

"I'm sorry," he said.

"You don't have to be sorry."

"I don't?"

"No, of course not. It's who you are. You're a city person. You're young. When people are young, excitement is a good thing. Living like I'm living now seems boring. Then you get older and you're wearing the scars of all that excitement you've chased after your whole life, and then what you used to call boring starts to look serene. Then you start to view boring as a lofty goal. But maybe you'll get to be my age and still love the city. Plenty of people do. The idea is that we get to do what suits us. The idea is not that what suits me has to suit you, too. If you can accept where I want to live, I can accept where you want to live. Has to be a two-way street, right?"

Lance smiled his trademark crooked smile. "And that's another thing. I like two-way streets. With more than one lane in each direction."

He fell silent, but Roseanna could hear his

breathing. It sounded loud and slow, as though every breath were a carefully planned sigh. As if he were doing exercises to clean out the inside of himself.

"That's a relief," he said.

"You shouldn't be afraid to tell me things like that."

"I try not to be."

"But you've been out at my place with me for so long now. And you never said a word. You never complained."

"We were getting to know each other," he said. "It was worth it. It was kind of nice."

They stepped out of the car in a parking lot at a shady state park.

"Leave the phone in the car," Lance said. But he handed it back to her. So at least it was more of a suggestion.

"But—" she began.

Before she could say more, she looked down at its display and saw the phone was getting zero bars of reception.

"So what was this you were saying about how I'd have cell phone reception all day?"

"I didn't say all day. I said mostly. And I said you have voicemail. I'm sure Franklin can handle voicemail."

Roseanna sighed deeply and locked the phone into the glove compartment of the Maserati.

They took off on foot, Roseanna following silently behind her son. She could hear the sound of running water. Maybe even falling water.

He seemed to know exactly where he was going, and he seemed to go there deliberately. More like there was an exact latitude and longitude to locate. Less like "This is a nice place. Let's poke around here."

She noticed he was carrying the spare pair of shorts with which he had threatened her. They were dangling from his left hand.

They walked along a shaded dirt path. Then the path bent suddenly and began to descend down stone steps, guarded on one side by a stone retaining wall. On the other side of the wall Roseanna looked down into a deep gorge carved by a running stream or river. The rock of the area had clearly been formed in horizontal shelf-like layers, now carved away by years of flowing water.

Lance was several steps ahead of her, so she hurried to catch up.

"This is near Ithaca," she said. "Isn't it?"

He stopped descending. Stood still to answer her.

"You've been here before?"

"No. But I've always known there were all these gorges around Ithaca. Your grandpa used to tell me about them. He went to Cornell, you know. Well, yes, of course you know. He only dropped it into every other sentence. He used to come out here with his college buddies, and they'd drink beer and dive off cliffs into the deeper pools."

"Grandpa? Got drunk and dove off cliffs?"

"Well, we were all young once, honey."

"Not Grandpa," Lance said.

Another crooked smile from him. Then they began to descend the stone steps again, more together this time.

"He always said he'd take me out here and show me the gorges," Roseanna said. "But of course he never did."

"Now *that* sounds like Grandpa," Lance said.

They crested the lip of a steep drop. On her right, Roseanna saw the water fall off into a stepped cascade, spreading out like a white bridal veil over thin layers of rock. It was a lovely sight, but she could not help but turn around and look back the way they had come. All these steps they were descending would have to be climbed again to get back to their car. That would be no small task.

"Why did you choose this particular gorge?" Roseanna asked, raising her voice to be heard over the falling water.

Lance only shrugged.

"Have you been here before?"

"Once," he said. "Neal and I explored this whole

area once. I thought this was the nicest waterfall. I figured you'd like a good waterfall. Being a nature person and all."

"Actually, it's more of a cascade. Sorry if that sounds like splitting hairs."

"What's the difference?"

"My understanding is that a waterfall involves free-falling water. When it tumbles over rocks at an angle like this, I think it's more of a cascade."

"The name of the park has the word *waterfall* right in it."

"Well, that's the park service for you, honey. Haven't you noticed they never use apostrophes on their signage? Clouds Rest in Yosemite? Angels Landing in Utah? They've apparently never heard of a possessive. They are clearly not the department of English grammar."

"We're stopping here," Lance said.

And he stopped.

They stood at the bottom of the gorge now. Or, at least, the bottom of this gorge. Whether there were more gorges downstream, Roseanna could not see. But they stood at the very edge of the water, which had now formed a wide pool with a high stone wall behind it. She craned her neck back to see the top of the gorge, from where they had come.

"You realize we'll have to walk back up there," she said.

Lance looked up. As though elevation were fresh news to him.

"All the more reason you should go in for a swim. It's getting hot. You want to be refreshed before we do the big walk out."

"You have *got* to be kidding me."

"What's so weird about wading into a pool of water and swimming on a hot day?"

"My legs are all pasty white. And how am I supposed to change into shorts anyway? We're in the open out here."

"And who are you thinking is going to see you?"

Roseanna looked around. She saw a group of three people descending the stairs above them, but they looked like ants from this distance. She pointed at them.

"They would," she said.

Lance shielded his eyes against the sun and looked where Roseanna had pointed. "Seriously?"

"Yes, seriously."

"They're a little far away to see much, don't you think?"

"But they're getting closer."

"Better hurry up and change then. You have on underwear, right?"

"Of course I have on underwear. What kind of question is that?"

Lance unbuttoned his light print shirt.

"Here," he said, taking it off. Baring his hairless, strong-looking chest to the dappled sun. "I'll hold this in front of you."

"But my legs are all pasty and white. Even after I'm done changing."

"You know . . . if you wore shorts once in a while, they wouldn't be."

"But I don't. And they are."

"So hurry up and change and then jump in. And then your legs will be underwater. And no one will see."

Roseanna opened her mouth to argue. But it was hot, and would only get hotter. And she knew she would regret the missed opportunity if they continued to be surrounded by people for the rest of their time here.

So she cursed under her breath, more or less nonstop. But she changed behind Lance's shirt.

Roseanna held her nose and let herself sink. The pool was shallow where she swam, and she had to bend her legs so they wouldn't touch bottom. She wrapped her arms around her knees and allowed her head to dip below the waterline.

She felt the icy coldness of it surround her head and face.

Then she popped up again and shook water out of her hair.

"I hate to admit it," she said to Lance, who floated on his back a few feet away, "but this is very pleasant."

Lance smiled but offered no comment. Then again, maybe no comment was needed.

Roseanna treaded water with her knees bent, and looked around.

The three people who had come down the stairs after them had long ago descended to this level and kept going. Moved downstream. Everybody wanted a pool to themselves, she decided.

Just on that thought she noticed the young man who apparently didn't.

He was in the water, and swimming toward them. Right toward them. It made her uncomfortable, the way it would if a stranger sat down next to her in an empty movie theater. He was breaking the rules that were universally observed by strangers. And those rules were there for a reason. Everybody knew it.

She watched him swim closer with a growing sense of alarm.

He was slightly built, with dark blond hair wetly slicked back along his head. He wore wire-rimmed glasses, even in the water, and swam in something that looked like a cross between a butterfly stroke and a dog paddle to keep his head above the surface. Probably to keep his glasses dry.

Roseanna swam the few feet to Lance and poked him hard in the ribs.

He bent in the middle, sank like a stone, then came up sputtering.

"That's not funny," he said, blowing water out of his nose.

"It wasn't a joke. That guy is coming right toward us. Why is he doing that?"

Lance looked around.

Then, much to Roseanna's surprise, he smiled broadly. He fell forward into a smooth-looking swimmer's stroke and headed straight for the intruder.

They met in the middle, where both tested the depth of the water by putting their feet down. They were able to stand, though Lance stood a good head taller. Whether the bottom was uneven or Lance was much larger, Roseanna could not know. But she hoped for the latter.

The two young men embraced.

Roseanna stood in the shallow water with her mouth open, vaguely thinking, *What is happening?*

A moment later they were headed in her direction, side by side. More or less walking. The water came up to Lance's chest and the other man's chin. They held each other's hand high, above the surface of the pool.

"Mom," Lance said when they arrived, "this is Neal. Neal, Mom."

Roseanna said nothing for an awkward length of time. Then she sputtered out a few words.

"Well, when you said *surprise* you really meant surprise."

"I hope you don't feel like we broadsided you," Neal said.

"Not at all. I'm happy to meet you."

She reached out one awkward hand to shake Neal's. Then she realized this was the old pattern. The old Roseanna. Keeping her distance out of formality and fear.

Instead she pulled her hand back and plunged forward two or three steps through the water to throw her arms around the young man.

He seemed surprised, but not unhappy.

"I've been wanting to meet you, too," he said into her ear.

"I'm off to find a restroom," Lance said a few minutes later. "You two get acquainted."

"An actual restroom?" Roseanna asked. "Like all the way up at the parking lot?"

She was attempting to gauge how long he would be gone. Because, truthfully, it was a little soon to be alone with Neal, and the prospect made her uneasy.

"That's a long way to go," Lance said. "I was thinking more like the men's room behind a big tree."

Then he swam to the shore and climbed out.

"Sorry," Neal said. "He probably should have told you."

"It's not a problem," she said, though it clearly was a little bit of one. "I just don't deal all that well with surprises."

"Which is why he should have told you."

He had a gentle voice. Patient, like a person

who takes the time to speak kindly to a child. Up close she decided he looked a bit more like a math or science nerd than the way Roseanna had imagined him.

"My family lives in Ithaca," Neal said. "Well, my dad. He's all the family I've got left now. So this is someplace I like to go. So we thought we'd meet here. Lance wanted this to be a de-stressing sort of a day for you, and I guess he thought if you knew this would be our first meeting . . . well, that maybe that would just make you nervous. And he figures you're nervous enough right now. What with all that's going on."

Roseanna said nothing in reply. Just mulled over the fact that Neal knew all about her. Because people talk to their partners.

She half stood, half floated in the water, absorbing the totality of Lance and Neal having so much shared history. So much life with each other that Roseanna knew nothing about. It felt as though someone had been watching her through one-way mirrored glass while staying safely anonymous and hidden himself. It also meant there was a great deal of her son's life that she had missed, but that much she'd known already. It just hurt to get a good look at it in retrospect.

Meanwhile the silence was seeming to make him uncomfortable.

So she said, "You've been very patient about having him away so long."

"I'm the one who kept encouraging him to patch things up with you."

For a split second, Roseanna took umbrage at the phrasing. It was not as though she and her son had had some huge, sudden falling-out. But the problem was only semantic, she decided. She consciously let it go.

"Really? You were encouraging it?"

"Strenuously," he said.

Another brief moment of umbrage. Was he saying someone had to hold a gun to Lance's head before he would agree to get near her again?

She took a deep breath and decided to make an effort in the opposite direction, away from umbrage.

"I guess I should thank you, then."

"You don't need to thank me. I just have some experience with mothers."

"Don't we all?"

Roseanna laughed. Neal didn't.

"I meant more like . . . I have some experience with the fallout from doing it wrong. My mother died while I was at Cornell." He treaded water for several long, silent moments, as though he never planned to go on with the story. Then he went on with the story. "I don't usually talk about this, but you're Lance's mom, so . . . here goes. It was almost midterms, and I was stressing about my grade point average. All I wanted to do was study. My mom asked me to come to the house to see her. She didn't say why. But I didn't go. I told her I needed to study. She died of a heart attack that night. I have no idea if she knew it was coming. My dad said no, she didn't, but it's also possible she knew but didn't tell him. She had a way of knowing things before they happened, but he never believed in that. I never found out what she wanted to say to me. I know it's kind of cliché—how a thing like that happens and it gets to be something of a personal crusade. Going through life telling everybody not to make the same mistake you made. But Lance was always acting like he had plenty of time to patch things up with you. That's dangerous thinking."

"Yes," Roseanna said. "It is."

Alice's frightened eyes appeared in her head, but she pushed them out again.

"I'm hungry!" a big voice shouted.

Roseanna whipped her head around to see that Lance was back. Standing at the edge of the pool. Waving to them to come ashore.

He cupped both hands around his mouth for another big shout. "We're taking you to lunch in Ithaca!"

Roseanna treaded water in silence for a moment. Neal looked into her face. She looked back.

"Please go over there," she said in a measured tone, "and tell your significant other that I'm not getting out of the water, because if I do, my . . . son-in-law, for lack of a better term, will see how pasty and white my legs are. And then for the rest of time, every Christmas and every Thanksgiving, I'll put on my finest clothes and share a meal with you, but all you'll see is the blinding white of those pasty legs. Once you see it you'll never be able to unsee it again. And I'll never live it down."

"I could tell him all that," Neal said, a genuine-looking smile playing on his lips for the first time since they'd met. "But maybe it would be easier if I just made a trip to that local men's room myself."

Chapter Twenty-Three

Done Deals, and How They Don't Exist

Roseanna broke the silence when she realized all three of them had been staring at their unusually handsome college-aged waiter for just a little bit too long.

"So, Neal," she said. "You went to Cornell, too."

His eyebrows jumped. As though he couldn't imagine how she knew that.

"Too? Are you a Cornell woman?"

"No, my father was."

"Oh, that's right. I knew that. Lance says he found a way to work it into every other sentence. I try not to do that. I try not to bring it up unless I'm asked. But I must've . . . oh yeah. It's all coming back to me now. It was when I was telling you about my mother."

That seemed to wake Lance from something akin to a deep, open-eyed sleep.

"You told her about your mother?"

"It fit the moment," Neal said. "If you'd been there, you would have understood."

"Where was I?"

"Peeing behind a tree."

Then the conversation died for an awkward length of time.

Roseanna looked around the restaurant and tried to make peace with her surroundings. But the establishment was healthy to the point of being hippie, and the college-town atmosphere felt jarring. Or maybe just being around so many people felt jarring. It made her want to raise a force field around herself and huddle inside it to stay safe.

The handsome waiter brought three glasses of water and the freshly squeezed juices they had ordered. Roseanna had had no idea what to order, being thoroughly unfamiliar with the juicing trend, so had allowed Neal to choose for her. He had chosen a blend of celery, carrot, and lemon.

She sipped it tentatively, as though it might bite back. It was surprisingly pleasant. She relaxed some, accepting that every new food experience might not be the death of her.

"How long have you two been together?" she asked when the waiter had left again.

They glanced sideways at each other, then down at the table.

"I'm sorry," Roseanna said. "Was that a bad question?"

"No," Lance said. "Of course not. Not at all. We're coming up on a year and a half."

A deadly silence fell. Roseanna worked hard to digest the information so as to improve their chances to go on making polite conversation. It worked poorly.

"I know, Mom," Lance said. "I know. It's pretty pathetic. It's a long time to have something going on in my life that I don't even bother to share with my own mother. But we're doing better now, and isn't that the main thing? Can't we put that away and just be happy for where we are now?"

Roseanna took a deep, bracing breath and decided she could. Because she just would.

She raised her juice glass to them in a toast, and they met her gesture with their own.

"To where we are now," she said as the glasses clinked together. Then she added, "And to never doing stupid crap like that ever again."

"Your thoughts on the city," Roseanna said to Neal during dessert.

They were all three slumped back in their chairs. Full, and finally more relaxed.

"*My* thoughts?" Neal asked.

"Yes. Yours. I already know *his*." She gestured vaguely in the direction of her son. "He told me on the drive down here that he loves the city and hates where I live. Which is okay, I suppose. Not everybody has to like it. Hell, I should be grateful everybody doesn't agree on that. I'm already overrun by people who love it as much as I do. But I must admit it was a little disappointing, because it's been so wonderful having him there. I guess part of me didn't want it to end. I didn't literally think he'd stay. I mean . . . it doesn't

377

make any sense when you think about it. There's no real place for him there. But it just made me realize that he'll be packing up and going home soon. And that made me sad. If I'm being totally honest."

"Not that soon, Mom," Lance said. "Not till you get through this whole legal thing."

"Right. Yes. Thank you for that."

Roseanna set down her fork. There was still half a slice of carrot cake on her plate, but she suddenly realized she couldn't stomach another bite of it. She slid her phone out of her pocket and glanced at it, surprised she had been able to forget it for so long.

There were no voicemails. No missed calls.

After an awkward pause, Neal jumped in.

"Me and the city. Okay. I like the city, but I don't love it the way he does. It's just useful to me. But I grew up near all this natural beauty, and I miss it. So I guess I'm more of a half-and-half guy. I have this dream that when I get older, I'll build a house out in the country and use it as a getaway."

"You could build it on my land," she said without thinking. Clearly without thinking, because who would say such a thing after thinking it through? "Never mind, scratch that," she said. "After all, I don't even know yet if I get to keep the place."

But there was a bigger reason why she should

not have said it. It was a plan that hinged on the two young men staying together. And, according to Lance, that was anything but a given.

She stole a glance at her son's face. The deep discomfort she saw there made her look away again.

She talked over the awkwardness of the moment.

"I think I only mentioned it because Nelson asked me recently if he could do a thing like that. Build something on my property. Not to live in indefinitely, as though he were family. Not that I'm saying you're family . . . ," she added in the vague direction of Neal. Roseanna felt her face redden. She kept talking, for lack of a better plan. "I'm also not saying you're not. Well, at this point it should be painfully obvious that I have no idea what I'm saying. Anyway, if he does, and then if he and Patty move to their own place, at least I'd have something like a guesthouse. Because it would be nice if you two would come visit after Lance goes home."

"Of course we'll come visit," Neal said.

"Nelson and Patty?" Lance asked, sounding amazed.

"I don't know if that's a done deal," Roseanna said.

"I didn't know it was any deal at all."

"I guess I wouldn't have, either, except that Martin told me. Right before he . . ."

She trailed off into nothing and stopped talking.

"Relationships are never a done deal," Neal said. "There's always hard work involved."

It was a statement that stopped the conversation dead for an embarrassing length of time. Nobody seemed to have anything they wanted to add to an observation like that one.

"So," Roseanna said, turning to Neal while Lance paid the check. "I never asked you what you do for a living, Mr. Cornell Graduate."

"I'm an attorney," Neal said.

"*Are* you? Isn't *that* interesting?"

In her peripheral vision she watched her son blush slightly. She didn't go on to say why she found it so interesting, so as not to embarrass him further.

"I'm sorry for what I said back there," Roseanna said on the drive home. "I should have thought before I shot off my mouth."

She powered her passenger seat back into a more reclined position. Lance had offered to drive again, and she had taken him up on it. Not because she didn't know where they were going, but because she was tired and a little bit sleepy.

"You mean the thing about building the house?"

"That very thing."

"It's okay."

"I doubt that."

"Well . . . ," Lance began. "It's okay *enough*.

You meant well, and it was a very nice offer. Just that . . ."

"You're not even sure you're going to stay with Neal."

"I'm surer than I was a couple of weeks ago."

"Good. I like him."

"Do you? That's interesting. I wanted to ask your impression of him, but I didn't want to put you on the spot."

"My impression. Let's see. He wasn't the way I'd pictured him."

"How did you picture him?"

"Well. You're a big, handsome guy. Of course, that's your mother talking, but we both know that objectively I'm right. I'm not saying Neal's not handsome. He is. But in a different way. I guess I was expecting a big, handsome guy who was more . . . you know. Hunky. Neal seems to have most of his good qualities on the inside. He's smart, and he seems to know what to value. He has some depth, from what I can tell. I suppose I wouldn't have guessed that as your type."

"It's not," Lance said, pulling over to the shoulder of the road to briefly study the navigation screen. "It's totally not my type. I've always gone with big and hunky, just like you pictured." He pulled back into the traffic lane of the deserted state route. "So I have this discomfort, I guess, because it's unfamiliar. I keep thinking I want to back away because he's not my type, and then I start remembering all the guys who were my type. Not that it was that enormous a crowd or anything, but . . . I guess what I'm saying is . . . I look back and I get it that my type never did me much good. Never got me anywhere I really wanted to go."

"His depth makes you uneasy," Roseanna said. It was not a question.

"Pretty much. It just makes the whole thing so damned . . . real."

"You could do worse than real."

"I suppose I could."

"I trust you to do the right thing."

"Do you? I wish I did."

"Trust me, kid. Nobody knows you like your mother."

Roseanna popped awake, surprised she had even fallen asleep. She was still in the passenger seat of the car, and Lance was turning into the dirt driveway of home.

Well, her home, anyway.

Well. Hopefully her home.

She had been sleeping with her face pressed against the glass, and she rubbed her cheek to bring blood back into it.

Then she remembered her phone.

She whipped it out of her pocket.

It showed a voicemail.

She stared at it while Lance pulled the car into

the barn. Her face tingled—not just the part that had been pressed against the window glass, but all of it. She felt frozen all over, but coldest in her face and lower intestines.

Lance turned off the engine and glanced over at her. She never raised her eyes to him, but in her peripheral vision, she could see his reaction. She could watch him take the situation in.

"What?" he asked. "Did someone call?"

"Yes, but now it's too late to call voicemail. You need reception for that."

"You can call your voicemail from the landline. Now aren't you glad I made you get a landline? Who called?"

"I don't know yet."

"You just go to 'recents' and it'll show the number."

"I know that," Roseanna said, sounding more annoyed than necessary.

"Then why aren't you doing it?"

"I don't know," Roseanna said. "I mean, it's a little hard to explain. Nothing works."

"The phone is not working?"

"No. Me. I'm not working."

"Want me to do it for you?"

He reached out for the phone. Roseanna tried to meet him halfway, but her hand and arm never received the signal. Lance gently slid the phone out of her hand.

She turned her head away. Watched Earnest,

who stood in his stall in the corner. He was bobbing his head up and down, as if affirming something. A yes answer to a question he couldn't possibly know.

Then she realized they had arrived home late for his afternoon feeding, and he was impatiently requesting that service.

"It was Franklin," Lance said.

Roseanna realized she had known that. Known it in some part of herself that knew things it rarely shared with the balance of herself.

Meanwhile she said nothing. Just watched Earnest nod with increasing determination.

"Want me to go inside and call your voicemail from the landline?"

"Yes, would you?" Roseanna asked, sounding fully functional to her own ears. "I'm just going to take a minute to feed the horse."

She opened the passenger door, and Buzzy set his head on her lap, tail whipping.

"And the dog," she added.

She looked up to see Lance standing in the doorway of the open barn. The late afternoon sun slanted through a high window on the far side of the barn and fell on him the way a spotlight falls on a lone actor on a stage.

She felt as though she might explode if he didn't speak, despite the fact that hardly more than a second had passed.

"So here was the message," he said. "Franklin called to tell you that Jerry called him today. To tell you that 'due to extenuating circumstances,' he's decided to accept your offer."

"Wait. Which offer? The first offer, that I can actually afford? Or the counteroffer I just made that'll more or less break me?"

Lance's eyes shifted down toward the dirt.

"Well, now, I feel a little guilty about this. Because you warned me that we could get a call while we were away, and we'd miss it, and then you wouldn't know for a day what the answer was, and you'd crack like an ice shelf. I tried to call him back. But Jill told me he's already left the office for the day."

"Oh," Roseanna said.

Earnest broke his concentration on the hay feeder for just a moment, which was rare for him. He swung his head around and bumped Roseanna on the shoulder with his nose, causing her to stumble a few steps. She had no idea why he would do such a thing. It was as though he were telling her to snap out of it.

Or maybe she was telling herself that, and got the two messages confused.

The horse resumed munching on his dinner.

"I'm sorry," Lance said.

"Don't be. I actually had a nice day. I didn't expect to. But, surprisingly, I did. I'll find out in the morning. And in the meantime . . ."

In the meantime she would be deeply uncomfortable. And, also, she would have a chance to learn to let things like that be. Because, really . . . how was she ever going to be happy if she couldn't learn to let things like that be?

"In the meantime," Lance said, "he's accepted one of your offers or the other. And either offer lets you keep this property. Right?"

"Yes, that's true. The difference is the comfort of my lifestyle. And whether I get to keep the car."

"So you know you can keep living here."

Roseanna sucked in air, almost involuntarily, then let it out in a loud, deep sigh.

Earnest turned to glare at her, as if to say, "Could you keep it down, please? I'm trying to eat."

"Yes," she said. "And that's the most important thing, isn't it?"

"I'd say."

And with that, Roseanna felt herself thaw. Her stuck body unstuck itself. Just that easily.

She walked to where Lance stood in the open doorway. Into that beam of light made for one actor only. Asked it to spotlight two.

She took his hand and squeezed it firmly.

"Thank you for not being mad at me," he said.

"Let's go play a few hands of cards before dinner," she said. "It'll give us something to keep our mind off things."

And they walked to the house—the house that Roseanna would continue to call home—hand in hand.

Roseanna stepped out of the shower and wrapped herself in a bath sheet, then walked out into her living room. Lance was nowhere around.

For a few minutes she waited for him. Stayed up for his return. But it had been a long, tiring day, and she was more than done with it. More than ready to put it—and herself—to bed.

She lit a candle for him and left it on the steamer trunk coffee table. The way she had that first night.

He slipped in quietly about half an hour later. Right around the time Roseanna was accepting that her exhaustion would not necessarily translate to the sleep she so desperately needed.

"I'm awake," she said, because she could tell he was trying hard to be quiet.

"Oh. I guess that makes sense. Under the circumstances. But I'm sorry you can't sleep." He came into her room and sat on the edge of her bed. "I hope you don't mind. I told Patty and Nelson that you get to keep the place."

"That was thoughtful. I guess I probably should have done it myself."

"You had a lot on your mind. But they've been nervous about it and I knew it. They didn't want to let on. To you, I mean. They wanted to stay positive for your sake, and they understood that it was a much bigger deal for you than it was for them. But it's been weighing on their minds."

"I don't doubt it."

They sat in silence for a moment or two, Rose-anna watching through the window as a huge, yellowish full moon rose to the right of CPR Hill. Or, at least, the former CPR Hill. Maybe now it was just a hill like any other. Pretty enough, but with no real relevance to her life. Ignorable, as all good hills should be.

"Wait a minute," she said. "You went all the way down that giant slope and across the creek to talk to Nelson in the pitch dark?"

"No. He's not down there. He's at Patty's."

"Oh, *he's at Patty's,*" she repeated. "That's interesting. So that's an actual thing?"

"I hate to shoot off my mouth and try to say. I'm not even positive what's an actual thing in my own life. But that's where he was all right."

Another silent moment of moon watching. This time she looked at her son's face in the soft light. He seemed to be watching the moon rise as well.

"I guess I'm off to bed," he said. "Though I still can't get the hang of sleeping this early."

"Don't go yet. There's something I need to say."

He had been halfway to his feet, bent at the waist and rising. He froze, stayed bent for a moment. Then he sank back down onto the edge of the bed. The light whump of him touching down and the sinking movement of the mattress reminded Roseanna that excessive solitude is not a proper goal. So many of the little things served as reminders these days.

"I should have said it when you first gave me Franklin's message. But my brain was going a lot of different directions."

"Mom, I know," he interjected. "I'm sorry."

"If you're sorry, then you don't know." She waited a moment to see if he cared to interrupt again. But he only waited in return, so she plunged on. "I should have said thank you, right away. But I'm saying it now, which is the next best thing."

"For . . . ?"

"*For?* You don't know what you did? You saved the most important thing I own. You talked Jerry out of taking it away from me."

"We don't know for a fact that my little talk was the reason he backed down."

"Oh, come on, Lance. 'Extenuating circumstances'?"

"Yeah. I guess I see your point. It was dicey, though. It was a risky thing to do."

"Life is dicey," Roseanna said. "But if it's a win, you just shut up and take it. Now give your old mom a kiss before you go off to bed."

And he did. Enthusiastically. Right in the middle of her forehead.

Chapter Twenty-Four

Go the Hell Home

Roseanna knew Lance had wakened up for the morning because he sat up on the couch and looked around until he located her. She was sitting on the floor, staring at the phone receiver, which she had set on the floorboards in front of her. She saw him rise up in her peripheral vision, without once taking her eyes off the receiver.

She met his gaze briefly.

He rolled his eyes dramatically and flopped back down.

"What time is it?" he asked in a voice dulled and muddled by sleep.

"A little after seven."

"And how long have you been staring at that phone?"

"About three hours."

"Because you honestly thought it would ring at four in the morning?"

"No. I'm just waiting for it to be late enough so I can call Franklin back."

"And you figure that'll come faster if you stare at the phone?"

"I had nothing else to stare at. It was dark pretty much everywhere else."

Lance sat up again. Shook his head and then placed his forehead in the palms of both hands.

"Let's gather the facts here," he said without undoing the facepalm. "Franklin's office opens at nine. Like every other office in the whole freaking—"

The phone rang.

It was so loud, so unexpected, that it made Roseanna jump, even from a seated position. She lurched away from the sound, which almost caused her to fall over backward.

She grabbed up the phone.

"Hello?"

"Roseanna?"

Franklin had a deep speaking voice and a telephone manner that was wonderfully calm. It never failed to comfort her. *Which is a good quality in a person who narrates the various lawsuits against you,* she thought.

"Franklin. I'm so glad you called."

"It's awfully early. I hope I didn't wake you. But I just got up and there's this text on my phone from Jill. She said Lance called the office yesterday afternoon and was quite keen to know which offer. So I figured you might be on pins and needles waiting to hear. But then I also figured you might be asleep."

"Sleep? What's that?"

It was in her nature to joke at a time like this, so she did. Despite the fact that she was in serious danger of imploding if he didn't get to the point, and fast.

"I owe you an apology, Roseanna," he said. "It never once occurred to me that you wouldn't know which offer I meant. It's the second one. There was really no way he was going back to that first offer you made. Frankly, I'm amazed he backed down at all. I don't know what 'extenuating circumstances' he's referring to, and of course I don't need to, but I would have voted him the man most likely to wring every cent he could get out of you. His change of heart was a surprise, to say the least."

Roseanna glanced over at Lance, who was staring at her intensely. She gave him a thumbs-down as an answer and watched his shoulders slump in a sort of human deflation.

"One of those mysteries of life," Roseanna said into the phone.

"But, really, Roseanna . . . I know this hits pretty hard. It's a big number. But if he'd gone for the number he wanted, and then all the legal fees you would have been on the hook for if we'd played this thing out to the bitter end . . . it's really not a bad outcome for you, based on the outcomes we had on the table. I think you lucked out, my friend."

"I think I did, too," she said.

"We'll draw up some papers and send them out for you to sign."

"Thank you. Oh. One other thing."

"Yes?"

But then Roseanna stopped, and did not go there.

"No. Never mind. Thanks for calling, Franklin."

She hung up the phone and sat looking at the hardwood boards of the floor. Processing where life had just taken her.

Lance came over and sat on the floor near her in his pajama bottoms. He draped an arm over her shoulder. Then he pulled her in close and kissed her firmly on the temple.

"Sorry, Mom. Could've been better."

"Could've been worse."

"True. What were you going to ask him there at the end? And then you didn't."

"Oh. That. I had it in my head to ask for one other bit of legal help. I wanted his office to look into the zoning around here. See if anybody can make us take down the metal zoo. I heard some locals were going to make a stink about it, and I wanted to know where I stood, but there's just been so much other, more important stuff going on."

"So why didn't you ask him to do it?"

She looked up into Lance's face, knowing he would see everything. That she was giving away the key to how all this was hitting her. She did it anyway.

"Because I can't afford it."

"Oh."

"And it was kind of a shock. To realize that. Like, this is my new reality, hitting home. Every time I turn around I'll need something, and then it'll dawn on me that I can't afford it. I've kind of adjusted to the idea that in a minute I'll only own a pickup truck, and I can't get it that bumper sticker that says, 'My Other Car Is a Maserati.' But for some reason I didn't see this bigger part coming."

"Got it," he said, and squeezed her shoulders more tightly.

It helped.

"I'm not feeling sorry for myself. Or I'm not trying to, anyway. It's just an adjustment."

"I get it," he said.

"I know people all over the world are getting by knowing there are tons of things they can't afford, but—"

"Mom, you don't have to apologize for what you're feeling."

They sat in silence for a time. How long a time would have been hard for Roseanna to judge. A minute or two, most likely.

Then Lance said, "You know . . . we have an attorney in the family."

"It's really not worth it to me to—"

"I was referring to Neal."

"Oh. Neal. Are you saying you think he'd look into my zoning problems for me?"

"I'm thinking he probably would. Because he really, *really* wants you to like him."

"But I already do like him."

"Well . . . how about we just don't tell him that until after he's finished the work?"

They turned to look at each other, both at the exact same time. Then they both burst out laughing.

It felt good to laugh.

"I'm laughing," Roseanna said, "but I'm also hoping you're kidding."

"I'm kidding. But I'm still pretty sure he'll do it."

Nelson came knocking shortly after ten a.m., right around the time the sun drove Roseanna back indoors. Lance was out, but she didn't know where.

She opened the door and smiled to see the young man standing on her doorstep. Her smile was not forced or painted on. It wasn't even fully on purpose. He just brought a smile to her face, a natural and unplanned reaction.

He held his hat in his hands and fidgeted with its brim, his eyes cast down to her welcome mat.

"Mind if I come in for a talk, miss? I won't waste too much of your time."

"You're not prone to wasting my time, Nelson. That's why you're still here."

She stepped back out of the doorway, and he

came in and stood in the middle of her living room as if about to recite a memorized speech.

"Hope you don't mind, miss. Your son told us the outcome of your legal case. And I just came here to tell you . . . I think I told you this once before, or something very close to it. But I need to spell it out real plainly now. You don't be worrying about anything when it comes to money, miss. That's not to say you'll have it coming out of your ears, because *we* don't. But you'll never be in it alone, we can say that for a fact. Not only are we prepared to help out financially, with a little actual cash money, but we'll be bringing trout from the creek, and eggs from our laying hens, and food from the vegetable garden we've been planting. You made what was yours ours, and now's the time when we pay you back for it, and you're going to be just fine, miss. Just fine. We plan to see to that."

He glanced up from her wooden floorboards to see how his oration was being received. Then he cast his gaze down again.

" 'We' being you and Patty?"

She watched his face flush almost crimson.

"Yes, ma'am. That's the 'us' I had reference to."

"So it's going well between you two?"

The red of his face deepened, if such a thing were possible.

"So far so good, miss."

"Well, I'm glad. And I appreciate what you just said. This is very good timing for being told I'm not in this alone."

"No, you're not, and you never will be if you don't want to be. We'll both be working a job just as soon as Willa's in kindergarten this fall. That's how come Patty's not here with me now to tell you all this. She's in Walkerville on a job interview. And I've been looking, too. We figure we'll pay you some rent, and that'll be a help to your situation. Maybe not a big rent like somebody else might charge us, but it'll be enough for you to eat on, and if you own the roof over your head and have enough money to feed yourself, well, that's the main thing, right?"

He still would not look at her. So he didn't see her cross the room to him. She figured he must have caught the movement in his peripheral vision. Still, he seemed surprised when she wrapped him into a hug. Surprised enough that it took several beats for him to unlock his limbs and hug her in return.

"Thank you, miss," he said, a light mumble against her ear.

She broke away and regarded him.

"Where's Lance?"

"Chopping wood."

Roseanna sighed audibly. "Why does he do that? I keep telling him he doesn't have to."

"He doesn't want you getting cold when the winter rolls around. You know. After he's gone."

"I'll have to go have a talk with him," she said.

Nelson broke his statue-like pose and headed for the door, the soles of his boots making a scuffing sound on the floorboards.

"Before you go, honey," Roseanna said.

He paused with his hand on the knob.

"Yes, miss?"

"That question you asked me a while ago . . ."

"Which question was that?"

"The one that involved new construction."

"Oh, right. That one."

"The answer is yes."

His head shot up and he looked directly into her face for the first time since arriving that morning.

"Really?"

"Really."

"You're sure?"

"I've never been more sure of anything in my life, honey. It'll be winter in a few months, and I have to figure out how to keep myself warm. I've never even lived in a place where I was responsible for my own snow removal. I don't want to be in this all by myself."

"You're not, miss. You're not."

And with that, he plunked his hat back on his head and left her alone.

And yet not alone. Not in any of the ways that counted.

• • •

She found Lance around the corner of the barn. He was stacking and covering firewood, which explained why she hadn't heard the familiar thump of the splitting maul.

He had his earbuds in, the wires running into his shirt pocket. When he saw her he pulled out one earbud and allowed it to dangle.

"I keep explaining to you how you don't have to do that," she said.

"That you do, Mom. That you do."

"And you always do it anyway."

"I don't want you to freeze. Well, actually . . . you're not going to freeze. You're getting a nice big propane heater that can sit outside the house and vent into your bedroom. It's a present from Neal and me, and Nelson's going to install it. But smart people have a backup. In a big storm you might run out of propane, and the trucks might not be able to get through to deliver. A good fire in the woodstove'll keep you from freezing."

They stood a moment, neither quite looking at the other, Roseanna pondering just how painful a long, snowy winter would prove to be.

Then she decided it didn't matter. She would deal with that situation when it arrived, and come out the other side. Every year millions of people managed it. She would manage, too. And besides, she realized, she had a son thoughtful enough to make sure she had a propane heater.

Then she chastised herself for putting those thoughts in the wrong order of importance.

"I came to ask two big things of you," she said.

"Okay." He pulled out the other earbud. Slid the phone out of his shirt pocket and tapped the screen to silence the music. "Shoot."

"Number one. I love you like crazy. I love you more than I love my own life. But I'm saying this in spite of that . . . no, I'm saying this *because* of that. You need to go the hell home now."

"I do?"

"Yes. You do. You have a life there. Right?"

"Something that passes for one," he said, a small smile tugging at one corner of his mouth.

"You have that nice young man waiting for you. And, as he so eloquently pointed out, there's a lot of work involved in relationships. I worry that . . . I mean, at the bottom of the thing, Lance, are you really still here just to help me at this point? And I ask that with no lack of gratitude, but I still have to ask. Or has it started to feel safe here because you're postponing doing that relationship work?"

"Hmm," Lance said, and sat down hard on an uncut round of tree trunk. "That's a tricky question." He sat still and pondered it for a time. "I guess the honest answer would be . . . yes. To both. Okay. Here's what I'd be willing to do. I'll pack up and go home today. Get my feet wet in the business again and catch up with what I

400

missed. Then come the weekend, I'll drive back out and see how you're doing."

"Fair enough. I'm wondering if you might take the train out, though. I could pick you up in Albany or Utica."

"Because . . . ?"

"I was hoping you'd drive the Maserati back into the city. And . . . you know. It's silly, but it's even a little hard for me to say it. Sell it for me. I'm embarrassed to admit it, but it would hurt me to do it myself. I can't really even really bring myself to watch it go. Gosh, I'm humiliated to say that."

"Don't be," Lance said. "Consider it done."

Roseanna had been back in the house for fifteen or twenty minutes after Lance's big departure, thinking no real thoughts, so far as she knew.

Then, with little if any forethought, she picked up her new phone.

She dialed a cell phone number she still knew by heart.

After five rings the call went to voicemail.

"Nita Langley," Nita's elf-like voice awkwardly said, sandwiched into the space in that pre-recorded voicemail message. The blank in which the user is supposed to identify herself and her mailbox.

Roseanna waited for the beep.

"Nita. It's Roseanna. Surprise. I was wondering if you wanted to have lunch sometime. You could come out here to the farm if you want, but I understand if you don't want to. It's such a long drive. Oh, wait. You don't have a car. Duh. That's typical me, right? You could take a train to some point in between and I could meet you. Catch up over a meal. Only if it sounds like a good idea, though. Even if you don't do it, I wanted you to know you're invited to. I just figured . . . just because we don't work together anymore doesn't mean we need to act like strangers. We'll never be strangers, now will we?"

She read off the first three numbers of her landline, the area code. Then she stopped and laughed at herself.

"Never mind," she said. "You have it on your cell phone now. Well, that's all. Hope you're well."

But before she could disconnect the call, she was struck with a strange and uncomfortable thought.

"Wait," she said, "that's not all. I'm not sure if you're still with the firm, but if you are . . . no matter what you may have heard around the watercooler, this is an offer of friendship only. Totally aboveboard. Okay. *That's* all. 'Bye."

She hung up the phone.

She knew if Lance were here, they would smile together over that last bit of the message.

But he wasn't.

So she smiled on her own, to herself. And that was also okay.

THREE YEARS AFTER THE MOVE

Chapter Twenty-Five

Paddling into Eternity

The hard clang of the bell at the gate brought Roseanna upright. She had been napping on her back on the floor of her living room, much the way she and Lance had always done—and occasionally still did. She had honed the skill of being able to nap, barely, despite the considerable din of small-scale construction.

She rose and looked out the window.

A young man was standing at her gate. Cleancut. Maybe Lance and Neal's age. He looked around in every direction, even above himself. He seemed to be waiting for something to happen, and open to the possibility that the event could come from anywhere at all. Even from the sky.

Roseanna sighed and walked out to see what he wanted.

As she plodded down her own dirt path, and was able to see him better, she developed a nagging sense that she might have seen him before. But she wasn't positive, and no context sprang to mind.

"What can I do for you?" she asked, a bit irritably, when she reached the gate.

"You don't remember me," he said, "do you?"

"You look vaguely familiar, but . . . I'm sorry."

"Evan Maxwell."

"Max? My reporter friend? Or enemy, as the case may be?"

"The very one. And I have to say this right now before I say anything else—I'm relieved to hear you call me your friend. Even with that little qualification that came afterward. I thought I might find myself looking down the business end of a shotgun if I ever came back around here."

She held the gate open for him, and he walked in.

She expected him to walk with her to the house. Instead he made a beeline for the field of sculptures.

"This has grown a lot," he said as they moved from metal animal to metal animal. And from metal animal to metal person. "I halfway thought your neighbors might have pressured you to take them down by now. I talked to a few of them, and there was quite a split as to whether the zoo was a delight or an eyesore."

"Yes, well, the law is the law," she said. "And my son-in-law is an attorney."

"*You're* an attorney," he said, stopping near the Martin sculpture.

"No, I'm an ex-attorney."

"Still on the bar?"

"Technically, yes. But I'd sooner move the

statues than go back into practicing any kind of law, even just for my own purposes. The backup plan was to haul them down by the creek where they couldn't be seen from the road. But, as it turned out, there was no ordinance to prevent me having them up here. So here they are in all their glory. Like I said, the law is the law."

Evan stood looking into the round sphere of what would have been Martin's face, if the statue had been given one.

"This reminds me of that old guy who used to chop wood here. The high-top sneakers. The scraggly hair sticking out underneath the hat. What was his name again?"

"Martin."

"Right. Martin."

He set off walking, headed for the only other sculpture that was not of the animal kingdom. Roseanna followed.

"What's all that noise?" he asked, looking up and around as he walked. Much the way he had at the gate. "Neighbors building? That must drive you crazy. I remember how you felt about your silence."

He stopped in front of the statue and stared into its face. This one had a face.

"Not neighbors," she said. "It's Nelson—you remember him—and my son. Nelson is building onto that tiny guest shack to make it big enough for a family. He already added one big room a couple of years ago, but then he and Patty had another baby. So the thing keeps expanding. And my son and his partner come up every weekend and work on their guesthouse. Lance is here working on it now. It might never be done at this rate, but at least it has walls and a roof now, so they can camp out in it. They don't need a tent anymore."

While she spoke, Evan continued to stare into the face of the statue. As if it might break down and tell him who it was.

"It's not the weekend, though," he said. Distantly. "It's Friday."

"Sometimes Lance comes up on Thursday or Friday and Neal drives out on Friday night."

"So basically there's been nonstop company and construction going on here since I last saw you," he said, still staring.

"Pretty much."

"And the noise doesn't drive you to distraction? You were so adamant about silence."

"Yeah. I still am, pretty much. But it just never does me a damn bit of good. Stuff happens no matter how I might feel about it."

Evan smiled without taking his eyes off the statue.

"And who is *this?*" he asked.

"That's Alice."

"Oh, *that's Alice,*" he repeated, his emphasis on the words sounding nearly reverent.

Alice, in iron, came up only to about the chest of Evan Maxwell. Not because she was not life size, but because she was seated in an iron canoe, paddling.

"We all worked together on this one," Roseanna said.

"I'm not surprised. It's different from the others. More detailed."

"Right. It's a real sculpture. We sculpted metal. Rather than just welding together a bunch of pieces to suggest a shape. It took ages. It was quite a project. I can't help noticing you're not taking notes about any of this. Is it safe to assume you're not planning a follow-up story?"

He looked over at her, his eyes breaking away from Alice for the first time since he'd seen her. He seemed genuinely surprised by the question.

"I'm not even a reporter anymore," he said. "Haven't been for quite some time now."

"Because . . . ?"

"I just don't think I was cut out for it. Oh, but maybe that's not the right way to put it. I'm not saying I was bad at it. I just didn't like it very much. It wasn't making me happy."

"Then you were smart to move on."

"I left not too long after I did that story about you, so I've always wondered if you might have had some influence on me." His eyes flickered back to Alice. "So Alice was a paddler?"

"No. Not at all. Never. Not in any way. She

hardly ever got out of the city. Never took vacations. All work and no play."

"But you've immortalized her until the end of time in a canoe."

"Right," Roseanna said. "We did. It's the closest we could get to giving her that much-anticipated retirement she missed out on. It was her own fault for not choosing a retirement hobby while she was alive. So I chose for her, and when I see her again, if stuff like that happens, I'll be brooking no complaints."

They walked together toward the sound of all that commotion.

As they rounded the house, Roseanna saw Mikey playing with the dogs. Buzzy ran away from the toddler in a circle, tail whipping, and the massive Hector loped along behind, afraid—as always—of being left out. Lance was up on a ladder attaching storm drains at the edges of the new guesthouse roof. Patty sat on the porch of her and Nelson's home, supervising Mikey's play.

"I must admit I was curious about who all still lived here," Evan said. "That's part of the reason I drove out. I would think about you from time to time and wonder if all those squatters were still living here, or if you'd followed through with putting them off your land."

"I put Melanie and Dave off. Well, I had Lance

410

do it. Probably the cowardly way out, but it got the job done."

"And Martin."

"No. I didn't evict Martin."

"He's still here?"

"No."

They stopped walking and just stood, half facing each other. Roseanna watched his face as he absorbed her meaning.

"Oh," he said after a time. "So there's a reason that wood chopper statue reminded me of Martin."

They walked again. Roseanna didn't answer because there was no need.

They passed the din of Lance's guesthouse construction, Roseanna wincing more dramatically than necessary at the noise, and continued on toward the barn. There Evan stopped suddenly, his eyes fixed to the handcarved wooden marker on the downhill side, which stood angled out over the valley.

"Is Martin buried on your property?" Evan asked.

"No, that's not him. Turned out he had a prepaid cemetery plot next to his wife."

"So who's this?" he asked, tentatively moving closer. "Earnest," he read out loud. "Who was Earnest? Another squatter?"

"No. Earnest was a horse."

"I didn't even know you had a horse."

"He wasn't living here yet when you came out to do that story. He showed up later."

"He didn't live very long, then."

"Oh, yes he did. He was thirty-seven or thirty-eight when he showed up. We're pretty sure he lived to see forty. A horse can't ask for more good years than that. Too bad you didn't get to meet him. He was quite a character. We all miss him. Which, frankly, I never thought I'd hear myself say about a horse. Especially a very old, very smelly horse. Turns out old and smelly are not deal breakers when it comes to affection. Who knew? That's likely to be a boon to me in my own later years, which are coming up fast."

They stood looking out over the valley together. It riveted Roseanna, that view. It always had, and it still did. She had once assumed it would lose its pull and become more commonplace. She had assumed wrong.

The dogs came up to join them, then stopped and stood transfixed, as if also enjoying the view. Hector sat, his head quite purposely underneath Roseanna's right hand. She patted it. The hulking beast half closed his eyes and sighed.

Behind them, Roseanna heard the dejected wail of the toddler, Mikey, brokenhearted because the dogs no longer cared to play. Inconsolable as only a two-year-old can be.

"You have two dogs now," Evan said over the din.

"This big guy is Lance's dog. All his life he wanted me to get him a dog. So I finally did. When he was thirty."

"Why didn't he get one on his own when he grew up?"

"He felt guilty about leaving a dog alone all day while he worked. So I went and got this guy when he was on his last day at the pound. Hours away from that room at the end of the hall, and the poor guy seemed to know it. He was so stressed he couldn't stop drooling. I told Lance if he couldn't handle the guilt of leaving him alone, he could keep the dog here and visit him on the weekends. But it didn't take my son long to figure out that the dog was just so grateful to have a home. Everything else paled in comparison. So what was the other reason?" she added suddenly, turning the conversation in a whole new, unexpected direction.

"Excuse me?"

"You said part of the reason you came back was to see if I had thrown the squatters off the place . . ."

"Oh. That. Right. Well . . . the main thing is . . . I've always felt a little guilty. Ever since I wrote that piece. You didn't want me to. You tried to tell me that. You didn't want your family or your law partners finding you and trying to force you home. You had a lot to lose. I've tried to put it out of my mind all this time. But finally I had to come back and see how things turned out."

"Not too badly," she said. "Things turned out okay. Rocky for a time. But family finding me was the best thing that could possibly have happened, and I owe you one for that. The law partner thing was dicey, but it passed. And I didn't lose anything I couldn't afford to lose."

"Well, that's a relief," he said.

"He would've found me anyway. You just speeded up the process."

They turned around and walked back into the fray together.

"So what do you do now?" she asked him. "Now that you're not doing the reporter thing anymore? I forgot to ask."

"I'm a musician."

"Sounds like a potential improvement. What do you play?"

"Guitar and bass. A little piano. I'm in a band. It's pretty hand to mouth. I'm not making nearly as much money as I was before."

"That's overrated," Roseanna said.

"Making lots of money, you mean?"

"Yes," Roseanna said. "That."

Lance came down from his ladder when he realized there was someone new on the property. The blessed silence rang out loudly, if such a thing were possible. He wiped his hand with a rag before he stuck it out in Evan's direction. It still looked plenty dirty.

"Lance," Roseanna said, "this is Evan Maxwell. Max, my son Lance. There's a reason I call him Max. Once my back is turned he might start complaining about it, and then you'll hear the story. The short version is, it serves him right."

Lance stood scratching his nose for a moment, seemingly lost in thought. Roseanna could see a streak of dirt he'd left on the bridge of his nose in the process.

"Evan Maxwell," Lance said. "Why does that sound so damn familiar?"

Then he got it. Made the connection. It was evident to Roseanna by the changes to his face.

"Oh, *Evan Maxwell,*" Lance repeated. "The reporter. Interesting. Between you and me, you were smart to wait a few years before you came back. She was pretty damn miffed at you for a while there. But she looks like she's over it now. To me, anyway. How does she look to you? But those first couple months. Hoo boy. First I showed up and more or less never left. Not full-time left, anyway. Then her old law partner showed up and served papers on her and took most of the money she planned to live on for the rest of her life. She almost lost this property. But she didn't. Everything else, but not that. And she's mellowed some these last couple years. Lucky thing for you."

He smiled that crooked smile of his, then climbed up his ladder again with a slight wave.

"That was interesting," Evan said.

"He tends to be a bit direct. Gets it from his mother's side of the family."

"You told me you hadn't lost anything you couldn't afford to lose."

"I didn't. Look at me. Am I dead?" She patted her solid belly. "Do I look like I miss too many meals?"

"But you could've lost this place."

"But I didn't. And even if I had, it would have been worth it to get my son back. This place is my favorite material thing in the world, but it's still a thing. It's not a son. So now I have both. The property and the son. If I were to ask for anything more than that, I think it would come off as downright greedy."

She walked him to the gate, and then his car.

"Was it worth the drive?" she asked him just before he climbed in.

"More than. I feel better. But now I kind of regret that I'm not in a position to do a follow-up story. Three years later and only two squatters put off the place. That's a hell of an update. After all this time, still two left who aren't blood family or in-laws. No, wait, three! Or maybe we should say two and a half. I forgot about the little girl. Where's the little girl?"

"School."

"Oh. Right. School. She's not as little as she used to be."

"Who *is?*"

He laughed. Unlocked the car doors with a beep of his smart key.

"But anyway," Roseanna said, "you got the math wrong."

"Right. The new baby. Four."

"Still wrong."

"Three and a half? Two and three-quarters?"

"Not even close."

"Okay, fine," he said, squinting into the sun and sheltering his eyes with one hand. "You tell me."

"Zero. Zero squatters. Everybody left is family."

He dropped his hand and nodded for one thoughtful moment.

"I guess that was a kind of math only you could do. So, look. The thing about the noise. How much you hate it. I've been watching you. And I think that might not be true anymore. You still say that. But I'm not sure I think you still mean it."

Roseanna stared into his face for a moment. He demurred and looked down at the road.

"We don't pay you to think, Max," she said in her best Roseanna-from-the-olden-days voice.

Then she turned back toward home, following all that construction din straight into the heart of ever-present chaos.

She glanced briefly over her shoulder before opening the gate. Evan Maxwell stood still, as if lost in thought. On his face was a crooked but distinct smile.

Heaven Adjacent
Book Club Questions

1. Roseanna is a high-powered attorney living a successful life in the city. When faced with a moment of crisis, she drives off and leaves everything behind. Do you think this was a rash decision or something that had been brewing for a long time?

2. Why does the inciting incident of Alice's untimely death affect Roseanna so deeply in ways other life experiences she had encountered had not?

3. No sooner does Roseanna think she has found peace and quiet away from everything and everyone than she discovers people squatting on her new property. As time goes on more uninvited guests appear and ask to stay. This also includes a lost and aging horse. Even though she protests their presence, Roseanna allows them to stay. In what ways did her relationship with these tenants transform over the course of the book?

4. Roseanna has an estranged relationship with her son, Lance. When he shows up looking for her following her disappearance, it creates both conflict and opportunity in their relation-

ship. How does their mother-son bond grow and shift over the course of the book?

5. One of the memories Lance brings up to his mother is how he'd always wanted a dog as a child. How did the author use this unresolved desire to bring their relationship closer? Why do you think her son ultimately decides to stay for a while?

6. Inspired by the little girl living on her property, Roseanna creates an "iron zoo," which attracts a lot of attention from the town and eventually a reporter. Discuss ways these sculptures end up touching and inspiring others. Do you think they helped Roseanna as well?

7. After Roseanna walks out on her business partner, Jerry, he files an expensive and emotionally draining lawsuit against her. Because of her choice to leave the past behind, Roseanna faces the possibility of losing almost everything she has left. Do you agree with her son's intervention into the matter, and the ultimate outcome?

8. At one point the reporter from the *New York Times* who first revealed Roseanna's location returns to see how she's doing. He reminds her, "You told me you hadn't lost anything you couldn't afford to lose." What do you think Roseanna meant when she said those words?

9. For the sculpture of Alice, which Roseanna called "a real sculpture" sculpted from metal, why do you think Roseanna chose to portray Alice paddling in a canoe?

About the Author

Catherine Ryan Hyde is the author of thirty-three published books. Her bestselling 1999 novel, *Pay It Forward*, adapted into a major Warner Bros. motion picture, made the American Library Association's Best Books for Young Adults list and was translated into more than two dozen languages for distribution in more than thirty countries. Her novels *Becoming Chloe* and *Jumpstart the World* were included on the ALA's Rainbow List; *Jumpstart the World* was also a finalist for two Lambda Literary Awards and won Rainbow Awards in two categories. *The Language of Hoofbeats* won a Rainbow Award. More than fifty of her short stories have been published in many journals, including the *Antioch Review*, *Michigan Quarterly Review*, the *Virginia Quarterly Review*, *Ploughshares*, *Glimmer Train*, and the *Sun*, and in the anthologies *Santa Barbara Stories* and *California Shorts*, as well as the bestselling anthology *Dog Is My Co-Pilot*. Her short fiction received honorable mention in the Raymond Carver Short Story Contest, a second-place win for the Tobias Wolff Award, and nominations for *Best American Short Stories*, the O. Henry Award, and the Pushcart Prize. Three have also been cited in *Best American Short Stories*.

Hyde is the founder and former president of the Pay It Forward Foundation. As a professional public speaker, she has addressed the National Conference on Education, twice spoken at Cornell University, met with AmeriCorps members at the White House, and shared a dais with Bill Clinton. An avid equestrian, photographer, and traveler, she lives in California.

Books are produced in the United States using U.S.-based materials

Books are printed using a revolutionary new process called THINKtech™ that lowers energy usage by 70% and increases overall quality

Books are durable and flexible because of Smyth-sewing

Paper is sourced using environmentally responsible foresting methods and the paper is acid-free

Center Point Large Print
600 Brooks Road / PO Box 1
Thorndike, ME 04986-0001 USA

(207) 568-3717

US & Canada:
1 800 929-9108
www.centerpointlargeprint.com